The Curved Blades

By Carolyn Wells

Originally published in 1916

The Curved Blades

Published by Resurrected Press

This classic book was handcrafted by Resurrected Press. Resurrected Press is dedicated to bringing high quality classic books back to the readers who enjoy them. These are not scanned versions of the originals, but, rather, quality checked and edited books meant to be enjoyed!

Please visit ResurrectedPress.com to view our entire catalogue!

ISBN 13: 978-1-937022-31-0

Printed in the United States of America

OTHER RESURRECTED PRESS MYSTERIES

By Carolyn Wells
Raspberry Jam
The Man Who Fell Through the Earth
In The Onyx Lobby
Vicky Van

By Louis Tracy
The Strange Case of Mortimer Fenley
The Albert Gate Mystery
The Stowmarket Mystery

By J. S. Fletcher
The Orange-Yellow Diamond
The Middle Temple Murder

By A. A. Milne
The Red House Mystery

By Agatha Christie
The Mysterious Affair at Styles

By Arthur Griffiths
The Passenger from Calais
The Rome Express

From the Dr. John Thorndyke Series
By R. Austin Freeman
The Red Thumb Mark
The Eye of Osiris
The Mystery of 31 New Inn
John Thorndyke's Cases
The Cat's Eye

By Arthur J. Rees
The Hampstead Mystery
The Mystery of the Downs

Visit RessurectedPress.com to see our entire catalog.

FOREWORD

Carolyn Wells was a successful humorist and poet before turning to writing mysteries in 1910. Her works had appeared in many of the magazines of the day and she had had a number of books published. But once she began writing mysteries, she did so with a vengeance, writing over a hundred in the following three decades, many of them featuring the detective Fleming Stone.

At a time when most writers of detective fiction were either British or emulated the British fashion, Wells developed a distinctly American style, more domestic than her English contemporaries and focused on the rising urban middle class of the East Coast.

While it is true that her plots were never as intricate as those of Agatha Christie and her puzzles rarely as clever as the authors of the "Golden Age" of British mysteries who wrote during the 20's and 30's, there was one area in which she excelled. Rather than being concerned with the details of the crime and the methods of detection, she was much more centered on the interactions between the various characters surrounding the victim, many of whom were suspects. The feelings of her characters toward each other as suspicion falls on first one than another form the heart of many of her works.

In this respect, *The Curved Blades* is one of Wells' better mysteries. Jealousies and class and nationalistic prejudices have full play. The victim, the wealthy middle-aged spinster, Lucy Carrington, was not well liked by those around her. Petulant and overbearing, she bred resentment amongst those who depended on her generosity, and once she is dead, that resentment that becomes aimed at the other potential suspects.

There are plenty of clues, but many seem pointless or contradictory, and the statements of the witnesses are all suspect as their motivation seems more to throw suspicion on others rather than to solve the crime. Fleming Stone uncharacteristically appears rather early in the book as opposed to his usual mode of coming in a few chapters from the end. Uncharacteristically, too, the normally detached detective becomes personally involved to the point where he questions his ability to maintain his objectivity.

Wells has been accused, with some justice, of not always playing fair with her readers by introducing the critical clue to the mystery's solution only at the end. It should be noted, however, that the concept of fairness really only took hold several decades after the book was written. There are plenty of false leads in *The Curved Blades* but nothing is deliberately concealed from the reader and there is no architectural secret as there are in so many of Wells' books.

Carolyn Wells was a popular and successful writer of mysteries in her day and her books give useful insights into the time and class that she wrote about. They also can be highly entertaining, and in this *The Curved Blades* is one of her better works. It is with pleasure that Resurrected Press offers this new edition of *The Curved Blades*.

About the Author

Carolyn Wells, June 18, 1862 March 26, 1942 was an American writer and poet. She was best known for her books of poetry and humor until around 1910 she read one of Anna Katherine Green's mysteries and took up the genre. Many of her mysteries featured the detective Fleming Stone. She was married to Hadwin Houghton, heir to the Houghton-Mifflin publishing company. She was a collector of poetry by other authors, and, upon her death, she bequeathed her collection of the works of Walt Witman to the Library of Congress.

Greg Fowlkes
Editor-In-Chief
Resurrected Press
www.ResurrectedPress.com

TABLE OF CONTENTS

CHAPTER 1: MISS LUCY CARRINGTON

"GARDEN Steps" was one of the showplaces of Merivale Park, Long Island. In summer it was an enchanting spot, and the dazzling white marble steps which led to the sunken gardens justified their right to give the place its name. Other stone steps gave on terraces and flower banks, others still/led to the Italian landscape gardens, and a few rustic steps of a wooden stile transported one to an old-fashioned garden, whose larkspur and Canterbury bells were the finest of their sort.

The house seemed an integral part of this setting. Its wide verandahs, or more often loggias, were so lavishly furnished with flowering plants, its windows so boxed with them, that the whole effect was that of a marvellously well-planted horticultural exhibition. But all this was of the summer. In winter—for it was an all-round-the-year home—only the varied and extraordinary collection of evergreens shared with the steps the honor of making picturesque and beautiful the view from the house windows.

And now, in January, one of the all too seldom enjoyed white snow storms had glorified the whole estate. Wind-swept drifts half hid, half disclosed the curving marble balustrades, and turned the steps to snowy fairyland flights. And, for it was night, a cold, clear, perfect winter night, a supercilious moon looked down, a little haughtily and condescended to illumine the scene in stunning, if a bit theatric, fashion. "Ripping picture, eh?" said Gray Haviland, as he held back the heavy curtain for the golden-haired young woman at his side to look out.

"Oh, isn't it a wonderful sight!" And as Anita Frayne took a step forward, toward the casement, Haviland let the curtain fall behind him and the two were alone in the deep embrasure of the wide bay-window.

"Not nearly such a wonderful sight as you are!" Haviland swung her round to face him, and stood gazing at the pretty, doll-like face that half laughed, half frowned into his own.

"Me! I'm not like a moonlit landscape!"

"No, you're just a golden morsel of summer sunshine—" Haviland's eulogy was interrupted by a petulant voice calling shrilly:

"Where are you two? I hear you talking; come on. I'm waiting."

"Oh, Lord! come on," and, holding the curtain aside, he let Anita pass and then followed her.

"Here we are, Cousin Lucy, all ready for the fray. Good evening, Count."

Count Charlier bowed Frenchily, and Anita gave him the bright, flashing smile that she kept on hand for mankind in general, and which was quite different from that she used on special occasions or for special friends.

Annoyed at the duration of this delaying smile, Miss Lucy Carrington tapped impatiently on the bridge table, and looked her impatience most unmistakably.

Mistress of Garden Steps, wealthy, well-born, of assured social position, capable and efficient, Miss Carrington lacked the one gift of Fate for which she would have bartered all else. She was not beautiful, and had not even enough pretension to good looks to think herself beautiful. Plain features, graying hair—dyed red—big, prominent light-blue eyes, and a pasty, pudgy complexion left no hope for the miracles worked by beauty doctors to avail in her case. Her figure was short and dumpy, the despair of her staymakers, and her taste in dress ran to the extremes in coloring and fashion.

Passionately fond of all beauty, Miss Carrington felt keenly her own lack of it, and to this lack she attributed the fact that she was a spinster. Those who knew her felt there might be other reasons why her suitors had been few, but, as a matter of fact, the acidity of her disposition was a direct result of her disappointed, loveless life, and even yet, though nearing fifty, Miss Lucy Carrington had by no means laid aside all thoughts of matrimonial adventure. Heiress to immense wealth, there had been fortune-seekers who asked her hand, but Lucy Carrington would none of these. Aristocratic and high-minded, she had unerring perception of motives, and the men who had been willing to marry her face as well as her fortune had been of such unworth that the lady scorned them. But now, looming on her hopes' horizon was a welcome possibility. Count Henri Charlier, a visitor of a neighbor, seemingly admired the mistress of Garden Steps and had fallen into the habit of frequent calling. Courteous and polished of manner, he flattered Miss Carrington in such wise that his attitude was acceptable if not indubitably sincere. Her closest scrutiny and most challenging provocation failed to surprise any admission of her lack of perfection in his eyes, and his splendid physique and brilliant mind commanded her complete approval and admiration. There had been hints that his title could not be read entirely clear, but this was not sufficient to condemn him in Miss Carrington's eyes.

To be sure, the Count had as yet said no word that could be construed as of definite intention, but there had been certain signs, deemed portentous by the willing mind of the lady in question.

Bridge was Miss Carrington's favorite diversion, and, as the Count also enjoyed it, frequent evenings were devoted to the game. It was, perhaps, a mistake that Miss Carrington should have allowed this, for her temper, always uncertain, lost all restraint when she suffered ill-luck at cards. A poor hand always brought down violent objurgation on the head of her partner and sarcastic comment or criticism on her adversaries. These exhibitions of wrath were not good policy if she wished to charm the French visitor, but, as he invariably kept his own temper, his irate hostess made little effort to curb hers.

"What are you doing, Anita?" cried Miss Carrington, petulantly, as they settled themselves at the table. "You know I always play with the blue cards, and you are dealing them!"

"Sure enough! Pardon me, Lady Lucy, I will take the red ones."

"Then, pray, wait till I make them up. There. No, let the Count cut them! Have you no notion of bridge rules? You are quite the most inattentive player! Will you kindly concentrate on the game?"

"Yes, indeed," and Anita Frayne smiled as she deftly dealt the red cards. "I hope you have a good hand."

"You hope I have a good hand! A strange idea for an adversary!"

"But I know you like to win," and Miss Frayne hastily gathered up her own cards. "I do not like to have you want me to win! That's babyish. I like to win by superior skill, not merely by lucky cards!"

This was an awful whopper, and all at the table knew it, but it was ignored and the game began.

Miss Carrington—Lady Lucy, as she liked to be called—did not hold good hands. On the contrary, she had a run of bad luck that made her more and more irate with each hand dealt. Miss Frayne, who was her protégée and social secretary, watched with growing apprehension the red spots that appeared in Miss Carrington's cheeks, infallible danger signals of an impending outbreak.

It came.

"Another handful of blanks!" Miss Carrington exclaimed, angrily, and flung the offending thirteen cards across the wide room.

"There now, Cousin Lucy," said Gray Haviland, determined to keep the peace if possible, "that was a clever idea! It will certainly change your luck! I'll collect the pasteboards, and we'll start fresh."

Easily, the big, good-looking young chap sauntered across the room and gathered up the cards, chatting meanwhile. "You don't lose your deal, you know; so try again, Cousin Lucy, and good luck to you!"

In angry silence Miss Carrington dealt again, and examined her hand. "Nothing above a nine spot!" she declared, throwing them, backs up, on the table.

"Too bad!" murmured Miss Frayne, carelessly picking up the hand. "Why, you didn't look closely! Here's an ace and two queens and—"

"They're nothing! How dare you dispute my word? I say the hand is worthless!" She fairly snatched the cards from the girl and turned them face down again.

"But mad'moiselle," began the Count, "if you have an ace and two queens, I could have played a no-trump hand grand,—ah, splendid!"

"Yes, you could have played it! You want to play all the open hands! You want me to sit here a dummy, a figure-head, every time!"

"Now, now, Lady Lucy—" and Anita Frayne laughed pleasantly.

"Be quiet! You're worse yet! You want to deal me good hands to humor me! I believe you would cheat to do it! I don't want good cards that way!"

"Ah," begged the Count, seeing Anita flush, "do not tell the young lady she cheats! Do not do that!"

"I'll tell her what I choose! Gray, say something! You sit there like a mummy, while these people are insulting me right and left! Tell Anita that I am right in not wishing her to deal me good cards purposely."

"But she didn't," declared Haviland; "you know she didn't. Why, she couldn't, even if she wanted to!"

"Oh, yes, she could!" and Miss Carrington gave a disagreeable sneer. "She's quite clever enough for any deceit or treachery."

"Stop, Cousin Lucy! I can't let you talk so about Miss Frayne in my presence!"

"Oh, you can't, can't you? And, pray, what right have you to defend her? Go away, both of you! I'll play with you no longer. Go away and send Pauline and Mr. Illsley in here. They, at least, will play fair."

Anita Frayne rose without a word. Haviland rose too, but talking volubly. "Let up, Cousin Lucy" he said sternly. "You've no right to treat Miss Frayne so. You ought to apologize to her for such rudeness."

"Apologize!" Miss Carrington fairly shrieked; "she'll do the apologizing, and you, too, my foolish young cousin. You little know what's going to happen to me! To-morrow you may sing another song!"

Haviland looked at her in astonishment; the Count, thoughtfully. The same idea was in both their minds. Could she mean that she was expecting the Count to propose to her that evening?

"Nothing nice can happen to you unless you learn to control that temper of yours," and Haviland swung away after Anita.

He found her in the next room, nestled in the corner of a big davenport, weeping into a sympathetic sofa-cushion.

"Go and find the others," she whispered, as he came near her. "Make them go and play with her!"

Obediently, Haviland went. In the glassed sun-parlor he found Pauline Stuart, Miss Carrington's niece, and Stephen Illsley, one of the most favored of Pauline's many suitors.

"For goodness' sake, people," he began, "do go and play bridge with the Lady of the Manor! She's in a peach of a fury, and you'll have to take your life in your hands, but go!"

"I won't," said Pauline, bluntly; "It's Anita's turn to-night. She said she'd do it."

"She did! But she came off second best, and she's weeping buckets on the best Empire embroidery sofa-cushions! I'm going to comfort her, but you must go and keep the gentle Lucy from pulling the house down about our ears! She's sure queering herself with his nibs! He can't admire her sweet, flower-like soul after this night's exhibition."

"I don't want to go a bit, but I suppose we'll have to," and Pauline smiled at her guest.

"Oh, go on," said Haviland, as he turned to leave them; "and, for Heaven's sake, give her all the good cards. Can you manage that, Illsley?"

"I am afraid not. Her eyes are too sharp."

"Well, if her luck stays bad, get her to play mumble-peg or something, instead of bridge."

Haviland disappeared and Pauline rose unwillingly. "I do so hate to play with Aunt Lucy," she said, "but it must be done. Are you willing to sacrifice yourself?"

"For you? Always!" And the two went to the cardroom.

Pauline Stuart, tall, dark, graceful, was a striking-looking girl. Only twenty-four, she carried herself with the dignity and poise of a duchess, and her heavy, dark brows gave her face an expression of strength and will-power that contrasted forcibly with the delicate Dresden china beauty of Anita Frayne. The two girls were not especially friendly, though never definitely at odds. Anita was envious of the more fortunate Pauline. The latter, Miss Carrington's niece, would inherit a goodly part of her aunt's large fortune, while the humble position of the secretary commanded only a liberal, not munificent, salary.

The girls, however, were at one in their dread of Miss Lucy's ebullitions of temper and their resentment of the biting sarcasms and angry diatribes she flung at them in her frequent spasms of fury.

Illsley, a well-set-up chap of good address, followed Pauline into her aunt's presence. "You waited long enough," grumbled Miss Carrington. "Sit down. It's your deal now, Pauline."

Matters went well for a time. Miss Lucy held good cards, and once or twice she triumphed through a mistake of her adversaries, which she fortunately did not discover was made on purpose.

Count Charlier's little bright black eyes darted inquiringly from aunt to niece, but he made no comment. All four played well, and when at last Miss Carrington made a grand slam her joy was effervescent.

"Good play," she flattered herself. "You must admit, Count, that it was clever of me to take that difficult finesse just at that critical point."

"Clever indeed, mademoiselle. You have the analytical mind; you should have been a diplomat. Also, Fortune favors you. You are beloved of the fickle goddess."

"Let us hope so," and for a moment Miss Carrington looked grave.

And then, with the perversity of that same goddess, the card luck changed. Pauline and Illsley held all the high cards, Miss Lucy and the Count only the low ones.

Storm signals showed. Whiter grew the stern, set face; tighter drew the thin, wide lips; and rigid muscles set themselves in the angry, swelling throat. Then, as she scanned a hand of cards, all below the ten, again they went in a shower across the room, and she cried, angrily:

"A Yarborough!" reverting to the old-fashioned term.

"Never mind, Aunt Lucy," and Pauline tried to laugh it off; "this is not your lucky night. Let's give up bridge for to-night. Let's have some music."

"Yes! because you love music and hate bridge! It makes no difference what I want. My wishes are never considered. You and Anita are just alike! Selfish, ungrateful, caring for nothing but your own pleasure. Mr. Ulsley, don't you think young girls should pay some slight attention to the wishes of one who does everything for them? Where would either of them be but for me? Are you not sorry for me?"

"Why,—I—you must excuse me, I am not sure I understand—"

"Yes, you understand, perfectly well. You know the girls slight me and snub me every chance they get. But it will not always be thus. To-morrow—"

"Come, Aunt Lucy," pleaded Pauline, "let us have some music. You know there are some new records, just arrived to-day. Let us hear them."

"Are there new records? Did you get the ones I wanted?"

"Some of them. We couldn't get them all."

"Oh, no, of course not! But if you had wanted certain records they would have been found!"

"But, Auntie Lucy, we couldn't get them if they aren't made, could we? Gray tried his best."

"Oh, tried his best! He forgot to ask for them, so he says he 'tried his best,' to excuse his carelessness. If Anita had wanted them—"

The starting of the music drowned further flow of the lady's grievances.

CHAPTER 2: A CLASH OF TONGUES

TRUE to its reputation for calming the impulses of the turbulent spirit, the music soothed Miss Carrington's ruffled temper, and she waxed amiable and even gay. Enthroned on her favorite red velvet chair, resplendent in an elaborately decorated gown of sapphire blue satin, with her bright auburn locks piled high and topped by an enormous comb of carved tortoiseshell, she dominated the little group and gave orders that must be obeyed.

She wore, among other jewels, a magnificent rope of pearls. So remarkable were these, that the Count, who had never seen them before, ventured to refer to them.

"Yes," agreed Miss Carrington, "they are wonderful. Practically priceless, I assure you. It took my agent years to collect them."

"And you grace an informal home evening with these regal gems?"

"Not usually, no. But you know, Count Charlier, pearls must be worn frequently to preserve their lustre. Laid away a long time, they grow dead and dull-looking."

"You keep them here? Is it safe, think you?"

"I don't keep them here all the time. Indeed, I got these from the Safe Deposit only this morning. I shall return them there in a few days. While here, I shall wear them all I can to liven them up."

"You brought a lot of your other jewels, didn't you, Aunt Lucy?" said Pauline, casually; "why did you? Are you going to a ball?"

"No: I wish to—to look them over and plan to have some reset."

"But are they safe?" inquired the Count again; "do you not fear thieves?"

"No, we never have such things as robbery in Merivale Park. It is a quiet, well-behaved neighborhood."

"But you have a safe?" went on the Count; "you take at least that precaution?"

"Oh, yes, I have a safe in my boudoir. There is really no danger. Count Charlier, would you like to hear me sing? Find one of my records, Gray."

Miss Carrington's singing voice had been a fine one and was still fair. She sometimes amused herself by making records for her phonograph, and Gray Haviland managed the mechanical part of it.

"Which one, Lady Lucy?" he asked, as he rummaged in the record cabinet.

"Any of those pretty love songs," and Miss Carrington glanced coyly at the Count.

"Here's a fine one," and Haviland placed a disk in the machine.

"Listen," he said, smiling; "don't miss the introduction."

The needle touched the record, and Miss Lucy's laugh rang out, so clear and true, it was difficult to believe it was a recorded laugh and not a sound from the lady herself. Then the recorded voice said: "This song is one of Carr's favorites, I'll sing it for him." And then, with only a few seconds' interval, Miss Carrington's voice sang, "Believe me, if all those endearing young charms."

It was well sung, and a perfect record, so that the incident of the singer listening to her own voice was interesting in itself.

"Capital!" applauded the Count, as it was finished. "It is indeed pleasant to preserve one's songs thus. May I not some time record my own amateur attempt?"

"Delighted to have you, Count," said Haviland, cordially. "Come over some morning, and we'll do up a lot of records."

"Since when have you been master here, Gray?" said Miss Lucy, with fine scorn. "I will give the invitations to my own house, if you please! Count Charlier, if you will come tomorrow afternoon I will instruct Mr. Haviland to make the records."

It was not so much the words as the manner of their utterance that was offensive, and Haviland set his lips in stifled anger. It was not at all unusual, this sort of rebuff, but he could not endure it as patiently as the two girls did. Haviland was a second cousin of Miss Carrington, and, while he lived with her in the capacity of a business secretary and general man of affairs, the post was a sinecure, for the services of her lawyer and of her social secretary left little for Haviland to do. His salary was a generous one and he was substantially remembered in her will, but he sometimes thought the annoying and irritating fleers he had to accept smilingly, were worth more than he was receiving. He was continually made to feel himself a dependent and an inferior.

These trials also fell to the lot of the two girls. Pauline, although her aunt's heiress to the extent of half the fortune, the other half to go to an absent cousin, was by no means treated as an equal of Miss Carrington herself. It seemed to give the elder lady delight to domineer over her niece and in every possible way make her life uneasy and uncomfortable. As to the social secretary, Miss Frayne, she was scolded for everything she did, right or wrong.

Often had the three young people declared intentions of leaving Garden Steps, but so far none of them had made good the threat. Vanity was the key-note of Lucy Carrington's nature, and, knowing this, they could, if they chose, keep her fairly sweet-tempered by inordinate flattery often administered. This proceeding hurt their self-respect, jarred their tempers, and galled their very souls, but it was that or dismissal, and thus far they had stayed. Matters were nearing a crisis, however, and Haviland 's patience was so sorely strained that he was secretly looking for another position.

Anita Frayne, whose pretty blonde doll-face belied a very fiery disposition, was on the verge of a serious break with her employer, and Pauline Stuart continually assured herself that she could not go on this way.

Pauline was the orphaned daughter of Lucy's sister, and had lived with her aunt for many years. Carrington Loria, the son of another sister, was engaged in antiquarian research in Egypt, where he had been since his graduation as an engineer. He, too, was an orphan and had lived with Lucy in his younger days, and he and Pauline were equal heirs to their aunt's wealth. The father of the three Carrington sisters, having become angered at his two daughters who married against his wishes, had left his entire fortune to Lucy, his only remaining child. Thus her niece and nephew were her only direct heirs, and, save for some comparatively small bequests, the Carrington estate would eventually be theirs.

Pauline well knew that if she left her aunt's roof it meant complete disinheritance, for Lucy Carrington was proud of her beautiful niece, and, too, was fond of her in her own way. But the ungovernable temper of the lady made her home an almost unbearable abiding-place. Since childhood years Carrington Loria had lived there only during his college vacations; but had been back occasionally for short visits from his now permanent Egyptian occupation. He had always come laden with gifts of Oriental products, and the rooms at Garden Steps showed many rare specimens of cunning handiwork and rich fabrics and embroideries.

To break the awkward pause that followed Miss Carrington's rude speech to Gray Haviland, Pauline picked up an antique scarab from a side table and drew the Count's attention to its inscription.

He expressed a polite interest, but cast furtive glances at his hostess, as if afraid of a further outbreak.

Nor were his fears unjustified. Miss Carrington administered a scathing reproach to Pauline for intruding herself upon the Count's attention, and bade her put aside the scarab and hold her tongue.

"Don't speak to me like that, Aunt Lucy; I am not a child!" And Pauline, unable to control herself longer, faced her angry aunt with an air of righteous wrath.

"I'll speak to you as I choose, miss! It is for you to mend your tone in addressing me! If you don't, you may have cause to regret it. Count Charlier came here to see me, and I refuse to countenance your clumsy attempts to engage his interest in your silly babble!"

"But—I insist—" stammered the greatly embarrassed Count, "allow me, madame, let me say, I call on you all—all—"

"Nothing of the sort!" declared Miss Lucy; "you came, Count, to play bridge with us. Our opponents behaved so rudely and played so badly it was impossible for us to continue the game. Nor can we enjoy music in this inharmonious atmosphere. Let us stroll in the conservatory, you and I."

She rose, trailing her heavy silks and flashing her sparkling jewels, and the Count, a little hesitatingly, followed her. They crossed the great hall, and, going through a reception room and the delightful sun-parlor, came to the warm, heavily-scented conservatory.

"Poor old Charlier!" said Haviland, as the pair disappeared; "he's in for it now! Do you suppose the palms and orchids will bring him up to the scratch? 'Nita, I'll bet you a box of gloves against a box of simple little cigarettes that he doesn't propose to the lady to-night?"

"Done!" cried Miss Frayne, who was sparkling again, now that the dread presence was removed. "I doubt he can help himself. She has him at her mercy. And he's too good-mannered to disappoint her wish."

"He'll propose," said Pauline, with an air of conviction. "He's a typical fortune-hunter, that man. Indeed, I am not sure he's a Count at all. Do you know, Mr. Illsley?"

"I know almost nothing of the man, save that he's a guest of the Frothinghams. That's not entirely in his favor, I think."

"Right you are!" agreed Haviland. "'Those people are,—well, they're to be queried. But I say, Polly, if the two do hit it off, it's grinding poverty for us, eh?"

"It may be a blessed relief, Gray. She'll give us something, of course, and send us away from here. I, for one, shouldn't be sorry to go. She is getting too impossible!"

"She is!" put in Anita; "every day she pounds us worse! I'd like to kill her!"

The fierce words and would-be menacing glance of the little blonde beauty were about as convincing as a kitten declaring himself a war lord, and even the stately Pauline smiled at the picture.

"She ought to be killed," declared Haviland, "and I say this dispassionately. I wouldn't do it, because killing is not in my line, but the eternal fitness of things requires her removal to another sphere of usefulness. She makes life a burden to three perfectly good people, and some several servants. Not one would mourn her, and—"

"Oh, stop, Gray!" cried Pauline; "don't talk in that strain! Don't listen to him, Mr. Illsley. He often says such things, but he doesn't mean them. Mr. Haviland loves to talk at random, to make a sensational hearing."

"Nothing of the sort, Polly. I do mean it. Lucy Carrington is a misery dispenser, and such are not wanted in this nice little old world."

"But perhaps," Pauline looked thoughtful, "the fault is in us. We don't like her, and so we see nothing good in what she does. Now, Carrington Loria adores her. She had a letter from him to-day—"

"Yes, Loria adores her!" interrupted Haviland, "because he doesn't live with her! She sends him love-letters and money, and he doesn't know the everlasting torture of living under her roof, year in and year out! But he caught on a little the last time he was here. He said,—well, in his quaint Oriental fashion, he said, 'Gee! she's the limit!' that's what he said."

"Well, she is," pouted Anita. "I can't do a thing to suit her. To-day I wrote a letter over six times before she was satisfied. And every change she wanted made was so foolish she wanted it changed back again. She nearly drove me crazy!"

"But I have to put up with her morning, noon, and night," sighed Pauline. "You have your hours off, Anita, but I never do. She even wakens me in the night to read to her, or to help her plan her new gowns."

"It is awfully hard for you," began Mr. Illsley, and then all stopped short, for the object of their discussion returned to the room.

It was plain to be seen Miss Carrington was in a state of suppressed excitement. She giggled almost hysterically, and tapped the Count playfully on the arm with her fan, as she bade him say good-night and go.

The interested ones watching her could not learn whether the Count had declared himself or not. The presumption was negative, for, had he done so, surely Miss Carrington would have told the good news.

Charlier himself was distinctly non-committal. Debonair as always, he made his adieux, no more demonstrative to his hostess than to the others, and went away. Illsley followed, and the household dispersed. The clock struck midnight as the ladies went upstairs.

Following custom, they all three went to Miss Lucy's boudoir. It was by way of reporting for to-morrow's orders, and was a duty never neglected.

The exquisite apartment, from which opened the bedroom and bath, was softly lighted and fragrant with flowers.

"How do you like Count Henri Charlier?"

Miss Carrington quickly demanded of her satellites.

"Charming," said the voluble Anita. "Just a typical French nobleman, isn't he? And how he adores our Lady Lucy!"

The whole speech rang false, but the vanity of the lady addressed swallowed it as truest sincerity.

"Yes," she returned, "he is infatuated, I have reason to think. But—we shall see what we shall see! Curb your impatience, girls! You shall know all in due time."

"Can I do anything for you, Auntie, to-night or to-morrow?" asked Pauline, and, though she tried to speak with enthusiasm, her tone did sound perfunctory.

"Not if you offer in that manner," and Miss Carrington looked at her niece coldly. "One would think, Pauline, that it must be an irksome task to do the smallest favor for your aunt and benefactor! Do you feel no pleasure in doing what trifles you can for one who does everything for you?"

"I would feel a pleasure, Aunt Lucy, if you were kinder to me. But—"

"Kinder!" shrieked her aunt; "kinder! Girl, have you taken leave of your senses? I give you a home, fine dresses, money, everything you can want, and you ask me to be kinder to you! Go! never let me see you again, after that speech!"

"Oh, auntie, don't! I didn't mean—"

"You didn't mean to exasperate me beyond endurance? No, of course you meant to stop short of that! But you have done it. I mean this, Pauline: to-morrow you go elsewhere to live. No longer will I give a home to such a monster of ingratitude!"

"But, Miss Carrington" —and Anita Frayne's soft voice implored gently "don't be hasty. Pauline didn't mean—"

"What!" and Lucy Carrington turned on her, "you take her part? Then you go, too! I want no ingrates here. Leave me, both of you. This night is your last beneath this roof! You are two unworthy girls, to scorn and slight the hand that has fed and clothed you and given you luxury and comfort such as you will never see again! Go, I've done with you! Send me Estelle. She, at least, has some small affection for me."

The two girls left the room. The scene was not without precedent. Before this they had been ordered to leave the house forever, but always forgiveness and reinstatement had followed. This time, however, the Lady Lucy had been rather more in earnest, and the girls looked at each other uncertainly as they turned toward their rooms.

Anita summoned Estelle, the French maid, and then told her to hasten immediately to Miss Carrington.

"Don't undress me," said the mistress as the maid appeared; "I'm not retiring at once. Get me out of this gown and give me a negligee and slippers."

"Yes, mademoiselle," and Estelle deftly obeyed orders and brought a white boudoir gown edged with swansdown.

"Not that!" cried Miss Carrington. "Bring the gold-embroidered one,—the Oriental."

"Ah, the green one, from Monsieur Loria?"

"Yes, the one my nephew sent me at Christmas time. My, but it's handsome, isn't it, Estelle?"

"Gorgeous!" declared the maid, and she spoke truly. Young Loria knew his aunt's taste, and he had sent her a typical Egyptian robe, of pale green silk, heavy with gold embroideries. In it Miss Carrington looked like one attired for a masquerade.

"Shall I take down mademoiselle's hair?" asked Estelle, lingering.

"No. I want to be alone. I will read awhile. You need not return. I will do for myself."

"There is your glass of milk, ma'mzelle, on the bed-table."

"Silly! I suppose I can see it for myself."

"Yes, ma'am. And you will have your tea at eight in the morning?"

"Of course, my tea at eight. As always. You might remember that much yourself. But nobody remembers things for my comfort."

"Pardon, but sometimes it is eight, and, again, it must be half-past."

"Eight! Now, will you go? You are most exasperating! Why do you stand there like a gibbering idiot?"

"The jewels, mademoiselle; the pearls! Shall I not put them in safety?"

"No! I will put them in the safe myself. Where is the key?"

"There, mademoiselle, on your dresser. But if I might—"

"You mayn't do anything except to get out and stay out! Do you hear? Shall I never be obeyed?"

"Yes, mademoiselle; good-night."

The soft tone was fully belied by the evil glare of the French girl's eyes, but that was not seen by Miss Lucy Carrington.

CHAPTER 3: THE TRAGEDY

THE house faced the east, and, built on an English model, was far wider than deep. A broad hall ran through the centre from front to back, and on either side there were successive rooms whose windows looked out on equally beautiful scenes, both front and back. On the right of the hall, as one entered, was the long living room, and beyond it, the library and music room. The other side of the hall was a reception room, opening into the sun parlor, and on to the conservatory, and back of these, the dining room and smaller breakfast room.

Breakfast was served at nine, and the members of the family were usually all present. Miss Carrington, herself, made a point of being on time partly from habit, and also because it gave her opportunity to chide those who were late.

When she was not in her place, on the morning after the stormy bridge game, Pauline expressed surprise, and Haviland echoed her words.

But Anita said scornfully, "She went to bed in an awful tantrum and probably didn't sleep well."

Miss Frayne was looking her prettiest, and her roseleaf face with its fluffy golden halo, was like a Greuze picture. She wore a frivolous little house gown of blue crepe de chine that just matched her forget-me-not eyes. Not especially appropriate garb for a secretary, but Miss Carrington preferred her household to be well-dressed, and really commanded pretty tints and fabrics for the two girls. Pauline was in white serge, of rather severe cut, but which suited her as no frills and flounces could. Her black hair was smoothly parted and coiled low over her ears, and her clear ivory-tinted skin was flushed faintly pink from the glow of the big, crackling wood fire.

"It's most unusual," went on Pauline, after a few moments more had passed, and the Lady Lucy had not appeared. "I'm going up to see if she is ill,—"

"Or merely in a tantrum extraordinary!" said Anita, her blue eyes full of laughing disrespect for her employer.

"'Nita," said Haviland, as Pauline disappeared, "hold your breakfast napkin up in front of your face, quick!"

"Why?" said the girl, wonderingly, as she did his bidding.

"Because, if you hadn't, I should have flown at you and kissed you! And I mustn't now, for Haskins is approaching with muffins."

Down came the shielding napkin and only the arrival of the muffin-laden Haskins saved the lovely laughing face from Haviland's impetuous caress.

The old butler fussed about, and several minutes passed, when Pauline called from above stairs, "Gray! Come here, at once!"

"Desperate case!" and Haviland rose, and unhurriedly left the room, pinching Anita's little ear as he passed her.

Another moment and Miss Frayne heard an exclamation from Haviland that made her rise from the table and go flying upstairs herself. The door of Miss Lucy's boudoir was open, and entering, she saw Pauline and Haviland with horror-stricken faces, gazing at a terrible sight. Miss Lucy Carrington, seated before her dressing-table, her face white and ghastly, her large eyes staring wide—staring horribly,—but, without doubt, unseeing. Nor was this all of the strangeness of the sight. She was robed in an embroidered Oriental-looking gown, and wore many jewels. Her red-dyed hair, dressed elaborately, as she had worn it the night before, was still crowned with the enormous comb of carved tortoise-shell, but the comb was broken to bits.

One portion, still standing upright, rose above the disordered coiffure, but the rest, in broken scraps, lay scattered over the puffs of hair,—over the white hands clasped in her lap,—and on the floor at her feet.

"What does it mean?" whispered Anita, shuddering, "is she—is she dead?"

"Yes," answered Haviland, briefly. He stood, hands in pockets, gazing at the startling figure.

"Who?—What?—" Anita's eyes riveted themselves on something else.

Around the neck of Miss Lucy was,—yes, it was—a snake!

With a low scream, Anita flung herself into Haviland's arms, but he put her gently away from him.

Aghast at this repulse, Anita put her hand across her eyes and turned to leave the room.

"Mind where you go, 'Nita!" called out Haviland, and the girl stopped just in time to save herself from stepping into a mass of debris.

"Why!" she cried, "why, it's Miss Lucy's tray!"

It was. The silver tray that had held the breakfast tea was on the floor, and near it a jumbled heap of silver and broken china that had once been a costly Sevres set. Dainty white serviettes were stained with the spilled tea and a huge wet spot was near the overturned silver teapot.

Hastily Anita ran from the room, but she sank down on a couch in the hall just outside the door, utterly unable to go further.

Fascinated by the beady eyes of the green snake, Pauline stared at it, with clenched hands.

Haviland stepped nearer and lightly touched it.

"Is it—is it alive?" gasped Pauline.

"It's paper," replied Haviland quietly. "A paper snake, a toy,—you know."

"But who put it there? Aunt Lucy is deathly afraid of snakes! Did fright kill her? Gray, is she—murdered?"

"Yes, Pauline, she has been killed. But could it be— fright? Impossible!"

"Not for her! You don't know her horror of snakes. Why, going through the Japanese department of a shop, I've seen her turn white and fairly fly from the counter where those paper things were displayed."

"But what else killed her? There is no wound, no shot, no blood."

"Get the doctor, Gray! Don't wait a minute. Telephone at once."

"He can do nothing, Pauline. She is dead." Haviland spoke like a man in a daze.

"But no matter, we must call him. Shall I?"

"No, I will."

"Go into her bedroom,—use that telephone by her bedside."

Obediently, Haviland went on to the adjoining room, the soft rugs giving forth no sound of his footfalls.

The door was ajar, and as he opened it, he called, "Come here, Pauline; look, the night lights are burning, and the bed untouched. She hasn't been to bed at all."

"Of course she hasn't. She has her hair as it was last evening. But her comb is broken."

"Broken! It's smashed! It's in tiny bits! She has been hit on the head,—don't touch her, Pauline! You mustn't! I'll call Dr. Stanton. You go out of the room. Go and find Anita."

But Pauline stayed. Turning her back to the still figure in the chair, she gazed curiously at the upset tray on the floor. She stooped, when Haviland's voice came sharply from the next room. "Don't touch a thing, Pauline!" he cried, as he held his hand over the transmitter.

She looked up, and then as she saw him turn back to speak into the instrument, she stooped swiftly and picking up something from the floor she hurried from the room.

She found Anita on the couch in the hall, and speaking somewhat sharply, Pauline said, "Where's Estelle?"

"Mercy! I don't know!" and Anita's blue eyes stared coldly. "How should I know anything about Estelle?"

"But she must have brought that tray an hour ago. Did she upset it, or who?"

"Pauline, why do you act as if I knew anything about this matter. Is it because you do?"

The blue eyes, cold like steel, and the dark ones, flashing fire from their shadows, looked steadily at each other.

Gray Haviland came hurriedly out to the hall.

"The doctor will be here at once," he said; "and he will call the coroner."

"Coroner!" screamed Anita; and ran away to her own room.

"Let her alone," said Pauline, contemptuously; "but Gray, we must nerve ourselves up to this thing. Don't you think we ought to—to put away the jewels? It's wrong to let any one come into a room where a fortune in jewels is displayed like that."

"But Doctor Stanton said to touch nothing, —nothing at all. You see, Pauline, in a murder case,—"

"Oh, I know; 'nothing disturbed till the Coroner comes,' and all that. But this is different, Gray. Doctor Stanton didn't know there are two hundred thousand dollars' worth of jewelry on that—that—on her."

"How do you know so exactly?"

"I'm not exact, but she has told me times enough that the rope of pearls cost one hundred thousand, and that corsage ornament she is wearing and her rings and ear-rings are easily worth the same sum. I tell you there will be policemen here, and it isn't right to throw temptation in their way."

"Besides," and Anita's voice spoke again as she reappeared in the doorway, "besides, Pauline, they are all yours now, and you should be careful of them!"

The tone more than the words conveyed a veiled insolence, and Pauline accepted it for such. With a sudden determined movement, she went swiftly to her aunt's side, and unfastened the long rope of pearls, the wonderful glittering sunburst, and a large diamond and emerald crescent that held together the glistening silk folds.

The rings and ear-rings she could not bring herself to touch.

"It is only right," she contended, as if trying to persuade herself, "these are too valuable to risk; no one could fail to be tempted by them."

"Why don't you finish your task?" said Anita, smiling unpleasantly, "why leave so much?"

"No one would attempt to take the rings or ear-rings," said Pauline, steadily, "and that scarab bracelet is not of great value."

"I thought that was a most valuable antique that her nephew sent her."

"She thought so, too," said Pauline, carelessly, "but Carr told me it was an imitation. Not one expert in a hundred can tell the difference, anyway."

As Pauline placed the mass of gems in the safe, the doctor came. "What does it mean?" cried the bewildered man, coming into the room. "Miss Carrington—"

Words failed him as he saw the astounding sight. For surely, no one had ever before seen a murdered woman, sitting before her dressingtable, staring but smiling, and garbed as for a fancy-dress ball!

Doctor Stanton touched the icy-cold hand, felt for the silent heart, and then turned his attention to the disheveled hair and broken comb.

"Fractured skull," he said, as his skilled fingers thridded the auburn tresses. "Killed by a sudden, swift blow on the head with a heavy, blunt,—no, with a soft weapon; a black-jack or sandbag."

"A burglar!" exclaimed Pauline.

"Of course; who else would deal such a blow? It was powerful,—dealt by a strong arm—it has driven bits of this broken shell stuff into the brain. But it was the force of the concussion that killed her. Here is a deep dent,—

and yet.—Tell me the circumstances. Why is she rigged out like this?"

"I've no idea," answered Pauline, taking the initiative. "When I left her last night, she had on an evening gown. But this negligee is not unusual; it is one of her favorites. Though why she has on that spangled scarf, I can't imagine."

"She seems to have been posing before the mirror, rather than engaged in making a toilette." Dr. Stanton was a pompous middleaged man of fussy manner. He did not again touch the body, but he stepped about, noting the strange conditions and commenting on them. "This paper snake,—tight round her neck! What does that mean?"

"What can it mean?" returned Pauline.

"She had an intense hatred,—even fear of snakes; I've never seen it before. Could it have been placed there to frighten her to death?"

"No; she didn't die of fright. See, her expression is placid,—even smiling. But the shattered comb and dented skull have but one explanation,—a stunning blow. Did she have on the comb last evening?"

"Yes; it is a favorite one with her. An heirloom, from a Colonial ancestor. It encircled the entire back of her head, when whole."

"At what time was she killed?" asked Gray Haviland. He had stood, till now, a silent listener to the conversation between Pauline and the Doctor.

"Oh, many hours ago," returned Stanton; "six or eight at least. Evidently she was preparing for bed, and trying the effect of some new finery."

"Those things are not new," put in Anita; "she has had them all a long time. But she must have been admiring herself, for when we found her she had on all her finest jewels."

"What?" cried Dr. Stanton; "where are they?"

"I took most of them off," replied Pauline, quietly, "and put them in the safe. If the police people must come,

I am not willing to have a fortune in jewels here to tempt their cupidity. And I have a right. It is no secret that my cousin Carrington and I are her heirs. But that snake perplexes me beyond all else. If you knew her aversion to them,—even pictured ones—"

"I do know it," returned the doctor; " I have often heard her say so. Ah," as he stepped carefully about, "she was adorning herself; see, here is powder scattered on the floor. She used this powder-puff, shaking it over the rug and floor."

"I saw that the first thing!" cried Pauline, excitedly; "and there was a " she stopped, looking in amazement at the white dust on the floor. For where she had seen a distinct footprint, as of a stockinged foot, there was now merely a blurred whirl! Some one had obliterated that footprint!

"A what? " asked the doctor, sharply. "Nothing. A—a lot of powder spilled,—I was going to say."

Gray Haviland looked at her. "Tell the truth, Pauline," he said.

"I have," she replied, with a calm quite equalling his own. "Must we have the Coroner, Dr. Stanton?"

"Yes, yes, of course; I will telephone at once. There will be police and detectives,—oh, it is a terrible case! Nothing must be touched, nothing! If there is any clue to this mystery, do not let it be disturbed."

"But you say it was without doubt a burglar who did it," said Anita, her wide eyes gleaming blue.

"It must have been."

"Then why were none of her jewels stolen?"

"Bless my soul!" and Dr. Stanton looked as if a bomb had exploded at his feet. "Sure enough! It cannot have been a burglar! Who, then? What other motive than robbery—"

"It was a burglar," declared Pauline, "and he was—he was frightened away by—by a noise something—"

"Not likely!" said Anita, "with all those gems in easy reach!"

"The Coroner and the police must get here at once!" and the doctor wiped his perspiring brow. "Never have I seen such an inexplicable state of affairs! Was—was Miss Carrington indisposed at all last evening? Did she say or do anything unusual?"

"Not at all," began Pauline, but Anita interrupted; "Yes, she did! She said, 'You little know what's going to happen to me! Tomorrow you may sing another tune!'"

"What did she mean by that?"

"I've no idea. Could it mean suicide?"

"No!" thundered the doctor;" her skull was fractured by some one bent on wilful murder! As there is no robbery, we must look for a deeper motive and a cleverer villain than any professional burglar!"

Chapter 4: A Paper Snake

ON the third floor was the bedroom of the maid, Estelle, and before its locked door stood Pauline and Anita, demanding admittance. There was no response from inside, until Pauline said sternly, "Unless you open this door at once, Estelle, the police will force it open."

The key turned, the door moved slowly ajar, and Estelle's face appeared, wearing an expression of amazement.

"What is it you say, Miss Pauline? The police? Why?"

The maid was making a very evident effort to appear composed, and was succeeding wonderfully well. Her eyes were reddened with weeping,—a condition which a hasty dabbing of powder had not concealed. She was nervously trembling, but her air of injured innocence, if assumed, was admirable.

"Estelle," and Pauline loomed tall and magnificent as an accusing angel, "what do you know of your mistress' death?"

Estelle gave a shriek and threw herself on her bed in apparent hysterics.

"Don't begin that!" ordered Pauline, "sit up here and tell the truth."

"But," and the maid sat up, sobbing, "I know nothing. How can I?"

"Nonsense! You took the tea-tray to her at eight o'clock. What did you see?"

Estelle shrugged her shoulders. "I saw Miss Carrington sitting before her mirror. She, I assumed, was engrossed in reverie, so I set down the tray on a tabouret and departed."

"You noticed nothing amiss?" said Anita, staring at the girl.

"No; I scarce looked at the lady. She reproved me harshly last night, and I had no wish, to annoy her. I set down the tray with haste and silently departed."

"You set it down? Who, then, overturned it?"

"Overturned? Is it then upset?" Estelle's manner was the impersonal one of the trained servant, who must show surprise at nothing, but it was a trifle overdone.

"Estelle, stop posing. Wake up to realities. Miss Carrington is dead! Do you hear? Dead!"

"Ah! Mon Dieu! Did it then kill her?" and Estelle's calm gave way and she screamed and moaned in wild hysterics.

"What can we do with her?" asked Anita, helplessly; "she must know all about the—the—"

"The murder," said Pauline calmly. "But she will tell us nothing. It is useless to question her. The Coroner will attend to it, anyway."

"The Coroner," and Anita looked frightened. "Will he question all of us?"

"Of course he will. And, Anita," Pauline whirled on her suddenly, "what are you going to say was the errand that took you to Aunt Lucy's room after one o'clock last night?"

"I! Nothing of the sort! I was not in her room after we left it together."

"I saw you. Don't trouble to deny it," and Pauline dropped her eyelids as one bored by a conversation.

"You did!" and Anita's flower face turned rosy pink and her blue eyes blazed with an intensity that Pauline's dark ones could never match. "Be careful, Pauline Stuart, or I shall tell what I know! You dare to make up such a story! It was I who saw you come from your aunt's room at a late hour! What have you to say now?"

"Nothing—to you," and Pauline swept from the room and returned slowly down the stairway to the second floor.

The sight of two police officers in the hall gave her a sudden start. How had they appeared, so soon? And how dreadful to see them in the palatial home that had heretofore housed only gentle-mannered aristocrats and obsequious liveried servants! The men looked ill at ease as they stood against the rich background of tapestry hangings and tropical palms, but their faces showed a stern appreciation of their duty, and they looked at Pauline with deferential but acute scrutiny.

Not noticing them in any way, the girl, her head held high, went straight to her aunt's room. Sergeant Flake was in charge, and he refused her admission.

"Coroner's orders, ma'am," he said; "he'll be here himself shortly, and then you can see him."

"Come away, Pauline," and Haviland appeared and took her by the arm; "where's Anita?"

"I left her in Estelle 's room. Oh Gray, that girl—"

"Hush!" and gripping her firmly, Haviland led her to a small sitting room and shut the door. "Now listen, Pauline; mind what I say. Don't give the least bit of information or express the slightest notion of opinion except to the chief authorities. And not to them until they ask you. This is a terrible affair, and a mighty strange one."

"Who did it, Gray?"

"Never you mind. Don't even ask questions. The very walls have ears!"

"Who upset that breakfast tray?"

"Estelle, of course."

"She says she didn't."

"She lies. Everybody will lie; why, Pauline, you must lie yourself."

"I won't do it! I have no reason to!"

"You may find that you have. But, at least, Pauline, I beg of you, that you will keep your mouth shut. There will be developments soon, —there must be,—and then we will know what to do."

The two returned to the boudoir. At first glance it seemed to be full of men. The beautiful room, with its ornate but harmonious furnishings and appointments of the Marie Antoinette period, was occupied with eager representatives of the law and justice hunting for any indication of the ruthless hand that had felled the owner of all that elegance.

Coroner Scofield was receiving the report of Doctor Moore, who had arrived with him. Dr. Moore agreed with Dr. Stanton that the deceased had been struck with a heavy weapon that had fractured the skull, but he admitted the wounds showed some strange conditions which could only be explained by further investigation.

The Coroner was deep in thought as he studied the face of the dead woman. "It is most mysterious," he declared; "that face is almost smiling! it is the face of a happy woman. Clearly, she did not know of her approaching fate."

"The blow was struck from behind," informed Dr. Moore.

"Even so, why didn't she see the approach of the assailant in the mirror? She is looking straight into the large glass,—must have been looking in it at the moment of her death. Why receive that death blow without a tremor of fear or even a glance of startled inquiry?"

Inspector Brunt stood by, gravely, and for the most part silently, watching and listening. "That might imply," he said, slowly, "that if she did see the assailant, it was some one she knew, and of whom she had no fear."

Gray Haviland looked up suddenly. A deep red spread over his face and then, seeing himself narrowly watched by the detectives present, he set his lips firmly together and said no word. Pauline turned white and trembled, but she too said nothing.

"Why is she sitting in this large easy chair?" went on the Coroner; "Is it not customary for ladies at their dressing tables to use a light sidechair?"

This showed decidedly astute perception, and the Inspector looked interestedly at the chair in question, which he had not especially noticed before.

Being tacitly appealed to by the Coroner's inquiring eyes, Pauline replied: "It is true that my aunt usually sat at her dressing-table in a small chair,—that one, in fact," and she pointed to a dainty chair of gilded cane. "I have no idea why she should choose the heavy, cushioned one."

"It would seem," the Coroner mused, "as if she might have sat down there to admire the effect of her belongings rather than to arrange her hair or toilette."

Absorbedly, all present watched Coroner Scofield's movements.

It was true, the quietly reposeful attitude of the still figure leaning back against the brocaded upholstery, and so evidently looking in the great gold-framed mirror, was that of one admiring or criticising her own appearance. Added to this, the fact of her bizarre costume and strange adornments, it seemed certain that Miss Carrington had come to her death while innocently happy in the feminine employment of dressing up in the elaborate finery that she loved.

But the snake! Carefully Coroner Scofield removed the inexplicable thing. He held it up that all might see. A Japanese paper snake, a cheap toy, such as is found together with fans and lanterns in the Oriental department of large shops.

"Could this have been placed round her neck after death?" Scofield inquired of the doctors. The two physicians agreed, that though that was possible, yet the appearance of the flesh beneath it seemed to indicate its having encircled the throat during life.

"Never!" cried Pauline, excitedly. "Aunt Lucy couldn't have sat there and smiled, with a snake anywhere near her!"

"That would seem so," and Dr. Stanton nodded his head. "I well know of my late patient's aversion to snakes. It amounted almost to a mania! It is not an uncommon one, many women feel the same, though Seldom to so great an extent."

"That deepens the mystery," said Coroner Scofield; "unless, indeed, the snake was put on after the crime. But that is even more mysterious. I shall now remove these valuable jewels, and give them to—"

He looked inquiringly at Haviland and Pauline, and the latter immediately responded: "Give them to me, Mr. Scofield. I am now mistress here."

Haviland said nothing, but he looked at Pauline as if in disapproval.

"Is this of great worth?" inquired Scofield, as he carefully removed the scarf from the shoulders it surrounded.

"Only moderately so," returned Pauline. "It is a Syrian scarf and was sent to her by her nephew who lives in Egypt. It is not new, he sent several to us about a year ago."

She took the long, heavy, white and silver drapery, and laid it in a nearby wardrobe. Then the Coroner unfastened the large pearls from their place as eardrops, and taking up one lifeless hand removed its rings. All these he handed to Pauline without a word.

"What is this?" he exclaimed suddenly; and opening the curled-up fingers of the other hand he drew forth a crumpled gray object. It was a glove, of soft suede, and so tightly had it been held that it was deeply creased.

"A man's glove!" said the Coroner, smoothing it out. "Will the wonders of this case never cease?"

He scrutinized it, but remarking only that it was of medium size and superior quality, he laid it carefully aside for the time. From the same arm he removed the scarab bracelet, also handing that to Pauline.

"The lady was fond of Oriental jewelry," he observed.

"Yes," returned Haviland, before Pauline could speak. "Her nephew sent or brought home much of it. But, as we informed you, Miss Carrington was also wearing pearls and diamonds of enormous value, compared to which these trinkets are as nothing."

"But scarabs, I am told, are of great price."

"Some are," returned Haviland. "That bracelet, however, is not genuine, nor of great value."

Then the Coroner, with delicate touch, removed the bits of broken tortoise-shell from the puffs of hair, and carefully laid them together on a small silver tray he appropriated from the dressing-table litter.

"I think," said Inspector Brunt, in his grave, slow way, "that it will be wise to photograph the whole picture from several points of view before the autopsy is performed."

Arrangements had been made for this, and Detective Hardy, a young man from Headquarters, stepped forward with his camera.

As those who were asked to left the room, Pauline and Gray went out together, and met Anita just outside in the hall.

"Oh, tell me, Gray! Who did it? What does it all mean?" she cried, and grasped him by the arm.

"Tell her about it, Gray," said Pauline, and leaving the two together, she went swiftly along the hall to her own room.

The alert eyes of the guarding policemen followed her, but also they followed the movements of every one else, and if they had, as yet, any suspicions, no one knew of them.

Meantime, the grewsome work of photography went on.

Surely never was such a strange subject for the camera! Denuded of her jewels, but still robed in her gorgeous dressing-gown, and still leaning back in her luxurious arm-chair, with that strange smile of happy expectancy, Miss Lucy Carrington presented the same air of regal authority she had always worn in life. Her eyes were widely staring, but there was no trace or hint of fear in her peaceful attitude of repose.

"There's no solution!" said Inspector Brunt, deeply thoughtful. "No one could or would crack a skull like that, but an experienced and professional burglar and housebreaker.And such a one could have but one motive, robbery, and the jewels were not stolen!"

"Inside job," observed Scofield, briefly, his eyes on his work.

"Maybe the burglar was frightened away at the critical moment."

"No. Whatever frightened him would be known to some member of the family."

"Maybe it is."

"Hey? Have you a theory?" and the Coroner looked up suddenly.

"Anything but! There's no possible theory that will fit the facts."

"Except the truth."

"Yes, except the truth. But it will be long before we find that, I'm afraid. It strikes me it's at the bottom of an unusually deep well."

"Well, you'd better find it. It'd be a nice how d' y' do for you to fall down on this case!"

"There's no falling down been done yet. And it may well be that the very fact of there being such strange and irreconcilable conditions shall prove a help rather than a hindrance."

And then, all being in readiness, the lifeless form of Miss Carrington, once the proud domineering autocrat, now laid low, was borne to a distant room, for the autopsy that might cast a further light on the mystery of her tragic death.

CHAPTER 5: A MAN'S GLOVE

INSPECTOR BRUNT and the young detective, Hardy, were interviewing the members of the household in the library, and the task was not an easy one. The two girls were distinctly at odds, and Gray Haviland, whether authoritatively or not, persisted in assuming a major role.

"It seems to me," Haviland said, "that it is the most remarkable mystery that has ever occurred in the experience of you police people. Now, I think the wisest plan is to call in a big detective,—no offence, Mr. Hardy,—but I mean a noted fellow, like Stone, say, and let him get at the root of the crime."

"I think, Gray," and Pauline looked very haughty, "that any such suggestion would come better from me. I am now mistress of the place, and it is for me to say what we shall do."

"I know it," and Haviland looked no whit abashed, "but you know Carr Loria is equally in authority, even if he isn't here, and you see—"

"I don't see that Carr's absence gives you any authority!"

"But it does, in a way. As Miss Lucy's man of affairs, I ought to look out for the interests of her heirs, at least, for the absent one. I'm sure Loria would want to do everything possible to find the murderer."

"Has this nephew been notified yet?" asked Inspector Brunt.

"Yes," returned Pauline; "we've telephoned a cablegram to the city to be sent to him in Egypt. But I don't know when he will get it, nor when we'll get a response."

"Where is he?"

"His permanent address is Cairo, but he is off in the desert, or somewhere, so much that sometimes he is away from communication for weeks at a time. Still I've sent it, that's all I can do."

"What did you tell him?"

"I made it rather long and circumstantial. I told him of Aunt Lucy's death, and that she was killed by a blow on the head by a burglar, which fractured her skull. I asked him if he would come home or if we should go there. You see, we were intending to sail for Egypt in February."

"Who were?"

"Myself, my aunt, Miss Frayne and Mr. Haviland. Carrington Loria has been begging us to make the trip, and at last Aunt Lucy decided to go. Our passage is engaged, and all plans made."

"And now?"

"Now, I do not know. Everything is uncertain. But if the burglar can be found, and punished, I see no reason why I, at least, shouldn't go on and make the trip. The others must please themselves."

Pauline looked at Anita and at Haviland with a detached air, as if now they were no longer members of the household, and their plans did not concern her.

Not so Haviland. "Sure I'll go," he cried; "I fancy Carr will be mighty glad to keep me on in the same capacity I served Miss Carrington. He'll need a representative in this country. I doubt he'll come over,—there's no need, if I look after all business matters for him."

"What does he do in Egypt?" asked the Inspector, who was half engrossed looking over his memoranda, and really took slight interest in the absent heir.

"He's excavating wonderful temples and things," volunteered Anita, for Pauline and Gray were looking, amazed, at a man who came into the room. He was the detective who had been left in charge of the boudoir, and he carried a strange-looking object.

"What is it?" cried Pauline.

"It's a black-jack." replied the detective."I found it, Inspector, just under the edge of the tassel trimmin' of the lounge. The fellow slung it away, and it hid under the fringe, out of sight."

Gravely, Inspector Brunt took the weapon. It was rudely made, of black cloth, a mere bag, long and narrow, and filled with bird shot.

"That's the weapon!" declared Brunt. "A man could hit a blow with that thing that would break the skull without cutting the skin. Yes, there is no further doubt that Miss Carrington was murdered by a burglar. This is a burglar's weapon; this it was that crushed the shell comb to fragments, and fractured the skull, leaving the body sitting upright, and unmutilated. Death was, of course, instantaneous."

"But the jewels!" said Detective Hardy, wonderingly; "why—"

"I don't know why!" said Brunt, a little testily; "that is for you detectives to find out. I have to go by what evidence I find. Can I find a broken skull and a black-jack in the same room and not deduce a burglarious assault that proved fatal? The thief may have been scared off or decided he didn't want the loot, but that doesn't affect the certainty that we have the weapon and therefore the case is a simple one. That burglar can be found, without a doubt. Then we shall learn why he didn't steal the jewels."

"But the snake?" said Pauline, looking wonderingly at the Inspector; "the burglar must have been a maniac or an eccentric to put that snake round my aunt's neck after he killed her, —and nothing will ever make me believe that she allowed it there while alive!"

"That's what I say," put in Haviland; "the whole affair is so inexplicable,—excuse me, Mr. Brunt, but I can't think it such a simple case as you do,—that I think we should engage expert skill to solve the mysteries of it all."

"That must come later," and Inspector Brunt resumed his usual gravity of manner which had been disturbed by the discovery of the black-jack. "Will you now please give me some detailed information as to the circumstances? Is the house always securely locked at night?"

"Very much so," answered Haviland; "Miss Carrington was not overly timid, but she always insisted on careful precautions against burglary. She had a house full of valuable furniture, curios, and art works besides her personal belongings. Yes, the house was always supposed to be carefully locked and bolted."

"Whose duty is it to look after it?"

"The butler Haskins, and his wife, who is the cook, had all such matters in charge."

"I will interview them later. Now please tell me, any of you, why Miss Carrington was arrayed in such peculiar fashion, last evening."

"I can't imagine," said Pauline. "My aunt was not a vain woman. I have never known her to sit before a mirror, except when necessary, to have her hair dressed. It is almost unbelievable that she should deliberately don those jewels and scarf and sit down there as if to admire the effect. Yet it had that appearance."

"But she wore the jewels during the evening, did she not?"

"Not all of them. She wore her pearls, because, as she told us, and as I have often heard her say, pearls must be worn occasionally to keep them in condition. But she added a large number of valuable gems—or, some one did,—after we left her last night."

"Whom do you mean by we?"

"Miss Frayne and myself. We were in her room, to say good-night to her, and we left at the same time."

"At what time?"

"About quarter past twelve, I should think, wasn't it, Anita? We went upstairs about midnight, and were with my aunt ten or fifteen minutes."

"Were your good-nights amicable?" asked the Inspector, and Pauline looked up in surprise.

Then, recollecting the last words of her aunt, she shut her lips obstinately and made no reply.

"Indeed, they were not!" declared Miss Frayne;" Miss Carrington told both Miss Stuart and myself that it would be our last night beneath this roof! That to-day we must seek some other home, for she would harbor us no longer!"

"Ah! And why did she thus treat you?"

"There was no especial reason," and Anita's lovely blue eyes looked straight at the Inspector with a pathetic gaze, "she was in a tantrum, as she frequently was."

"She didn't mean it," put in Pauline, hastily.

"She did!" asseverated Anita; "I've heard her threaten to send us away before, but never so earnestly. She meant it last night, I am sure. And, too, she knew something would happen to her last night,—she said so."

"What? what's that?"

"Do hush, Anita!" said Pauline; "those foolish words meant nothing!"

"Proceed, Miss Frayne," and the Inspector spoke sternly.

"She did," went on Anita "I don't remember the exact words, but she said I little knew what was going to happen to her, and she said 'to-morrow you may sing another song!' Surely such words meant something!"

"If they did," said Pauline, angrily, "they merely meant that she was going to dismiss you to-day!"

"Not at all," and Anita glanced at her, "she distinctly said something would happen to her, —not to me."

"You know better than to take things she said in a temper, seriously! If we are to repeat idle conversations, suppose I say that I heard you say last evening that you'd like to kill her!"

"I didn't!" shrieked Anita.

"You did," declared Pauline, calmly; "and Gray said she ought to be killed, too. I know you didn't mean to kill her, but I've just as much right to quote your foolish words as you have to quote hers."

"Nonsense!" said Haviland; "let up, Polly! You two are always at each other! As there is no question as to who killed poor Miss Lucy, why rake up our foolish words spoken under the intense provocation of her exhibition of temper,—which was specially trying last night. Inspector, can we tell you anything more of importance?"

So far the Inspector had been almost silent, and appeared to be learning some points from the conversation not addressed to him. Now, he changed his manner, and began briskly to ask questions.

"This glove," he said, holding it out, "was, as you know, found clasped in her hand. Is it yours, Mr. Haviland?"

"No," said the young man, as, after a close examination of the glove he handed it back; "no, it is a size smaller than I wear, and it is of a different make from mine."

"Have you any idea whose it can be? It is highy improbable the burglar left it."

"I've no idea," and Haviland shrugged his shoulders. "But if it was not left by the intruder, where could it possibly have come from? It is a man's glove."

"Could it be one of Cousin Carr's?" said Pauline. "Aunt Lucy was awfully fond of anything of his. She kept one of his caps in her drawer for months, after he left the last time."

"No," replied Haviland; "it isn't Loria's. He wears larger gloves than I do. My theory points to a sort of gentleman burglar, a 'Raffles,' you know, and I think he talked with Miss Lucy, before he struck that blow, and disarmed her mind of fear."

"What an extraordinary idea!" and Pauline looked thoughtful.

"But how else explain the glove?"

"And the snake! Did your gentleman burglar persuade her to wear that paper thing? Never! Gray, you're absurd!"

"Another thing," went on Inspector Brunt, returning the glove to bis roomy pocket-book; "In the bedroom we noticed a glass of milk and beside it an empty plate. Was it the lady's habit to have a night lunch?"

"Yes," said Anita; "but she rarely ate it. In case of insomnia, she had ready a light repast, but she almost never touched it."

"The glass of milk is still untouched," said Brunt, "but the plate is empty. What did it contain?"

"A sandwich, I think," said Anita. "That is what Estelle usually prepared for her. She will know,—Estelle, the maid."

"Miss Carrington's lady's maid?"

"Yes; though not hers exclusively. She was expected to act as maid for Miss Stuart and myself also, at such times as Miss Carrington didn't require her services."

"And she, then, brought the breakfast tray, that is upset on the floor?"

"Yes; Miss Lucy always had an early cup of tea, before she dressed for breakfast with the family."

"And the maid took it to her this morning? Did she not then discover the—the tragedy?"

"She says not!" cried Pauline; "but I'm sure she did! She says she saw Miss Lucy at the mirror, and thinking her engrossed, merely left the tray on the tabouret and went away."

"Ridiculous!" exclaimed Haviland; "What does Estelle mean by such lies? Of course she saw Miss Carrington's strange appearance, of course she was frightened out of her wits, and of course she dropped the tray and ran. But why not say so? And why not give an immediate alarm? She took that tray, probably, about eight. Pauline went up at nine. What was Estelle doing all that time? Why didn't she go in to dress Miss Carrington? I tell you, Mr. Inspector, there's a lot of queer work to be explained, and with all due respect to the force, I'm pretty sure you'll need expert service if you're going to get anywhere. And I'm sure, too, that if we can get word to Carrington Loria and back, he'll say spare no trouble or expense to avenge his aunt's murder. He is equally heir with you, Pauline, and he ought to be consulted."

"The will hasn't been read yet," said Miss Stuart; "we can't assume anything until that is done."

"Pshaw! you know perfectly well half of the bulk of the estate is yours and half Carr's. I have a small slice and Miss Frayne a bit. The older servants have small legacies, and there are a few charities. That, Mr. Brunt, is the gist of the will. Do you not agree with me, that as I was the man of business for the late Miss Carrington, I am justified, in the absence of Mr. Loria, in continuing my services, at least, until we can get definite directions from him?"

"Those matters are outside my province, Mr. Haviland. Miss Carrington's legal advisers will doubtless come here soon, and such things will be decided by them. Now, here's another point. I noted in the course of our investigation in the boudoir a quantity of powder fallen on the floor near the dressing table, in such relation to it that it would seem Miss Carrington was using the face powder as she sat there. Was this her habit?"

"Her habit? Yes;" said Anita, "Miss Carrington was in the habit of using face powder,—even cosmetics. It is not strange then, that such a proceeding was part of her night toilette."

"No, not at all," agreed Mr. Brunt. "But where the powder was thickest, on the hard floor, near the rug, was a muddled spot, as if some one had wiped out or swept up a mark or print. Can any of you explain this—"

No one spoke, and the stern voice went on. "I remember, Miss Stuart, that you began to say something bearing on this while we were in that room, and you suddenly stopped, appearing confused. I ask you why?"

Pauline hesitated, bit her lip, looked at Gray and then at Anita, and finally said, "I may as well tell. It is nothing. When I went to my aunt's room, and found what I did find,—I was so excited and nervous I scarce knew what I did. But I remember seeing a footprint in that powder, and in obedience to an impulsive instinct I —I obliterated it."

"With what?"

"With my handkerchief. I merely slapped at it, and the light powder flew about it."

"Why did you do this!"

"I don't know. I had no real reason. I was not thinking of what I was doing."

"Then you did not have a desire to shield some one from possible suspicion!" The words were shot at her so swiftly that Pauline gasped.

"Suspicion! What do you mean? Was it not the work of a burglar?"

"Was the impression of a foot that you saw, the foot of a man or a woman!"

"How can I tell? It was large, but as it was a bare or stockinged foot I could not judge. Might not the burglar have removed his boots, before entering the room?"

"He might, indeed, and that is just what he did do. For more prints of that stockinged foot have been discovered on the stairs, and there is no doubt that the tracks are those of the assailant of Miss Carrington. With your permission, Miss Stuart, I will now go to interview the servants. May I ask you to await me here, all of you? I shall not be very long."

As the Inspector and the detectives left the room, Haskins appeared to announce Mrs. Frothingham and Count Henri Chaxlier.

Chapter 6: A Neighbor's Call

"Oh, is it not terrible? What can I say to comfort you!"

Mrs. Frothingham's distressed tones and her air of eager, intense sympathy met with little response from Pauline.

Haviland had been called from the room on an errand and Anita's willingness to receive the neighbor's condolences did not seem acceptable. The overdressed, forward-mannered widow continued to direct her attention entirely to Pauline, and that young woman merely surveyed the visitor coolly and replied in monosyllables.

"Thanks," she said, and her icy air would have deterred a less determined intruder.

"I simply couldn't help running over as soon as I heard the dreadful news. For we are neighbors after all, though not so very well acquainted; and neighbors have a camaraderie of their own, I think."

"Yes?" said Pauline, and her eyelids fell slightly, with an expression of boredness.

"Yes, indeed," Mrs. Frothingham rattled on; "and I said to our dear Count, we must run over at once, there may be something we can do for the saddened ones."

"Thank you;" and had a marble statue been given vocal powers the effect would have been much the same.

"Dear friend," continued the unabashed visitor, "I know how overcome you must be—"

"I am not overcome at all," said Pauline, rising, and determined to hear no more; "and I must beg to be excused, Mrs. Frothingham, as I have many matters to attend to this morning."

"Ah, yes, of course, you have. We will not detain you. The Count and I merely called for a moment to inquire—"

"Yes, I quite understand. Miss Frayne will be pleased to answer your inquiries. Thank you both, and—good-morning."

With a polite but distant bow, Pauline left the room, and as Count Charlier sprang to hold the door open for her, he, after a moment's hesitation, followed her out.

"A moment, I beg, Miss Stuart," he said as they reached the hall; "You are offended at Mrs. Frothingham's intrusion, but have I not a right to call? Was I not such a friend of Miss Carrington as to justify this tribute of respect to her memory?"

"Certainly, Count," and Pauline grew a shade kinder, "but I am not sufficiently acquainted with your friend to receive her visits."

"Ah, no. That is conceded. But, I pray you, tell me of the sad affair. I have heard no details,—that is, unless you would rather not."

"No, I am not unwilling. You were a good friend of Aunt Lucy's—she was fond of you, and I am glad to talk to some one. Let us sit here."

Pauline indicated a recessed seat in the hall and the pair sat there. She recounted briefly the story of the tragedy and the Count was duly sympathetic. Pauline watched him closely, and discerned great interest but little grief or sorrow.

"A burglar, of course," said the Count hearing of the cruel weapon. "How could any one attack the charming lady! And the marvelous jewels she wore! They were, of course, stolen?"

"No; that's the strange part. They were not."

"Ah, how splendid!" and his absorbed air of satisfaction gave Pauline a thrill of disgust at his cold-bloodedness. "And now they are all yours? Those magnificent gems?"

"The property, most of it, is divided between my cousin and myself."

"Your cousin? Mr. Haviland?"

"No; he is but a distant connection. I mean my first cousin, Mr. Loria, now in Egypt."

"Ah, yes, I have heard Miss Carrington refer to him. He will come home?"

"I do not know. We have cabled of course. Count Charlier, do you remember hearing my aunt say, last evening, that she expected something to happen to her?"

"I remember, Miss Stuart."

"Have you any idea what she meant?"

"I? But how could I know?"

"Answer my question, please."

The Count's eyes fell, and he shifted his feet about uneasily. At last he said: "It is not pleasant to say such things, but since you ask, I may be permitted to assume that the late Miss Carrington had a regard for my humble self."

"And she expected, she—hoped that her regard might be returned?"

"It may be so."

"And that last night you might tell her so?"

"You honor me."

"Did you tell her so?"

"I did not, Miss Stuart. What might have happened had she lived I cannot say, but I did not, last evening, say any word to Miss Carrington of my aspiration to her hand."

"Did you say anything that could have been taken as a hint that some time, say, in the near future, you might express such an aspiration?"

"I may have done so."

"Thank you, Count Charlier. I had perhaps no right to ask, but you have answered my rather impertinent questions straightforwardly, and I thank you."

Pauline rose, as if to end the interview. In the doorway appeared Anita. "Pauline," she said, "I wish you would come back and listen to Mrs. Frothingham's story. It seems to me of decided importance."

"You have something to tell me?" asked Pauline, returning to the library and looking at the unwelcome neighbor with patient tolerance.

"Yes, Miss Stuart. Now, it may be nothing, —nothing, I mean, of consequence, that is, you may not think so, but I—"

"Suppose you let me hear it and judge for myself."

"Yes. Well, it's only this. I was wakeful last night, or rather early this morning, and looking from my bedroom window, which faces this house, I saw a man climb out of a window on the first floor and skulk away among the shrubbery."

"At what time was this?" and Pauline looked interested at last.

"About four o'clock. He was to all appearances a burglar—"

"How could you tell? Was it not dark at that hour in the morning?"

"No; the moon is past full, you know, and it shone brightly in the western sky."

"Enough for you to discern the man clearly?"

"I took a field-glass to assist my vision. He stealthily climbed out and skirting the bushes made his way swiftly toward the great gates."

"This is indeed an important bit of information, Mrs. Frothingham; I dare say you ought to tell it to the police who are here."

"Oh, I couldn't! I'm so timid about such things! But,— if you would go with me, Miss Stuart—"

"Miss Frayne will go with you," said Pauline, coolly; "You will find a policeman in the hall who will direct you where to find the Inspector."

Without another word Pauline bowed in a way to include the lady and the Count also, and went away to her own room.

"Stuck-up thing!" exclaimed Mrs. Frothingham, and Anita nodded her golden head in agreement.

Inspector Brunt instructed Hardy to hear the story of Mrs. Frothingham, and he devoted his own attention to Count Charlier, of whom he had heard as being a friend of Miss Carrington's. He quizzed the Frenchman rather pointedly as to his friendship with the unfortunate lady and the Count became decidedly ill at ease.

"Why do you ask me so much?" he objected; "I was a friend, yes; I may have aspired to a nearer relation, yes? That is no crime?"

"Not at all, Count," said Mr. Brunt; "I only want to find out if Miss Carrington's strange reference to something about to happen to her could have had any reference to you."

"It might be so; I cannot say. But all that has no bearing on the poor lady's death."

"No. At what time did you go away from here, Count Charlier?"

"At about midnight."

"You went directly home?"

"To Mrs. Frothingham's, where I am a house guest, yes."

"And you retired?"

"Yes."

"And remained in your bed till morning?"

"But of a certainty, yes! What are you implying? That I had a hand in this affair?"

"No, no; be calm, my dear sir. I ask you but one question. Is this your glove?"

The Inspector took the glove from his pocket and offered it to the Count.

The Frenchman took it, examined it minutely and without haste.

"No, sir," he said, returning it; "that is not my property."

"Thank you, that is all," and the Inspector put the glove back in his pocket.

"There is no doubt as to the main facts," said the Inspector, a half hour later, as, with the members of the family he summed up what had been found out from all known sources. "The assailant was most certainly a burglarious intruder; the weapon, this 'black-jack'; the motive, robbery. Why the robbery was not achieved and what is the meaning of the unexplained circumstances of the whole affair, we do not yet know. They are matters to be investigated, but they cannot greatly affect the principal conditions. You may be thankful, Miss Stuart, that the sad death of your aunt was undoubtedly painless; and also that the thief did not succeed in his attempt to purloin the valuable gems."

The Inspector's speech might seem coldhearted, but Brunt was a practical man, and he was truly glad for himself that in addition to finding the murderer he did not also have to recover a fortune of rare jewels.

"Now," he went on, "as to the maid, Estelle. I have talked with her, but she is so hysterical and her stories so contradictory, that I am inclined to the opinion that she has some sort of guilty knowledge or at least suspicion of the intruder. The man was stocking-footed, and it is a pity, Miss Stuart, that you erased that footprint on the floor! But it would have been of doubtful use, I dare say. We have found faint tracks of the powder on the steps of the staircase, and though the last ones are almost indiscernible they seem to lead through the butler's pantry, and to an exit by that window. But the window was found fastened this morning, so, if it was used as a means for the burglar's getaway, it must have been fastened afterward by some person inside. Could this person have been the maid, Estelle?"

"Sure it could!" exclaimed Haviland, who was an interested listener. "That girl is a sly one! I caught her this morning, trying to take away that glass of milk. I told her to let it alone."

"Why?" asked the Inspector.

"Because I thought if she wanted to get it away, there must be some reason for her to want it! What was it?"

"Nonsense!" and Anita looked scornfully at Gray; "naturally, Estelle would do up the rooms, and would, of course, remove the remains of Miss Lucy's night luncheon."

"But that's just it!" said Haviland, triumphantly: "she didn't take the plate that had had sandwiches on it! If she had, I should have thought nothing of it. But she took the glass of milk, in a furtive, stealthy way, that made me look at her. She turned red, and trembled, and I told her to set the glass down. She pretended not to hear, so I told her again. Then she obeyed. But she glared at me like a tigress."

"Oh, rubbish!" said Anita. "She was annoyed at being interfered with in her work, and perhaps fearful of being censured."

"All right," said Haviland, "then there's no harm done. If that girl is entirely innocent, what I said won't hurt her. But she looked to me as if on a secret errand and a desperate one."

"What puzzles me is," mused the Inspector, "why she persists in saying that she left the tray in good order in the room,—though it was discovered an hour later, upset,—when we know that Miss Carrington had been dead since, at least, two or three o'clock."

"Look here, Inspector," and Haviland frowned, "if the murder was committed at two or three o'clock, how is it that Mrs. Frothingham saw the intruder escaping at four or later?"

"There is a discrepancy there," admitted Brunt, "but it may be explained away. The doctors cannot be sure until the autopsy is completed of the exact hour of death, and, too, the lady next door may have made an error in time."

"Well, I'll inform you that Estelle did upset that tray herself," said Pauline with an air of finality.

"How do you know?" and Inspector Brunt peered at her over his glasses.

"It was while Gray was telephoning for the doctor," said Pauline, reminiscently, "that I looked carefully at that overturned tray."

"I know it," said Haviland, "I told you not to touch anything."

"I know that, but I did. I picked up from the debris, this;" and Pauline held up to view a tiny hairpin of the sort called 'invisible.'

"It is Estelle's" she said; "see, it is the glistening bronze color of her hair. Anita has gold-colored ones, and I do not use these fine wire ones. I use only shell. Moreover, I know this is Estelle's,—don't you, Anita?"

"It may be."

"It is. And its presence there, on the tray, proves that she let the tray fall in her surprise at seeing Aunt Lucy, and in her trembling excitement loosened and dropped this hairpin. Doubtless, she flung her hand up to her head—a not unusual gesture of hers—and so dislodged it."

Brunt looked closely at the speaker. "You've got it all fixed up, haven't you, Miss Stuart?"

Pauline flushed slightly. "I didn't 'fix it up,' as you call it, but I did gather, from what I saw, that the truth must be as I have stated; and in my anxiety to learn anything possible as to the mystery of this crime, I secured what may or may not be a bit of evidence. As Mr. Haviland has said, if Estelle is entirely innocent of any complicity in the matter, these things can't hurt her. But it would scarcely be possible for her to have been so careless as to drop a hairpin on the tray without noticing it, if she were not startled and flurried by something that took her mind and eyes entirely away from her duties."

"I think you are purposely making a great deal out of nothing," remarked Anita; "it seems unfair, to say the least, to condemn the poor girl on such trifling evidence."

The talk was interrupted by the entrance of the Coroner and the two doctors.

"It is found," said Coroner Scofield, "that the cause of Miss Carrington's death was not the blow on the head."

The Inspector looked his amazement, and the others sat with receptively blank countenances waiting further disclosures.

"No," went on Scofield, "we find in the stomach unmistakable traces of poison."

"Poison!" It was Anita's frightened whisper; "who would poison her?"

"What kind of poison?" asked Brunt.

"Aconitine; deadly and sure. It leaves little trace, but certain tests reveal it beyond all doubt. That is why we have been so long. The tests are difficult of performance. But, it is over, and we report that Miss Lucy Carrington was poisoned by aconitine, administered either by her own hand or another."

"Oh, she never would poison herself!" cried Anita; "who did it?"

"And the blow on the head? " said Inspector Brunt, looking deeply perplexed.

"Her death, from poison, occurred at or near two o'clock," asserted the Coroner; "the blow on the head was given after life had departed."

"Incredible!" said Brunt.

"It is, indeed, Inspector. But those are the facts. The heavy blow fractured the skull, but left no bruise or mark, nor was there any blood from the cut scalp. In addition we have the poison found in the system, and the death symptoms of quiet, placid dissolution which are consequent always on that particular poison."

"Could it have been self-administered?" asked Brunt.

"Not by Miss Carrington," said Doctor Stanton, decidedly. "The lady has been my patient for years, and she had an absolute abhorrence of all sorts of drugs or medicines. She made more fuss over taking a simple powder than a spoiled child. I have often prescribed for her, knowing full well she would not take my prescriptions because of her detestation of taking medicine. When remedies have been really necessary, I have had to administer them while with her, and a difficult task it was. Moreover, my patient was not of the temperament or disposition to seek death for herself, nor had she any reason to do so. No; the case is murder; the poison was administered by some one who wished for her death and deliberately set out to accomplish it,—and succeeded."

"Is the action of this poison instantaneous?" asked Brunt.

"No; death ensues about a half hour to an hour after the dose is taken into the system."

"Then, we gather that the poison was taken in the neighborhood of one o'clock, last night."

"Yes," agreed the Coroner, "about one o'clock."

"About one o'clock!" whispered Anita, in an awe-struck, gasping way, and her great blue eyes stared dazedly into the dark ones of Pauline.

Chapter 7: The Inquest

NEXT morning the inquest was proceeding. The great living-room at Garden Steps was crowded with listeners, drawn hither by sympathy, interest or curiosity. And each class found ample to satisfy its motive. The mere fact of being within that exclusive home, within those heretofore inaccessible doors, was enough to thrill and delight many, and observation and scrutiny were as well repaid as was the listening to the astounding revelations that were poured into their ears.

Coroner's Scofield's jury was composed of intelligent men, who were eagerly receptive to the appalling facts narrated to them and the curiously bizarre bits of evidence that became known as the witnesses were questioned. Dr. Stanton told of his being called to the house, and his discoveries and conclusions. He admitted that he assumed death was caused by the blow on the head, but claimed that it was a pardonable error in view of the fact that such a blow had been given. He affirmed, and Dr. Moore corroborated it, that the autopsy showed that death was caused by aconitine poison, administered, either by the deceased or another, at an hour not earlier than one o'clock, and probably soon thereafter. The terrible blow that had fractured the skull had been given after life had been for some time extinct.

Dr. Stanton asserted emphatically his late patient's detestation of drugs or medicines of any sort, adducing thereby the extreme improbability of the poison having been selfadministered. Moreover, the temperament and disposition of the late Miss Carrington entirely evinced a love of life and desire to prolong it by means of any device or assistance the doctor might give.

Pauline was called next, and a little flutter of excitement in the audience greeted her appearance.

Exceedingly dignified, but of a sweet, gracious mien, she at once received the silent approval of the crowd. Her black gown, its collar of sheer white organdy slightly open at the throat, well suited her pale, beautiful face and her dark hair and eyes. To-day, her eyes seemed fathomless. At times, gazing intently at the Coroner until they almost disconcerted him; and then, hidden by veiling lids, whose long lashes fell suddenly, as if to conceal further disclosures.

On the whole, Pauline was not a satisfactory witness. She told, in most straightforward way, of leaving the breakfast table to go to her aunt's room and of finding there the dead body. She told clearly all the circumstances of the upset tray, the spilled powder and the eccentric garb of Miss Carrington herself. But questions as to her opinion of these facts brought little response.

"You left Miss Carrington at half-past twelve?" asked Coroner Scofield.

"Not so late, I think," returned Pauline; "probably at quarter or twenty minutes past twelve,—I am not sure."

"How was she then dressed?"

"In the gown she had worn during the evening."

"And her jewels?"

"When I left my aunt, she was wearing her pearls and the other jewelry she had worn with her evening dress. Some brooches and rings and bracelets."

"But not so much as she had on when you discovered her in the morning?"

"Not nearly so much."

"How do you account for this?"

"I don't account for it. To me it is exceedingly mysterious."

"And the paper snake round her neck?"

"I have no idea by whom such a thing could have been brought to my aunt. But I am positive she never put it on herself. Nor can I think she would allow it to come near her if she were alive,—or conscious,—or, had power to scream for help. Any one knowing my aunt's fear and horror of anything reptilian will agree to this."

"It seems evident," said the Coroner, thoughtfully, "that some intruder entered Miss Carrington's room, at or near one o'clock. That this intruder in some manner induced Miss Oarrington to swallow the poison, whether conscious of her act or not. That the intruder subsequently, and for some reason, placed the snake round the neck of the victim, and, later still, brutally gave her a stunning blow with the black-jack which was found, and thereby fractured her skull. Granting these assumptions, can you, Miss Stuart, give us any information that would lead to discovery of the hand that wrought this havoc?"

"Not any," and Pauline raised her great eyes a moment to Scofield's face and slowly dropped them again.

"Then can you not express an opinion or suggest a theory that might account for such strange happenings, at least, in part?"

"No," said Pauline, slowly; "I have no idea, nor can I imagine why my aunt should be so elaborately arrayed and seated in an easy chair in front of her mirror. It is contrary to all her customs or habits."

"Could she have been killed first and could the jewels and adornments have been added afterward?" asked the Coroner of the doctors.

"No," replied Dr. Moore; "the whole condition of the body and clothing make such a theory practically impossible."

"Quite impossible," added Dr. Stanton; "and, too, what would be the sense of such a proceeding?"

"We are establishing the facts of the proceedings, not the sense of them," returned the Coroner, a little testily, for he was at his wits' end even to make a beginning in this strange case.

"At least," he went on, "we have the facts and the approximate time of the crime; have you, Miss Stuart, any suspicion of who the murderer can be?"

The question was shot out suddenly. If its intent was to startle the witness, it certainly succeeded. Pauline Stuart turned even whiter than she had been, and she caught her breath quickly and audibly as she flashed a frightened glance at Gray Haviland. It was by no means an accusing glance, though many who saw it, eager for a direction in which to cast their suspicions, took it for such.

But Pauline controlled herself immediately. "Certainly not," she said coldly. "That is, I can have no suspicion of the murderer's identity. It was, of course, a midnight intruder, of the criminal class. I have no individual acquaintances who use or possess the weapon that was employed in this crime."

"The black-jack is an auxiliary only. The poison may have been administered by one not versed in the ways of professional criminals. You admit that, I suppose?"

"It is no doubt true," said Pauline, icily, "that poison may be given by a person not belonging to the criminal classes. I fail to see, however, how that fact affects the matter in hand."

"It may well affect it. Since Miss Carrington was killed by a deadly poison, we must conclude that the black-jack assault was made with the intention of concealing the poisoning and making it appear that the blow caused the death. There seems to me no other way to account for the conditions that confront us."

A silence followed this. Its truth was patent to everybody. Clearly, the poisoner had delivered the blow, for no one else would attack a victim already dead. And a plausible reason would be the hope that the poisoning would pass unnoticed in view of the other apparent cause of death.

"And it points to the work of an amateur," went on Scofield; "a professional criminal would know that the autopsy would disclose the earlier crime."

Pauline lost her nerve. "I don't know anything about it!" she cried, and sank back into her seat, her face buried in her hands. Coroner Scofield was a man of tact. "It is entirely natural, Miss Stuart," he said, "that this thought should overcome you. But we must realize the fact that the theory of a professional burglar is practically untenable, because nothing was stolen. A burglar's motive could be only robbery, and this did not take place. Nor can we think that a burglar was frightened away, before he could appropriate the jewels. For, after giving the poison, and before the blow was given, sufficient time elapsed for a successful getaway to be made. Nor would the burglar have been at pains to cover up his poisoning work, for having achieved his end, he would have secured his booty and made escape. So, it is evident that the motive, not being robbery, is as yet unknown, and may be obscure and complicated."

"What could it have been?" asked Pauline, her composure regained, her voice low and even.

Scofield looked at her. "It is said, Miss Stuart, that the only motives for murder are love, revenge or gain. Can you imagine any one of these directed toward your aunt?"

Pauline replied tranquilly. Evidently she had fully recovered her poise. "I can think of no one who could have killed my aunt for love; it is improbable that she has ever done any one such wrong as to call for such a deed in revenge; as to gain, if you mean pecuniary gain, all the legatees mentioned in her will may be said to have that motive."

Pauline's manner and tones were so impersonal, so scathingly ironic as to amount to a disclaimer for all the legatees. Her way of suggesting it made it seem so far removed from possibility that it was far more emphatic than any denial could have been.

But Coroner Scofield was as unmoved as his witness.

"Quite so," he said coolly; "and therefore inquiries must be made. Did you, Miss Stuart, after leaving your aunt soon after midnight see or hear anything unusual or suspicious?"

"What do you mean by unusual or suspicious?"

"I mean did you see or hear anything, anything at all, that you could not explain to yourself as being in any way connected with the tragedy we are investigating?"

Before answering, Pauline looked in turn at all the members of the household. Haviland slowly turned his head as if to look at something across the room, and as slowly brought it back to its previous position.

"I did not," said Pauline, looking straight at the Coroner.

"That is all," said Scofield, briefly, and the next witness was called.

This was the maid, Estelle. Her eyes were red with weeping, but she was not hysterical now, or incoherent. She answered tersely questions as to Miss Carrington's habits and as to her words and actions during the maid's last interview with her.

"I left her at about quarter of one," the witness deposed; "I had given her the Oriental negligee, of which she is fond. I offered to take down her hair and put away her jewels, but she declined those services, and bade me leave her."

"She was wearing, when you left her, only the jewels she had worn during the evening?"

"Only those, sir. When I changed her evening gown for the boudoir robe, she bade me replace such jewels as I had already taken off her. She kept on her rings, bracelets and her long rope of pearls while I changed her costume."

"And then she dismissed you for the night?"

"Yes, sir."

"Where was she then? Sitting before the mirror?"

"No, sir. She stood in the middle of the floor."

"Was she in an amiable mood?"

"She was not. Because I offered to assist her further, she ordered me from the room in anger."

"Ah, in anger! Was Miss Carrington often angry with you?"

"Indeed, yes; as she was with everybody."

"Confine your answers to your own experience. You prepared a night luncheon for your mistress?"

"Yes, sir," and now Estelle's voice trembled and her eyes rolled apprehensively.

"What was it?"

"Two small sandwiches and a glass of milk."

"What sort of sandwiches?"

"Caviare, sir."

"Ah, yes. And why did you put a large dose of bromide in the glass of milk?"

"Did it kill her?" and Estelle screamed out her query. Pauline and Anita looked at one another. It was the same question Estelle had asked of them.

"An overdose of bromide may be fatal," parried the Coroner, not answering the question directly. "Why did you do it?"

"I didn't do it," and the French girl shrugged her shoulders; "why should I poison my mistress? She was quick-tempered, but I was used to that."

"Don't be stupid," said the Coroner; "the bromide didn't poison Miss Carrington, for, in the first place, she didn't take it. The glass of milk was found next morning untouched, though the sandwiches were gone. Therefore, the bromide in the milk was found. Why did you put it in?"

"I didn't do it," reiterated the maid. "Look higher up for that!"

"What do you mean?"

"I mention no names, but somebody must have done it, if bromide was found in that milk."

"But you tried to get the glass away next morning, without being seen."

"Who says I did?"

"Never mind that; you were seen. Why?"

"Well, sir, if I thought anybody was going to get into trouble because of it, I was only too glad to help, if I could, by removing it before it was noticed." Estelle spoke slowly, as if weighing her words, and her furtive glances at Pauline bore only one significance. It was palpably apparent that she suspected Miss Stuart of the deed, and out of kindness had tried to remove the incriminating evidence.

Pauline stared at her with a glance that went through her or over her or around her, but gave not the slightest attention to the speaker.

"Did you put bromide in your aunt's glass of milk, Miss Stuart?" asked the Coroner, and Pauline said, calmly, "Certainly not."

Mr. Scofield sighed. It was a difficult matter to get at the truth when the witnesses were clever women, in whose veracity he had not complete confidence.

He gave up Estelle for the moment, and called Gray Haviland.

The young man's appearance gave every promise of frankness and sincerity. He detailed the circumstances precisely as Pauline had told them. He denied having heard or seen anything suspicious during the night. He referred to the Coroner's list of motives for crime, and added that he agreed with Miss Stuart that the present case could scarcely be ascribed to love or revenge. If the murder was committed for gain, it was, of course, a formal necessity to question all the beneficiaries of Miss Carrington's will, but he was sure that all such inheritors were quite willing to be questioned. For his part, he believed that the criminal was some enemy of Miss Carrington, unknown to her immediate household, and he suggested that such a one be searched for.

"You've got that glove," he reminded, "that was found clasped in the hand of the murdered woman. Why not trace that; or endeavor to learn in some way the reason for the many peculiar circumstances; or discover, at least, a way to look for further evidence; rather than to vaguely suspect those who lived under Miss Carrington's roof?"

"I am not asking your assistance in conducting this inquiry, Mr. Haviland," and the Coroner spoke shortly; "but pursuing my own plan of obtaining evidence in my own way. Will you kindly answer questions without comment on them?"

"Oh, all right; fire away. Only remember, that we relatives and friends are just as much interested in clearing up this mystery as you are, and we want to help, if we can be allowed to do so intelligently."

Asked again if he saw or heard anything unusual in the night, Haviland replied, "You said 'suspicious' the other time. I did see something unusual. I saw Estelle go stealthily downstairs at three A.M. That's unusual, but I don't go so far as to call it suspicious."

CHAPTER 8: ANITA'S STORY

INSTEAD of showing surprise at this statement, the Coroner broke the breathless silence that followed it, by saying:

"Will you please explain what you mean by 'stealthily?'"

"Just what I say," returned Haviland, bluntly. "She went slowly, now and then pausing to listen, twice drawing back around a corner and peeping out, and then coming forth again; she wore no shoes and carried no light; she went down the big staircase in the manner I have described, and after about ten minutes, returned in the same fashion. That's what I mean by stealthily."

"What was your errand?" asked Scofield of Estelle.

"Nothing. I didn't go," she replied, coolly.

"She tells an untruth," said Gray, calmly. "She did go, just as I have described. But it was doubtless on an innocent errand. I have no idea she was implicated in Miss Carrington's death. I am sure it is of casual explanation,—or, I was sure, until Estelle denied it."

"How was it you chanced to see her?"

"I was wakeful, and I was prowling around to find something to read. I went out in the hall and got a magazine from the table, and had returned to my room and was just closing the door, when I saw a white figure glide across the hall. She passed through a moonlit space or I could not have seen her. She was wrapped in a light or white kimono thing, and I should never have thought of it again if it were not for what has happened."

"You knew it to be this Estelle?"

"Yes; her red hair was hanging in a braid."

"'Tisn't red!" snapped Estelle, but Mr. Scofield silenced her with a frown.

"Well, auburn, then," said Haviland, easily.

"You may as well own up, Estelle; what did you go down for?"

"I didn't go," repeated the maid, obstinately, and no cross-questioning could prevail on her to admit otherwise.

"All right," and Haviland shrugged his shoulders; "I suppose it doesn't matter, as the crime was committed about one o'clock. It's up to you, Mr. Coroner, to find some person who acted suspiciously nearer that time. And, by the way, as man of business of this estate, unless some worthwhile evidence is forthcoming pretty soon, I'm going to round up a detective or two who will get somewhere."

"Give us a little more time, Mr. Haviland," said Scofield, suavely, "this inquest is only begun."

"Well, get it over with, and then, if the truth hasn't come to light, I'll take a hand." Miss Frayne was called next, and Anita, with a look of importance on her pretty face, came forward.

Her evidence, at first, was merely a repetition of that already heard, and she corroborated Pauline's recital of the scene as the two girls bade Miss Carrington good-night.

"And then?" prompted the Coroner. "Then I went to my room, but I didn't retire. I sat thinking over what Miss Carrington had said to me. And as I thought about it, I concluded that this time I was really dismissed from her secretaryship. And that made me feel very sorry, for it is a good position and I've no wish to lose it. So,—after a time, I began to think I would go to Miss Carrington's room and if she were still up, I would beg her forgiveness."

"Forgiveness for what?"

"For any fancied grievance she might have against me. I have always tried to please her, but she was, er,— difficult, and it was not easy to do the right thing at all times."

"Did you go to her room?"

"I went to the door—"

"At what time?"

"Soon after one o'clock. Not more than five or ten minutes after."

There was a rustle of excitement. The poison was said to be administered at about one! Did this fair doll-like girl know the secret of the tragedy?

"Proceed, Miss Frayne; tell the story of anything you saw at that time."

"I saw nothing. But I heard a great deal."

"What was it?"

"The door of Miss Carrington's room was closed, and I was about to tap at it, when I heard talking inside. I paused, and I listened, in order to discover if her maid was still with her, or some one else. If it had been Estelle, I should have tapped for admittance. But it was not."

"Who was it?"

"I cannot say. The voice I heard distinctly was that of Miss Carrington herself. Her voice was high-pitched, and of what is called a carrying sort. The things she said were so strange, I lingered, listening, for I was so surprised I couldn't help it."

"First, I heard her say, quite plainly, 'Your face is the most beautiful I have ever seen! I wish mine were as beautiful.' I assumed, then, she must be talking to Miss Stuart, for surely she would not say that to her maid. Then she said, 'But, to-morrow, I shall be forever freed from this homely face of mine.'"

"Miss Frayne, this is very singular! Are you sure you heard correctly?"

"I am sure. But there is more. She next said, 'To-morrow you will be glad!—glad!' It was almost a scream, that. And she went on, 'To-morrow all these jewels will be yours,—if you—ah, but will you?' and then her voice trailed off faintly, and I could hear no more."

"You heard nothing more at all?"

"Yes; I waited,—oh, I admit I was eavesdropping, but it was so strange I couldn't help it,—there was silence. It may well be some one else was replying to her, but I could not make out any other person's words. A low voice would not be audible like a high-pitched one. But after a moment, Miss Carrington resumed; she said, 'I shall change my will. Not Carr's half, that must stand. But the other half shall never go to a niece who has no affection for me!' Again I heard nothing, for the responses were inaudible. Then Miss Carrington said, in a musing tone:

'I have already willed you ten thousand dollars of those United States bonds, but—' And then, after quite a long pause, Miss Carrington cried out, not loudly, but tensely, 'Henri, Henri! you are the mark I aim at!' That frightened me so, I ran swiftly back to my room, and locked the door."

"You assumed Henri to be Count Charlier?"

"I had no other construction to put upon the words."

"You thought the gentleman was in Miss Carrington's room?"

"I couldn't think that! And yet, it sounded as if she were speaking to him, not of him."

"This is a very strange story, Miss Frayne. Have you mentioned these things you overheard to any one before this?"

"No. I have thought them over, and concluded it was best to tell the story first to you."

"And quite right. It is, then, your opinion that there was another person in Miss Carrington's room, to whom she was speaking?"

"It seemed so to me."

"But you did not hear this other person's voice?"

Anita paused a moment and then said: "Not distinctly."

"Did you hear it at all?"

"I cannot say. When I did not hear Miss Carrington's voice clearly, there were sounds that might have been another person or her own voice speaking more inaudibly."

"Might it not be that she was merely talking to herself,—soliloquizing?"

"It could not have been that. She spoke definitely and decidedly to some one when she said 'Your face is beautiful,' and when she said, 'I have willed you ten thousand dollars,' indeed, every thing she said was as if spoken to some hearer; not as one who talks to herself."

"After you regained your room, did you leave it again?"

"No, I did not."

"H'm. Now, are you positive, Miss Frayne, that all these speeches were said just as you have repeated them? It is a great strain on the memory to repeat accurately a conversation as long as the one you have just rehearsed."

"The speeches I heard are burned into my brain. I could not forget them if I would. I may have erred in some minor or unimportant words, but the most of what I heard is precisely as I have repeated it. Indeed, so thoroughly was I amazed at it all, I wrote it down as soon as I reached my room. I had then no thought of —of what was going to happen, but Miss Carrington had made peculiar remarks during the evening about something happening to her, and in connection with that the words I heard seemed so remarkable,—not to say uncanny,—that I made a note of them. This is not an unusual habit with me. I often make notes of conversations, as it has been useful in my services as secretary."

"As how?"

"If a caller in a social or business way had conversation with Miss Carrington, and I was present, I often made a record, in case she asked me later just what had been said."

"I see. And how do you interpret the words, 'Henri, you are the mark I aim at?'"

"I can only think that Miss Carrington was in favor of considering a marriage between herself and the Count."

"You made use of the word 'uncanny.' Do you imagine that Miss Carrington had any foreboding of her approaching doom?"

"When I heard her say, 'To-morrow I will be forever freed from this homely face of mine,' and ' to-morrow all these jewels will be yours,' I couldn't help thinking,— after the discovery of her death,—that she must have anticipated it."

"Did her voice sound like the despairing one of a person about to die?"

"On the contrary, it sounded full of life and animation."

"Did she seem angry with the person to whom she was speaking?"

"At times, yes. And, again, no. Her voice showed varying emotions as she talked on."

"Her speech was not continuous, then?"

"Not at all. It was broken, and in snatches. But, remember, I could not hear all of what she said, and the other person or persons not at all."

"Did you not catch a word from the other voice?"

"I cannot say. Much, in a low tone, that I could not hear clearly, might have been Miss Carrington's voice or another's. The door was closed, and as soon as I realized there was some one there, not Estelle, I had no thought of knocking, and I soon went away. I ought to have gone away sooner, and would have done so, but I was so amazed and puzzled I stayed on involuntarily."

"Your story, Miss Frayne, is very extraordinary. Can you suggest, from what you heard, who might have been in the room with Miss Carrington?"

"I can not, nor do I wish to. I have told you what I heard, it is for you to make deductions or discoveries."

"I wish to say a word, Mr. Coroner," and Pauline Stuart, with her dark eyes blazing, rose to her feet. "I am sorry to say this, but I must ask you to hesitate before you put too much faith in the amazing tale you have just listened to. I am sure Miss Frayne could not have heard all that nonsense! It is impossible, on the face of it, that my aunt should have received any one in her room after her maid left her. It is incredible that she should have made all those ridiculous and meaningless remarks! And it is despicable for any woman to imply or hint that Miss Carrington was receiving a gentleman caller! I am surprised that you even listened to what must be the ravings of a disordered mind!"

Pauline looked at Anita like an avenging goddess. But the darts of scorn from her dark eyes were met and returned in kind from the big blue ones of the secretary.

"I resent your tone and your words," said Anita, deliberately; "but since you choose to adopt that attitude, I will go on to say, what I had intended not to reveal, that I saw you coming from your aunt's room, after the conversation I have told of took place."

"Wait a minute," said the Coroner; "you said that immediately after hearing the alleged conversation you went at once to your room, and did not leave it again."

"Nor did I. But a few minutes later, unable to restrain my curiosity, I opened my door, and looked out. My position then commanded a full view of the hall, and I saw Miss Stuart go from her aunt's room to her own."

Pauline looked at the speaker. Coldly her glance swept back to the Coroner, and she said: "I deny that I was in my aunt's room after leaving it at midnight in company with Miss Frayne. But she forces me to tell that I saw her going away from it at exactly quarter past one."

"How do you fix the time so accurately?"

"I was sitting in the upper hall,—it is really a sitting-room, at the bay-windowed end,—looking at the moon. I, too, had been disturbed at my aunt's attitude, and her threats to send me away to-day, and I had gone to the hall windowseat, a favorite haunt of mine, and had sat there for a half hour or more."

"Could any one going through the hall see you?"

"Probably not, as the draperies are heavy, and I was in the deep window-seat. I was thinking I would go to my room, and then I saw Miss Frayne come from my aunt's room and go to her own."

"Are you sure she came from the room?"

"She was closing the door, her hand was on the knob. She did not see me, I am sure, for I drew back in the window and watched her. And just then I heard the hall clock chime the quarter after one."

"You didn't see Miss Frayne when she went to Miss Carrington's room?"

"No; I suppose I was then looking out of the deep window."

"Nor did you hear her?"

"No, the rugs are thick and a light foot-fall makes no sound."

"What did you next do?"

"I went—I went straight to my own room."

The slight hesitation told against Pauline. All through her testimony, all through her arraignment of Anita,—for it amounted to that,—she had been cool, calm and imperturbable. But now a momentary hesitation of speech, added perhaps, to the circumstantial story of Anita Frayne, caused a wave of doubt,—not enough to call suspicion,—but a questioning attitude to form in the minds of many of the audience. To whom, if not Miss Stuart, could Miss Carrington's remarks about beauty have been addressed? It was well known that Miss Lucy adored beauty and had all her life lamented her own lack of it. This was no secret woe of the poor lady's. To any one who would listen, she would complain of her hard lot in having all the gifts of the gods except good looks. To whom else would she say 'To-morrow all these jewels will be yours,—if you—ah, but will you?' And yet, after all, it did not make sense. Was it not far more likely to be a figment of Miss Frayne's clever mind, for what purpose who might say? At any rate, their stories were contradictory and moreover were garbled.

The jurymen sighed. The case had been mysterious enough before, now it was becoming inexplicable.

Chapter 9: Further Testimony

COUNT HENRI CHARLIER was being questioned, and he was distinctly ill at ease. His French savoir faire was not proof against definite inquiries as to his intentions regarding the late Miss Carrington, and indefinite allusions concerning his movements on the night of her death. He had related, straightforwardly enough, his visit at Garden Steps that evening and his departure at or about midnight. He denied his engagement of marriage, but admitted that he had paid Miss Carrington such attentions as might lead her to suspect an attachment.

"You did not return to this house after leaving on Tuesday night?"

"Most assuredly not."

"You were not in Miss Carrington's boudoir at one o'clock or thereabouts?"

Count Charlier's black eyes snapped. But by a successful effort he controlled his indignation, and said, simply, "I was not."

"But she was heard to address you."

"Impossible, as I was not there."

"She distinctly declared that you were the mark she aimed at. What construction do you put upon those words?"

"It is not for me to boast of my attraction for a lady."

Count Charlier simpered a little, and Gray Haviland looked at him with a frown of undisguised scorn. Haviland had never liked the Count, indeed, he even doubted his right to the title, and especially had he feared a marriage between him and Miss Lucy. And, granting that this feeling was partly due to a consideration of his own interests, Haviland also distrusted the Frenchman and doubted Miss Lucy's happiness as his wife.

"Did Miss Carrington leave you a bequest of ten thousand dollars in United States bonds?" went on the Coroner.

"I—I don't know," and the Count stammered in an embarrassed way.

"You do know!" shouted Haviland; "the will has been read, and you know perfectly well that such a bequest was left to you."

"Why did you deny the knowledge?" asked Scofield, sternly.

"I'm—I'm not sure—"

"You are sure!" stormed Gray. "Now where were you when Miss Carrington spoke those words to you? If not in her boudoir, then on the balcony outside the window, perhaps."

"Absurd," said the Coroner.

"Not at all," said Gray; "that window opens on a balcony enclosed by glass. It is easily reached from outside by a small staircase, mostly used in summer, but always available. How could Miss Carrington speak to the Count concerning the bonds and concerning her infatuation for himself, which is no secret, unless he were there before her? And how could he be in the room—in her boudoir—unknown to the servants? Moreover, Mr. Coroner, I believe the glove found in Miss Carrington's hand to be the property of Count Charlier."

"But no!" cried the witness, excitedly; "I have repeatedly disclaimed that glove. It is not mine, I know not whose it is. I know nothing of this sad affair, whatever. If the money is left to me, as I have been told, it is a—a surprise to me."

"Surprise nothing!" murmured Haviland, but he said no more to the Count.

"If my story might be told now,—" ventured Mrs. Frothingham.

After a moment's hesitation, Coroner Scofield decided to let her tell it, as having a possible bearing on Count Charlier's testimony.

The rather stunning-looking widow was fashionably dressed, and she fluttered with an air of importance as she took the stand. She related again the story she had told of the supposed burglar, whom she saw leaving the living-room by way of a window, at four o 'clock on Wednesday morning.

"How can you be so sure it was a burglar?" asked Scofield.

"Oh, he looked like one. All huddled up, you know, and his face buried between a high coat collar and a drawn-down cap. And he walked slyly,—sort of glided among the shrubs and trees, as if avoiding notice. No man on legitimate business would skulk like that."

"Might it not have been Count Charlier?" asked the Coroner, bluntly.

"Certainly not!" and Mrs. Frothingham gave a little shriek. "The Count is a slim and elegant figure; this was a stocky, burly man; a marauder, I know."

"It may be," said the Coroner, wearily. "It may be that a burglar was concealed in the house, or let in by a servant, and that he attacked Miss Carrington as she was seated at her dressing table. It seems impossible that he should have administered poison to her, however, and the conjoined circumstances may indicate collusion between—"

"Between whom?" asked Inspector Brunt.

"I don't know," confessed Scofield. "Every way I try to think it out, I run up against an impassable barrier."

"That's what I say," began Haviland; "it is a most involved case. I shall cable Carrington Loria for authority to employ an expert detective."

"Why cable him?" asked Pauline; "I am equally in authority now. Carr and myself each receive half the residuary estate of Aunt Lucy, and, of course, I am as

anxious to find the—the murderer, as Carr can possibly
be."

"Well, somebody will have to authorize it who is
willing to pay for it. As man of business in this home, I
am willing to attend to all such matters, but I must have
authority."

"You seem to me a little premature, Mr. Haviland,"
commented the Inspector. "Perhaps when the inquest is
concluded, it may not be necessary to call on any other
detective than our own Mr. Hardy."

"Perhaps not," agreed Haviland; "but unless you
people all wake up, you're not going to get anywhere. I
admit the getting is difficult, but that's just the reason a
wise sleuth should be called in before the trails grow
cold."

And then the Coroner returned to his task of
questioning Mrs. Frothingham.

The widow was not definitely helpful. Her statements
were often contradictory in minor details, and when she
corrected them they seemed to lose in weight. She stuck
to the main points, however, that by the help of a strong
field-glass she had discerned, in the bright moonlight, a
man leave by way of the French window, at four o 'clock,
and had seen him make his way stealthily out by the
great entrance gates of the place. Cross-questioning on
this brought no variations, and the jurymen wagged their
heads in belief of her story.

But her accounts of her own doings on Tuesday
evening were vague and indefinite.

"I was in my own home all the evening," she said at
one time; and again, "I went out for a short walk at
eleven o'clock." This last in refutation of Haskins, the
Carrington butler, who deposed to having seen the lady
walk across the lawns of Garden Steps.

"Where did you walk?"

"Oh, just around my own place; and for a moment I
strolled over here because the Steps looked so beautiful in
the moonlight."

"You were alone?"

"I was. I have no house guests at present, save the
Count; and as my brother, who lives with me, is on a
Western trip, I was alone, and I walked about to kill time
until Count Charlier should return after his bridge game
over here."

"Did you walk near the house, while on the Garden
Steps' estate?" asked Scofield, scenting a possible
espionage of her titled visitor.

"Oh, no!" and the witness bristled with indignation;
"why should I! I was not really an acquaintance of Miss
Carrington, merely a neighbor."

"Beg pardon, ma'am, but I saw you on the
conservatory verandah," said Haskins, in a deprecatory
way.

"That is not true, Mr. Coroner," said the lady,
glancing scornfully at the butler. "I beg you will not
accept a servant's statement in preference to mine!"

"You are sure of this, Haskins?" said the Inspector
gravely.

"Yes, sir. Sure, sir." and the man looked doggedly
certain, though a little scared.

"And you deny it?" went on Scofield to Mrs.
Frothingham.

"I most certainly do! How absurd for me to be over
here, and how more than absurd for me to deny it if I
were!"

This seemed sensible. Why should she deny it? And
mightn't the butler be mistaken? Or deliberately
falsifying?

If there were collusion or criminal assistance by any
of the servants, surely the word of all of them must be
mistrusted unless proven. And, too, what could have
brought Mrs. Frothingham to the verandah of a home
where she was not an accepted guest? Or, could she have
been spying on the Count?

For it had slowly entered the Coroner's not very alert
mind that perhaps the volatile widow had her own plans

for the Count's future, and Miss Carrington did not figure in them. The manner of the witness bore out this theory. She was self-conscious and at times confused. She frequently looked at the Count and then quickly averted her gaze. She blushed and stammered when speaking his name or referring to him. In a word, she acted as a woman might act in regard to a man of whom she was jealous. And the situation bore it out. If Mrs. Frothingham had matrimonial designs on her distinguished guest, would she not naturally resent his visits to a rich neighbor? Mrs. Frothingham was not rich, and she may well have been afraid of Miss Carrington's charm of gold, which could cause many a man to overlook anything else that might be lacking.

Coroner Scofield was getting more and more tangled in the mazes of this extraordinary case. He was practically at his wits' end. At last he blurted out: "It is impossible, it seems, to get a coherent, or even plausible story from a woman! Is there any man present, who knows any of the details of the happenings of Tuesday evening and night!"

There was a moment's silence at this rather petulant speech, and then Stephen Illsley rose, and speaking very gravely, said: "It seems to be my unpleasant duty to tell what little I know of these matters."

The relieved Coroner heard this with satisfaction. Accepting his good fortune, he prepared to listen to Illsley's testimony.

"I was spending the evening here," the witness began, "and during my visit I was in the various rooms. At a late hour, perhaps something after eleven,—I was crossing the hall, and I saw Mrs. Frothingham on the stairway."

"On the stairway!" exclaimed the Coroner, in amazement.

"Yes," returned Illsley, his grave eyes resting on the face of the widow, who stared at him as if stricken dumb.

"Yes, I saw her distinctly. She was evidently coming downstairs, one hand rested on the banister, and she was looking upward at the ceiling."

"Did she see you—"

"I think not. If so, she made no sign. But she was not looking my way, and I went on into the reception room, where I was going in search of a scarf Miss Stuart had left there. When I recrossed the hall, the lady had disappeared."

"Did not this seem to you a strange circumstance?"

"I had no right to any opinion on the subject. It was not my affair what guests were at the house I was visiting, or what they might be doing."

"But Mrs. Frothingham asserts she was not an acquaintance of Miss Carrington."

"I did not know that, then; and even so, it gave me no right to speculate concerning the lady's presence there. Nor should I refer to it now, except that in view of the subsequent tragedy it is due to every principle of right and justice that all truths be known as to that evening. Mrs. Frothingham will, of course, recall the episode and can doubtless explain it."

"I should like to hear the explanation!" said Pauline, with flashing eyes. "As mistress here now, I am interested to know why a stranger should wander about this house at will."

Mrs. Frothingham sat silent. Her face showed not so much consternation or dismay as a cold, calculating expression, as if debating just what explanation she should offer.

At last she spoke. "I may as well own up," she said, and laughed nervously. "I was on the verandah, as the vigilant butler noticed. I did step inside the hall, as I had so often heard of the rare tapestries and paintings, and, in my ennui, I thought it no harm to take a peep. The great door was ajar, and I was a little chilled by my walk across the lawns. I said to myself, if I meet any one I will merely beg a few moments' grace and then run away. Yes,

I did take a step or two up the stair, to look at a picture on the landing. It was all innocent enough, perhaps not in the best of taste, but I was lonely, and the light and warmth lured me. In a moment I had slipped out and run away home, laughing over my escapade like a foolish child."

Her light laugh rippled out as she concluded her story. She looked ingenuous and truthful, but the Coroner distrusted feminine fairy-tales, and this was a little too fanciful to be true. Moreover, Mrs. Frothingham was looking at him sharply from the corner of her eye. Clearly, she was watching him to see how he took it.

He didn't take it very well. The acknowledged presence of an outsider in the house, for a not very plausible reason, was illuminating in his estimation. She had been on the stairway. Had she been to Miss Carrington's room? True, she said she went only to the landing,—but pshaw, women had no regard for the truth! Had she and Count Charlier planned between them to — bah, why did this woman want to kill her neighbor? Even if she were jealous of the Count's attention, would she go so far as crime?

No, of course not! He must question her further. And yet, what good would that do, if she would not tell the truth?

Well, she was in the house at half-past eleven, that much was certain, for Stephen Illsley's story and her own and also the butler's testimony all coincided as to that.

And then, Detective Hardy, who had just returned from a short errand, made a startling statement. He declared that the glove which had been found clasped tightly in the dead fingers of the late Miss Carrington did belong to Count Henri Charlier.

Mr. Hardy had been searching the Count's wardrobe, and though he did not find the mate to that particular glove, he found many others, some worn and some entirely unused, but all of the same size and made by the same firm as the one now in the Coroner's possession!

Thus cornered Count Charlier reluctantly admitted that it was his glove.

"I denied it," he thus excused himself, "because I have no idea how it came into Miss Carrington's possession, and I did not wish to implicate her in an affair with my unworthy self."

"H'm," thought Gray Haviland, fixing his attention on the Count and on the flustered Mrs. Frothingham; "A precious pair of adventurers! I expect Scofield is right, we won't need an expert detective."

There was more of the inquest. But its continuance brought out no developments not already here transcribed. There was much crossquestioning and probing; there was much rather futile effort to make all the strange details fit any one theory; there was variance of opinion; and there was more or less dissension.

But as a final result, the Coroner's jury brought in a verdict that Miss Lucy Carrington met her death by poison administered by a person or persons unknown, who thereafter, probably for the purpose of diverting attention from the poison, struck her a blow on the head. The jury in their deliberation felt that Count Henri Charlier was implicated. But not having sufficient evidence to make a charge, suggested to the detective force that he be kept under surveillance.

CHAPTER 10: BIZARRE CLUES

IT was Saturday. The funeral of Miss Carrington had been held the day before and the imposing obsequies had been entirely in keeping with her love of elaborate display in life. The casket was of the richest, the flowers piled mountain high, the music, the most expensive available; for the young people in charge had felt it incumbent on them to arrange everything as Miss Lucy would have desired it.

It was a pathetic commentary on the character of the dead woman that while all who mourned her felt the shock and horror of her death, they were not deeply bowed with sorrow. Pauline, as nearest relative, would naturally grieve most, but for the moment her affections were lost sight of in the paralyzing effects of the sudden tragedy.

Anita Frayne had practically "gone to pieces." She was nervous, and jumped twitchingly if any one spoke to her. Gray Haviland was reticent, an unusual thing for him, and devoted most of his time to matters of business connected with the estate. Estelle, the maid, had succumbed to a nervous break-down, and had been taken to a nearby sanatorium, where she indulged in frequent and violent hysterics.

The household was in a continual excitement. Lawyers and detectives were coming and going, neighbors were calling, and reporters simply infested the place.

Pauline and Anita, though outwardly polite, were not on good terms, and rarely talked together.

But this morning the two girls and Haviland were called to a confab by Hardy, the detective.

"They've arrested the Count," Hardy began, and Anita screamed an interruption:

"Arrested Count Charlier! Put him in jail?"

"Yes," returned the detective. "I found the other one of that pair of gloves, the mate to the one in the lady's hands,—where, do you suppose?"

"Where?"

"Rolled up in a pair of socks, in the Count's chiffonnier drawer; of course, to hide it, as it is not at all easy to destroy a thing like that while visiting."

"I know it," said Pauline, earnestly; "it is hard. I've often noticed that, when I've wanted to burn a letter or anything. You can't do it, unknown to the servants or somebody."

"Rubbish!" said Anita. "It would have been easy for the Count to dispose of a glove if he had wanted to. But he didn't. He never committed that crime! If a glove was found, as you say, somebody else put it there to incriminate an innocent man. It's too absurd to fasten the thing on Count Charlier! Do you suppose he went to the boudoir and gave Miss Carrington poison, and then shook hands good-evening, and left his glove in her grasp? Nonsense! The glove in her dead hand was put there by the criminal to implicate the Count, and the glove in the rolled-up socks for the same purpose and by the same person!"

"By Jove, Miss Frayne! You may be right!" cried Hardy. "Somehow I can't see the Count's hand in this thing, and yet—"

"And yet, he did it!" put in Haviland. "Have they really jailed him? I'm glad."

"I'm sorry," said Pauline, and her face was white; "Did he—did he—c-confess?" The girl's voice trembled, and she could scarcely pronounce the words.

"Not he," said Hardy; "he seemed dazed, and declared his innocence,—but he was not convincing. He takes it very hard and talks wildly and at random. But you know what Frenchmen are; liable to go off their heads at any time."

"But look at it," reasoned Anita; "why would the Count kill Miss Carrington? Why, he thought of marrying her."

"Not much he didn't!" and Hardy smiled a little. "I size it up this way. Matters had gone so far that he had to propose to the lady or clear out. He didn't want to clear out for then she would take back the little matter of ten thousand dollars already marked for him in her will. Moreover, he couldn't realize that tidy little sum, which he very much wants, so long as she lived. To be sure, he would have had far more, had he married her, but that was not in 'his nibs" plans. So he resorted to desperate measures. He's a thorough villain, that man! Outwardly, most correct and honorable, but really, an adventurer, as is also his friend, the dashing young widow."

"Mr. Hardy," and Pauline spoke calmly, now, "do you know these things to be true of Count Charlier, or are you assuming them?"

"Well, Miss Stuart, I know human nature pretty well, especially male human nature, and if I'm mistaken in this chap, I'll be surprised. But also, I've set afoot an investigation, and we'll soon learn his record, antecedents and all that. At present, no one knows much about him; and what Mrs. Frothingham knows she won't tell."

"It was very strange for Aunt Lucy to give him that money—" began Pauline musingly.

"Not at all," broke in Gray, "I know all about that. Miss Carrington had a certain bunch of bonds that amounted to just fifty thousand dollars. In one of her sudden bursts of generosity, and she often had such, she decided to give those bonds to five people. I mean, to devise them in her will, not to give them now. Well, four were Miss Stuart and Carr Loria, Miss Frayne and myself. And then, she hesitated for some time, but finally announced that the fifth portion should be named for the Count. I was there when the lawyer fixed it up, and Miss Carrington turned to me and said, laughingly, 'I may change that before it comes due!' Oh, she was always messing with her will. I'm glad there's a tidy bit in it for me, as it is. Her demise might have taken place when I was for the moment cut out."

"Was there ever such a time—!" asked Hardy.

"There sure was! Only last month, she got firing mad with me, and crossed me off without a shilling. Then she got over her mad and restored me to favor."

"You and Miss Frayne have other bequests than those particular bonds you mentioned!" asked the detective.

"Yes, we have each ten thou' beside, which was all right of the old lady, eh, Anita?"

"None too much, considering what I have stood from her capricious temper and eccentric ways," returned the girl.

"Your own temper is none too even," said Pauline, quietly; "I'd rather you wouldn't speak ill of my aunt, if you please."

What might have been a passage at arms was averted by the appearance of a footman with a cablegram.

"It's from Carr!" exclaimed Pauline, as she tore it open, and read:

Awful news just received. Shall I come home or will you come here? Let Haviland attend all business. Love and sympathy.
CABBINGTON LORIA.

"He's in Cairo," commented Haviland, looking at the paper; "that's lucky. If he had been off up the Nile on one of his excavating tours, we mightn't have had communication for weeks. Well, he practically retains me as business manager, at least for the present. And Lord know's there's a lot to be done!"

"I don't understand, Gray, why you look upon Carr as more in authority than I am," said Pauline, almost petulantly; "I am an equal heir, and, too, I am here, and Carr is the other side of the world."

"That's so, Polly. I don't know why, myself. I suppose because he is the man of the family."

"That doesn't make any difference. I think from now on, Gray, it will be proper for you to consider me the head of the house as far as business matters are concerned. You can pay Carr his half of the residuary in whatever form he wants it. I shall keep the place, at least for the present."

"Won't Mr. Loria come back to America?" asked Hardy.

"I scarcely think so," replied Pauline.

"There's really no use of his doing so, unless he chooses. And I'm pretty sure he won't choose, as he's so wrapped up in his work over there, that he'd hate to leave unless necessary."

"But won't he feel a necessity to help investigate the murder?" urged Hardy.

"I don't know," and Pauline looked thoughtful. "You see what he says; when he asks if he shall come home, he means do I want him to. If I don't request it, I'm fairly sure he won't come. Of course, when he learns all the details, he will be as anxious as we that the murderer should be found. But if I know Carr, he will far rather pay for the most expensive detective service than come over himself. And, too, what could he do, more than we can? We shall, of course, use every effort and every means to solve the mysteries of the case, and he could advise us no better than the lawyers already in our counsel."

"That's all true," said Haviland; "and I think Loria means that when he puts me in charge of it all. But after a week or so we'll get a letter from him, and he'll tell us what he intends to do."

"I shall cable him," said Pauline, thoughtfully, "not to come over unless he wants to. Then he can do as he likes. But he needn't come for my benefit. The property must be divided and all that, but we can settle any uncertainties by mail or cable. And, I think I shall go on the trip as we had planned it."

"You do!" said Gray, in amazement. "Go to Egypt?"

"Yes, I don't see why not. I'd like the trip, and it would take my mind off these horrors. Our passage is booked for a February sailing. If necessary I will postpone it a few weeks, but I see no reason why I shouldn't go. Do you?"

"No," said Haviland, slowly.

Hardy seemed about to speak and then thought better of it, and said nothing.

"Of course I shall not go," began Anita, and Pauline interrupted her with:

"You go! I should say not! Why should you?"

"Why shouldn't I, if I choose?" returned Anita, and her pink cheeks burned rosy. "I am my own mistress, I have my own money. I am as free to go as you are."

"Of course you are," said Pauline, coldly.

"Only please advise me on what steamer you are sailing."

"That you may take another," and Anita laughed shortly. "But I may prefer to go on the one you do. Aren't you rather suddenly anxious to leave this country?"

Pauline faced her. "Anita Frayne," she said, "if you suspect me of crime, I would rather you said so definitely, than to fling out these continual innuendoes. Do you?"

"I couldn't say that Pauline. But there are, —there certainly are some things to be explained regarding your interview with your aunt on Tuesday night. You know, I heard you in her room."

"Your speech, Anita, is that of a guilty conscience. As you well know, I saw you come from her room at the hour you accuse me of being there."

"Let up, girls," said Haviland; "you only make trouble by that sort of talk."

"But when an innocent man is arrested, Pauline ought to tell what she knows!"

"I have told, and it seems to implicate you!"

The impending scene was averted by Haviland, who insisted on knowing what word should be sent to Loria.

"May as well get it off," he said; "it takes long enough to get word back and forth to him, anyway. What shall I say for you, Polly?"

"Tell him to come over or not, just as he prefers, but that I shall be quite content if he does not care to come; and that I shall go to Egypt as soon as I can arrange to do so. Put it into shape yourself,—you know more about cabling than I do."

Haviland went away to the library, and Hardy followed.

"Look here, Mr. Haviland," said the latter, "what do these ladies mean by accusing each other of all sorts of things? Did either of them have any hand in this murder!"

"Not in a thousand years!" declared Gray, emphatically. "The girls never loved each other, but lately, even before the death of Miss Lucy, they have been at daggers drawn. I don't know why, I'm sure!"

"But what do you make of this story of Miss Frayne's about hearing Miss Stuart in her aunt's room?"

"She didn't hear her. I mean she didn't hear Miss Stuart; what she heard was Miss Carrington talking to herself. The old lady was erratic in lots of ways."

"Why do you all say the old lady? She wasn't really old."

"About fifty. But she tried so hard to appear young, that it made her seem older."

"She was in love with the Count, of course?"

"Yes; as she was in love with any man she could attach. No, that's not quite true. Miss Lucy cared only for interesting men, but if she could corral one of those, she used every effort to snare him."

"Is the illustrious Count interesting?"

"She found him so. And, yes, he always entertained us. She made that bequest to attract his attention and lure him on. And then—"

"Well, and then?"

"Oh, then he couldn't withstand the temptation and he shuffled her off, to make sure of the money now."

"You think he killed her, then?"

"Who else? Those girls never used a blackjack—"

"But the poison?"

"Had it been poison alone, there might be a question. But that stunning blow has to be remembered. And neither Miss Stuart nor Miss Frayne can be thought of for a moment in connection with that piece of brutality."

"But the snake? The queer costume?"

"The costume wasn't so queer—for a boudoir garb. The snake is inexplicable,—unless the man has a disordered mind, and used insane methods to cover his tracks. Then there's the glove, you can't get around that!"

"That glove might have been put in her hand by anybody."

"That's so! By a professional burglar, say! I really believe—"

"Oh, let up on that professional burglar business! No burglar is going off without his loot, when he has uninterrupted time enough to kill a person twice, with poison and then, to hide that, with a fractured skull! How do you explain, even in theory, those two murderous attacks?"

"Good Lord, man, I don't know! It's all the most inexplicable muddle. I don't see how any of the things could happen, but they did happen! You're the detective, not I! Aren't you ever going to discover anything?"

"I may as well own up, Mr. Haviland, I am beyond my depth. There is a belief among detectives that the more bizarre and amazing the clues are, the easier the deduction therefrom. But I don't believe that. This case is bizarre enough, in all conscience, yet what can one deduce from that paper snake and that squeezed-up glove? It was all up in a little wad, you know, not at all as if it were carelessly drawn from a man's hand, or pulled off in a struggle."

"There was no struggle. The features were composed, even almost smiling."

"I know it. That proves it was no burglar. Well, I'm up a tree. I wish you felt inclined to call in Fleming Stone. He's the only man on this continent who could unravel it all."

"I want to get him, but Miss Stuart won't hear of it. I'd have to have either her authority or Loria's."

"But Mr. Loria gave you full swing, in that cable."

"Yes, for ordinary business matters. But this is different. I 'd have to have assurance that he'd pay the bills before I engaged Stone. I've heard he's some expensive."

"I've heard that, too. But, by Jove, I'd like to work with him! Or under him. I say, I wish you could bring it about."

"I might cable Loria on my own, and not mention it to Miss Stuart until I get the permission."

"Do. For as you say, the two ladies cannot possibly be involved, and I, for one, don't believe that nincompoop Count ever pulled off such a complicated affair all by himself."

"What about the widow he's visiting?"

"Ah, there you have it! Those two are in it, but there's more mystery yet."

"I'd like to have it straightened out," saict Haviland, thoughtfully. "In a way, I feel responsible to Loria, since he has put me in charge. And if he wants me to get Stone, I'll be glad to do so. As you say, it can't affect the girls,— that stuff Anita made up was only to bother Pauline. You see, Pauline came back at her with a counter accusation. They're both unstrung and upset, and they scarcely know what they're saying."

"Then there's that French maid."

"Oh, Estelle. She's a negligible quantity. She's hysterical from sheer nervousness, and she lies so fast she can hardly keep up with herself."

"Well, think it over, and if you see your way clear to call in Stone, I'll be mighty glad. If the Frenchman is the guilty party, Stone will nail him and prove it beyond all doubt. And if not, we surely don't want an innocent man to swing."

"That we don't," agreed Haviland.

CHAPTER 11: FLEMING STONE

"YES, I have often heard the idea expressed that the more bizarre the clues appear, the easier the solution of the mystery. And this is frequently true."

Fleming Stone looked from one to another of the interested group of listeners. They sat in the library,— Pauline, Anita, Gray Haviland and the young detective, Hardy.

Haviland had carried out his plan of cabling Carrington Loria for authority to employ Mr. Stone, and had received a reply to use his own judgment in all such matters and charge the expense to Loria's account.

Pauline had been opposed to the idea of calling Fleming Stone to the case, but as she seemed unable to put forth any valid objections, Haviland had insisted until she gave her consent. So arrangements had been quickly made, and the great Detective had reached Garden Steps on Wednesday afternoon, just a week after the discovery of the murder.

Previously unacquainted with Stone, the whole household was interested in his personality, and this preliminary conversation was by way of introduction.

A man of nearly fifty, Fleming Stone was tall and well proportioned, with a carriage and bearing that gave an impression of strength. His clear-cut face and firm jaw gave the same character indications as are seen in portraits of Lincoln, but his features were far more harmonious than those of our rugged-faced president. Stone's hair, thick and dark, was slightly grayed at the temples, and his deep-set eyes were now lustrous, and again, shadowed, like the water of a dark pool. His lean jaw and forceful mouth made his face in repose somewhat stern, but this effect was often banished by his delightful

smile, which softened his whole countenance and gave
him a distinct air of friendliness.

His manner was full of charm, and even Pauline
became fascinated as she watched him and listened to his
talk.

Fully at ease and skilfully directing the conversation,
while he seemed merely sharing it, Stone was studying
and classifying the new elements with which he had to
deal. Not yet had he inquired as to the details of the case
in hand, he was discussing detective work in general,
much to the gratification of Tom Hardy, who listened as a
pupil at the feet of Gamaliel.

"Yes," went on Stone, settling back sociably in his
easy chair, while the others unconsciously fell into more
informal postures, "Yes, bizarre effects do often point the
way to a successful quest. Why, once, a man was found
dead, with his feet in a tub of cold water. It was
discovered that his feet had been immersed after death
had taken place. Obviously the tub of water had been
used as a blind, to fog up the case. But the very character
of the clue led at once to a man who was known as a 'cold
water fiend,' and a fiend indeed he was. He was the
murderer. You see, he was clever, but not clever enough.
He had wit enough to think of the queer circumstance of
the tub of water, but not enough to realize that the clue
would lead directly to his own undoing."

Everybody looked thoughtful, but it was Hardy who
spoke; "Yes, Mr. Stone," he said, "but that clue was put
there on purpose. Do you think these strange effects
connected with Miss Carrington's murder were
deliberately arranged?"

"That I can't tell now, Mr. Hardy. In fact, I have not
heard a connected and circumstantial account of the
discoveries, as yet. Suppose we go over the case, leisurely,
and let me get a complete account by means of a general
conversation. I will ask questions, or you may volunteer
information, as seems most enlightening. Tell me first of

the character and characteristics of Miss Carrington. Was she timid, or fearful of burglars?"

"Not at all," said Haviland. "She was careful to have the house locked up at night by the servants, but she had no burglar alarms or anything of that sort."

"If a marauder had appeared, would she have been likely to scream out in affright?"

"No, I don't think so," volunteered Anita.

"She would more likely demand to know what he wanted and order him out."

"Yet the black-jack clearly indicates a burglar," went on Stone; "I can't imagine an ordinary citizen, of any calling, owning or using such a weapon."

"Have you examined the thing?" asked Haviland.

"No; I should like to see it."

Tom Hardy at once produced it, having brought it with him from Police Headquarters for the purpose.

"H'm," said Fleming Stone, as he fingered the not very alarming-looking affair. In fact, it was merely a long, narrow bag, made of dark cloth and filled with shot. The bag was tied tightly at one end with a bit of twine to prevent the escape of the contents.

"Home-made affair," Stone went on. "Made probably by a professional burglar, but an amateur murderer. See, it is merely a bit of heavy cloth, cut from an old coat sleeve or trouser leg, sewed up in a bungling manner to make a bag. It is stitched with coarse black thread and the stitches are drawn hard and firm, evidently pulled through by a strong hand. Then, filled with shot, it is tied with a bit of old fish-line, which also is pulled and knotted by muscular fingers. And—" Stone paused abruptly.

"And—" prompted Anita, breathlessly, her eyes fixed on the speaker.

"Nothing much," and Stone smiled; "only I should say the burglar lived in a house recently remodeled."

Hardy nodded in satisfaction. This was the sort of deduction he was looking for. Next he hoped for the color of the man's hair, and the sort of cigar he smoked. But he was doomed to disappointment.

"We seem to have drifted from the subject of Miss Carrington," Stone said. "The evening before her death was she in her usual spirits? Evidently no premonition of her fate?"

"On the contrary," said Gray, "she remarked during the evening that something would happen to her that night which would surprise and astound us all. She said distinctly that 'tomorrow everything would be different.'"

""What did you understand her to mean by that?"

"We couldn't understand it at all. It was most mysterious. Nor do we yet know what she meant. For surely she had no thought of dying. She spent the evening playing cards and listening to music, and conversation with the family and guests, quite as usual."

"In amiable mood?" asked Stone.

"No," replied Pauline, taking up the talk; "on the contrary she was exceedingly irritable and ill-tempered."

"You saw her after she went to her room for the night?" and Stone turned his whole attention to Pauline.

"Yes; Miss Frayne and I always went to her room with her, to say good-night and to receive possible orders or suggestions for the next day's occupations."

"And you say she was unamiable?"

"That is a mild word," and Pauline smiled a little. "She was in a high temper, and she told us both that we were to leave this house the next day."

"You both left her in that mood?"

"Yes, we were obliged to do so. She dismissed us peremptorily and ordered us from the room."

"And you saw her next, Miss Stuart, when?" asked Fleming Stone gently.

Pauline hesitated for a perceptible instant, then she said, with a slight air of bravado, "next morning."

"I have been told the main facts," went on Stone, "but I want to learn certain details. Please tell me, Miss Stuart, exactly how she then appeared."

"Oh, I can't!" and Pauline flung her face into her hands with a short, sharp cry.

"I should think you couldn't!" exclaimed Anita, and her voice was distinctly accusing. This seemed to rouse Pauline, and she looked up haughtily at the speaker. "I don't wonder you think so!" she cried. "But since you ask, Mr. Stone, I will do the best I can. My aunt was seated at her dressing-table, but not in her usual chair,—or indeed, as if she were in any way attending to her toilette,—but in an easy chair, more as if she were sitting there in contemplation."

"Was she given to such indications of vanity?" asked Stone, in a gentle way.

"Not at all. My aunt was not a beautiful woman, and she had no illusions about her personal appearance. I have never known her to look at herself in a mirror more than was necessary for her dressing. Her maid will tell you this."

"Go on, please, Miss Stuart."

"When I saw my aunt, she was sitting placidly, even smilingly,—and I did not, for a moment, imagine she was not alive. Then I noticed her large tortoise-shell comb was broken to bits, and I noticed, too, her rigid, staring face. The next few moments are a confused memory to me, but I know I touched her hand and felt it cold, then I called to Mr. Haviland and he came."

"Tell me of your aunt's garb. I understand it was most unusual."

"Only in the accessories. The gown she had on was a negligee of Oriental make and fabric, elaborate, but one of which she was fond and which she had worn several times. Round her shoulders was a scarf, one of those heavy Syrian ones, of net patterned with silver. Then, she had on quantities of jewelry. Not only her pearls, and a few pins, which she had worn during the evening, but she had added many brooches and bracelets and rings of great value."

"She was wearing, let us say, a hundred thousand dollars' worth of jewelry?"

"Far more than that. Her pearls alone are worth that amount. Her diamond sunburst is valued at fifty thousand dollars and her emerald brooch is equally valuable. My aunt believed in gems as an investment, and though she usually kept them in a safe deposit vault, she had recently taken them from there, and had them all in the house."

"A strange proceeding?"

"Very. I have never known such a thing to occur before unless for some especial social occasion."

"And the paper snake, of which I have been told—"

"That is the strangest part of all! My aunt was not only afraid of live snakes, but she had also a perfect horror of any picture or artificial representation of them. She could never, in her right mind, have placed that paper snake about her own neck, nor would she have allowed any one else to do it, without screaming out in horror. Yet, the doctors declare it must have been placed round her neck before death. Therefore, it is to me entirely unexplainable."

"Is not that a bizarre clue that should make the case an easy one?" asked Anita, with an inquiring glance at Stone.

"It may be so," he replied, with a thoughtful look at her. "Where could such a snake have come from?"

"It was brought by the burglar, of course," said Pauline, quickly.

"I don't mean that; but where could it be bought?"

"Oh, at Vantine's or any Japanese shop," said Pauline, "or at some of the department stores."

"Could you, by inquiry, find out if Miss Carrington purchased it herself at any of those places?"

"I could inquire; but I am sure, Mr. Stone, that Aunt Lucy never bought such a thing."

"It would simplify matters somewhat if you would kindly find out," and Stone nodded at her, as if to stamp this suggestion a definite request. The conversation went on, and no one noticed that so deftly did Fleming Stone guide it that only facts were brought out. No sooner did any one begin to formulate an opinion or theory than he skilfully turned the subject or changed the drift of the discussion.

He gathered from facial expressions and manners much that he wanted to know, he learned the attitudes of the various members of the household toward each other, and he came to the conclusion that as Gray Haviland had engaged him, and as he stood as business head of the estate by authority of Carrington Loria, to Haviland should his reports be made.

"Tell me more of Mr. Loria," Stone said, at last, after many matters had been discussed. "He and I are children of Miss Carrington's two sisters," said Pauline. "Our parents all died when we were young children and Aunt Lucy brought us both up. Carr, as we call him, lived with us, except for his college terms, until four years ago. Then he had an opportunity to go to Egypt and engage in excavation and ancient research work. He is absorbed in it, and has been home only twice in the four years. It was planned that my aunt and I should go to Egypt next month on a pleasure trip, and both he and we looked forward eagerly to it. Miss Frayne was to accompany us, and Mr. Haviland also."

"Is it your intention to abandon the trip?"

"Speaking for myself, Mr. Stone, no," and Pauline looked determined. "I cannot answer for the others, but it seems to me that such a visit to my cousin would be not only right and proper for me, but the only way for me to find relief and distraction from these dreadful scenes."

"You won't go, I assume," said Stone, gently, "until the murderer of your aunt is apprehended with certainty?"

"I cannot say," and suddenly Pauline flushed rosily and looked distinctly embarrassed.

"Bather not!" declared Anita, with an unpleasant glance, and Fleming Stone made haste to introduce a new phase of the subject.

Chapter 12: Estelle's Story

AT the invitation of Haviland, Fleming Stone was a house guest at Garden Steps. Pauline had raised objections to this, but with Carr Loria's authority back of him, Gray had insisted, and Pauline unwillingly consented.

Stone himself recognized the fact that Pauline disliked him, or at any rate disliked having him on the case, but he ignored it and showed to her the same gracious manner and pleasant attitude that he showed to all. Anita, on the other hand, seemed charmed with Stone. She lost no opportunity to talk with him, and she used every endeavor to attract his attention to herself. In fact, she tried to flirt with him, and much to the surprise of the others, Stone seemed ready to meet her advances and respond to them. The morning after his arrival, breakfast over, Stone announced his intention of making a thorough examination of Miss Carrington's rooms, and asked that he be permitted to go alone for the purpose.

"If Mr. Hardy comes, send him up," he ordered, as Haviland unlocked the door to give him admittance.

Stone passed through the boudoir to the bedroom and from that to the elaborate dressing-room and bath. Quickly he noted the obvious details. Everything had been left practically untouched, and his rapid, trained gaze took in the bed, turned down but not slept in; the toilet accessories laid ready in the bathroom; and the fresh, unused towels, that proved the unfortunate victim had not prepared to retire, but had, for some reason, donned her jewels at that unusual hour.

Back to the boudoir Stone went and made there more careful scrutiny. Carefully he examined the white dust of powder on the floor.

At Hardy's orders, this had not been swept away, and
Stone stood, with folded arms, looking at it. He saw the
place where the powder had been smeared about,—he
had been told of this,—but he saw other places where
faint footprints were to his keen eye discernible. Not
sufficiently clear to judge much of their characteristics,
but enough to show that a stockinged foot had imprinted
them.

"Well, what do you make of the tracks?" asked Hardy,
coming in upon his meditations.

"Their tale is a short one but clear," returned Stone,
smiling a greeting to the younger detective. "As you see,
they go out of the room only, they don't come in."

"Proving?"

"That the intruder came in at the door, accomplished
his dreadful purpose, and then, stepped around here in
front of his victim,—here where the powder is spilt, and
then went straight out of the room. Why did he do this?"

"He heard something to frighten him off?"

"He saw something that frightened him. I doubt if he
heard anything. But he dropped his black-jack and fled.
Did you bring the photographs of the scene?"

"Yes, here they are." Hardy handed over a sheaf of
the gruesome pictures, and Stone scanned them eagerly.
Yet their gruesomenesslay largely in the idea that the
subject of them was not a living person,—for in
appearance they were by no means unpleasant to look at.
The face of Miss Carrington was serene and smiling, her
wide-open eyes, though staring, were filled with a life-like
wonder, not at all an expression of fright or terror.

"You see," volunteered Hardy, "she was sitting here,
admiring herself, and happily smiling, when the villain
sneaked up behind her and gave her that crack over the
head."

"But she was already dead when she was hit on the
head."

"So the doctors think, but I believe they're mistaken. Why, there's no theory that would account for hitting a dead person!"

"And yet, that is what happened. No, Hardy, the doctors are not mistaken about the hour of death, and about the poison in her system and all that. But the most obvious and most important clue, for the moment, is that black-jack. Just where was it found?"

"Right here, Mr. Stone, under the edge of this couch. Hidden on purpose, of course."

"No, I think not. Dropped by the burglar, rather, when he was startled by something unexpected. You see, he doubtless stood here, where the powder is dusted about, and to drop the thing quickly, it would fall or be flung just there where it was found."

"Yes, but what scared him, if he didn't hear anything?"

"Something that frightened him so terribly that he fled without taking the jewels he had come for! Something that made him make quick, straight tracks for the door and downstairs and out, by the way he had entered."

"Good lord! Say, Mr. Stone, you think it was that make-believe Count, don't you?"

"Why make-believe?"

"Oh, somehow, I feel sure he's a fake. He's not the real thing,—or I'm greatly mistaken!"

"Let me see that glove found in her hand. Have you it with you?"

Hardy had brought some of the exhibits held by the police, and, taking the glove from his bag, he handed it to Fleming Stone.

Stone looked at the glove hastily, but, raising it to his nose, smelled of it very carefully.

"No," he said, returning it, "no, the Count is not the man who wielded the black-jack. I'm fairly certain of that."

"Well, I'm blessed if I can see how you know by smelling! By the way, Mr. Stone, I suppose you heard all about the conversation that Miss Frayne related as taking place in this room after one o'clock that night?"

"Yes, I've read the full account of it What do you think about it?"

"Oh, I think it was the Count, talking to Miss Carrington before he killed her. He has a very low voice, and speaks almost inaudibly always. Then, you see, he is down in her will for ten thousand dollars of those bonds, and he's very fond of pearls—"

"What's that? Who said he was fond of pearls?"

"Oh, maybe you didn't hear about that. Why, Miss Frayne remembered afterward, that another sentence she heard Miss Carrington say was, 'I know how very fond you are of pearls.' She forgot that speech in her evidence, but found it afterward in the written account she had of what she overheard at the door. And his Countship is fond of pearls. He talked a lot about those the lady wore that last evening. He says himself pearls are a hobby with him."

"So you really think the Count was in this room that night?"

"Surely I do. It's no insult to the lady's memory to say so. She had a right to receive him in her boudoir if she chose to do so. It's no secret that she was trying to annex him, and he was not entirely unwilling. You see,—the way I dope it out,—she had him up here to show off her stunning jewels, and so tempt him on to a declaration that she couldn't seem to work him up to otherwise. You know she said, 'Tomorrow these may all be yours, if you will only—' or some words to that effect. What could all that mean, except as I've indicated? And she said, 'You are the game I'm after,'—those weren't the words, I know, but it meant that."

"However, I can't think the Count struck that awful blow that fractured her skull. Villain he may be, even a murderous one, but that black-jack business, to my mind, points to a lower type of brain, a more thick-skinned criminal."

Stone spoke musingly, looking about the room as he talked.

"Could it be," he went on, "that she was talking to herself? or, say, to a picture,—a photograph of somebody? I don't see any photographs about."

Both men looked around, but there were no portraits to be seen.

"Funny," said Hardy: "most women have photographs of their family or relatives all over the place. Not even one of Miss Stuart or of her nephew, Loria."

"No, nor any of absent friends or schoolmates." Stone looked over all the silver paraphernalia of the dressing-table and other tables for even a small framed photograph that might have escaped notice, but found none. On the walls hung only gilt-framed water colors or photographs of famous bits of art or architecture in dark wood frames. Many of these were of old world masterpieces, Italian cathedrals or Egyptian temples. Others were a well-known Madonna, a Venus of Milo, and one at which Hardy exclaimed, "She's a sure enough peach! Who's she?"

"That's Cleopatra, starting on her Nile trip," said Stone, smiling at Hardy's evident admiration.

"'Tis, eh? Then Loria brought it to her. He's daffy over anything Egyptian. And he's mighty generous. The house is full of the stuff he brings or sends over; and it's his money, Mr. Stone, that pays your damages. Miss Stuart, now, she's none too free-handed, they say."

But Fleming Stone paid little heed to this gossip. He was studying the photographs of the dead lady as being of far more interest than pictures on the boudoir walls.

"Where's that maid?" he said suddenly; "the one who brought the breakfast tray—"

"She's in the sanatorium," returned Hardy; "we told you that, Mr. Stone."

"Yes, yes, I know. But where? Can I see her? Now, at once!"

"Yes, I suppose so. It's right near here. A small private affair, only a few patients. They needn't really have sent her, but she carried on so, Miss Stuart wouldn't have her about any longer."

"Come, let us go there." As he spoke, Fleming Stone left the room, and without waiting for the hurrying Hardy, ran downstairs, and was in the hall, getting into his great coat when the other joined him.

So great was Hardy's faith in his superior, and so anxious was he to watch his methods, that he donned his own overcoat without a word, and the two set forth.

It was only a short walk, and on the way, Stone looked about in every direction, asking innumerable questions about the neighboring houses and their occupants.

After passing several large and handsome estates, they came to a district of less elaborate homes, and after that to a section of decidedly poorer residences. At one of these, Stone stared hard, but not till they were well past it, did he inquire who lived there.

"Dunno," replied Hardy; "it's a sort of boarding-house, I think, for the lower classes."

"Is it?" said Stone, and they went on.

At the sanatorium they found Estelle. She was not hysterical now, but was in a sort of apathetic mood, and listless of manner.

Stone spoke to her with polite address, and a manner distinctly reassuring.

"It will be much better for you, Estelle," he said, pleasantly, "if you will speak the truth. Better for you, and better for you know whom."

His significant tone roused her, "I don't know who you mean," she exclaimed.

"Oh, yes, you do! somebody whose name begins with H, or B, or S."

"I don't know any one beginning with S," and Estelle frowned defiantly.

"But some one with—" Stone leaned forward, and in the tense pause that followed, Estelle's lips half formed a silent 'B'.

"Yes," went on Stone, as if he had not paused. "If you will tell the whole truth, it will be better for Bates in the long run."

Estelle began to tremble. "What do you know?" she cried out, and showed signs of hysteria.

"I know a great deal," said Stone, gravely, "and, unless assisted by what you know, my knowledge will bring trouble to your friend."

"What do you want me to tell you?" and Estelle, now on her guard, spoke slowly and clearly, but her fingers were nervously twining themselves in and out of her crumpled handkerchief.

"Only your own individual part in the proceedings. The rest we will learn from Bates himself."

"How do you know it was Bates?"

"We have learned much since you left Garden Steps," and now Stone spoke a little more sternly. Hardy looked at him in wonder. Who was this Bates, clearly implicated in the murder, and known to Estelle?

"You see, Mr. Haviland saw you go down to open the window for him to come in," Stone went on, as casually as if he were retailing innocent gossip. "Did you go down again and close it?"

"I haven't said I opened it yet," and Estelle flashed an irate glance at her questioner.

"No, but you will do so when you realize how necessary it is. I tell you truly, when I say that only your honesty now can save your friend Bates from the electric chair." Estelle shuddered and began to cry violently.

"That only makes matters worse," said Stone patiently. "Listen to me. This is your only chance to save Bates' life. If I go to the police with what I know, they will convict him of the murder beyond all doubt. If you tell me what I ask,'—I think, I hope, between us, we can prove that he did not do it."

"But didn't he?" and Estelle looked up with hope dawning in her eyes.

"I think not. Now there's no time to waste. Tell me what I ask or you will lose your chance to do so. You opened the living-room window for Bates to come in, at about three o'clock?"

"Yes," admitted the girl.

"And went down and closed and fastened it at —"

"Five o'clock," came in lowest tones.

"Not knowing that Miss Carrington was dead?"

"For Bates went there only to steal the jewels?"

"Yes."

"And so, when you took the breakfast tray, and fonnd the lady —as you did find her —you were frightened out of your wits, and dropped the tray?"

"Yes."

"And so, to shield Bates, who you thought had killed her, you lied right and left, even trying to incriminate Miss Stuart?"

"Yes, sir."

"Have you seen Bates since?"

"No, sir."

"And until now you have thought he killed your mistress?"

"I didn't know."

"Another thing, Estelle; you put bromide in the glass of milk in order that Miss Carrington might sleep soundly, and not hear Bates come in?"

"She didn't drink that milk!"

"But you fixed it, thinking she would?"

"Yes."

"That's all. Come on, Hardy." and somewhat unceremoniously, Stone took leave, and made for the nearest telephone station.

After that, matters whizzed. Stone had called the Police Headquarters and asked that an officer be sent with a warrant for the arrest of Bates.

"How do you know where he is?" asked Hardy, nearly bursting with curiosity.

"I'm not sure, but at least I know where to start looking for him," Stone replied, as the two went back the way they had come.

Stone stopped at the boarding-house he had noticed on the way to the sanatorium, and rang the bell.

Sure enough, Bates lived there and Bates was at home.

At Stone's first questions he broke down and confessed to the assault with the black-jack.

"But I didn't kill her!" he cried, "she was already dead! Oh, my God! can I ever forget those terrible, staring eyes! The saints forgive me! I was half crazy. There she was, dead, and yet smiling and happy looking! Oh, sir, what does it all mean?"

CHAPTER 13: BATES, THE BURGLAR

BROUGHT before the magistrate, Bates told a coherent though amazing story.

It seems he was Estelle's lover, and had long ago persuaded her to let him know when Miss Carrington had a quantity of jewelry in the house, that he might essay a robbery. The plan was simple. Estelle had promised to slip downstairs at three o'clock and raise a window for his entrance, and later, but before any one else was about, she was to slip down and lock it again. In the meantime, they assumed, the burglary would be quietly accomplished, their supposition being that Miss Carrington would be asleep in her bedroom, and the boudoir easy of access.

"You entered by the window, then, at what time?" asked Stone, who was doing most of the questioning.

"At quarter of four in the morning," replied Bates, and all noted that this was shortly before the hour when Mrs. Frothingham saw through her field-glass a man leaving by the same window.

"You went directly up the stairs?"

"Yes; Estelle had often told me the lay of the rooms, and I went straight to the lady's boodore."

"You carried with you a 'black-jack.' Did you have murder in your heart?"

"That I did not! I took that, thinkin' if the lady woke up and screamed, I'd just give her a tap that would put her to sleep without hurtin' her at all, at all. I'm no murderer, Sir, and I'm confessin' my attempt at burglary, and—and assault, so I won't be accused of a greater crime."

"That's right, Bates, it'll be better for you to be perfectly truthful. Now, what did you see when you entered the room?"

"I had stepped inside and shut the door before I saw anything, and then, I turned to see the lady's face, but in the mirror. I was behind her, and in the glass I saw her smilin' face, and of course, I thought she was alive, and that she saw me. I knew she'd scream in a minute, and the sight of all the jewels gleamin' on her neck drove me fair crazy with greed, I suppose, and I up with my sandbag, and hit her head, not meanin' to hit hard enough to kill her, but only to knock her unconscious-like."

"And then?"

"The blow smashed the big comb she was wearin' but she didn't move nor fall over. She was leanin' back in her big chair, and she jest sat there, and kept on smilin'. My knees shook like the ague, for I thought it was magic, or that my eyes was deceivin' me. There was no sound anywhere, and I stood starin' at that smilin' face and she starin' back at me! I nearly screamed out myself! But I bucked up, and thinkin' that she was struck unconscious so quick, her face didn't change, I made to take off some of the jewels I was after. I touched her neck and it was cold! The lady was dead! Had been dead some time, I was sure, 'cause she was so cold and stiff. I trembled all over, but my only thought then was to get out. Not for a million dollars would I touch them sparklers! There ain't often a burglar who is ghoul enough to rob a corpse! Leastways, I'm not. I wouldn't. I wouldn't! I'm a tough and a bad egg generally, but I wouldn't steal from no corpse! Not I!"

"So you left the house at once?"

"That I did, as fast as my tremblin' legs could get me downstairs. I was clean daft. I couldn't make it out and I didn't try. I thought it was the Devil's own work, somehow, but how, I didn't know. My mind was full, makin' my escape. I ran like the old boy was after me, and reachin' home, I hid under me bedclothes and groaned all night. Full a week went by, and I begun to breathe easy, thinkin' I'd never be suspected of a hand in it, when up conms this gentleman, and says I done it. Well, I've told the truth now, and I'm relieved to get it off my chest."

Bates heaved a deep sigh, as of a man eased of a great burden. His whole story bore the stamp of truth, and his manner of telling was straightforward and earnest. Nor was there reason for doubt. Though a startling tale, it entirely explained many of the strange conditions that had seemed so bewildering. It would never have occurred to Bates nor to any one to make up such a yarn, and what else could have deterred him from the contemplated robbery but the superstition that makes even the most hardened criminals refuse to steal from a dead person? Therefore, the narrative was accepted as probably true, and Bates was taken to the Tombs to await further proceedings against him.

"You're a wonder!" said Gray Haviland, as, that same afternoon, he discussed the matter with Fleming Stone. "Would you mind telling me how you went straight to the criminal and walked him off to jail?"

"That was practically a bit of luck," and Stone smiled. "It was the black-jack that gave me the clue. If the fellow hadn't dropped that in his fright, we might never have traced him. Though we would perhaps have found him eventually, through the maid, Estelle. She is not good at keeping things secret. However, he did drop the weapon, and it led straight to him."

"But how?"

"Well, the thing smelled strongly of creosote. Now, it was made from a bit of old cloth that looked like a piece of some discarded garment,—a man's coat, say. If the odor had been camphor or moth balls, I should have assumed a garment laid away in storage, but creosote is not used for that purpose. So I deduced a house recently remodeled by use of a certain kind of shingles. I know that the odor of those shingles clings to everything in the house for months. It is almost ineradicable. So I looked about for a house lately reshingled."

"Why not a new house?" asked Hardy, who was present.

"A point well taken," said Stone, nodding approval, "but in a new house the odor often is dispelled before the people move in. In a remodeled house, the furnishings stay there during the work and so are deeply impregnated with that unmistakable smell of creosote. At any rate, I worked on that, and when I found that a newly shingled old house was a boardinghouse of the type Bates would be likely to live in, I went there to see, and found him."

"Yes, but how did you know there was such a person as Bates? Where did you get his name?"

"From your cook," returned Stone, simply. "I concluded there was no doubt that Estelle had let the man in and relocked the window afterward. So I deduced a friend of the girl's so dear to her that she would do this for him. I asked the cook, Mrs. Haskins, as to Estelle's admirers and learned that there were two, Bates and Higgins. Mrs. Haskins couldn't say which one Estelle more favored, so I decided to try both. Bates—the cook told me—lived in a boarding-house near here, and Higgins over in New York. So when I asked Estelle a few leading questions I pretended to greater knowledge than I really had. I spoke of a name beginning with either B, H, or S. She fell into the trap and said quickly that she knew no one initialed S. Then I said, 'but beginning with ' and waited; she said no name, but involuntarily her lips form a silent 'B,' and I knew she had Bates in mind. The rest was easy. Bates, the boarding-house and the shingles formed a combination too indicative to be merely coincidence. And so we found him. And I, for one, believe his story. I know the strong superstition that imbues those people concerning a corpse, and the unexpected discovery that he had attacked one was enough to make that man beside himself. Indeed, it's a wonder that he didn't himself make an outcry in his terror and fright."

"I have heard of your prowess in these matters," said Haviland, "but I didn't look for such quick work as this. Why, you hadn't even interviewed Estelle when you came to your conclusions about Bates."

"No, but remember, I have seen a full account of all the evidence, not only at the inquest, but all that has been gathered by the police and by Mr. Hardy here. Last night I read all this carefully, and it was enlightening on these points that led up to to-day's work. But, now, I don't mind telling you, Mr. Haviland, that a much more difficult and complicated problem faces us, to discover who gave to Miss Carrington the poison that killed her."

"Have you any suspicions?" and Gray looked the Detective straight in the eyes. "I have not, as yet," and Fleming Stone returned the steady gaze. "Have you?"

Gray Haviland hesitated. Then he said: "I would rather not answer that question, Mr. Stone. If I should have suspicions, and they should be unjust or ill-founded, is it not better to leave them unmentioned, even to you? You are here to discover the criminal. I can not think my suspicions, if I have any, could help you, but they might easily hinder you by wrong suggestion."

"Very well, Mr. Haviland, just as you please. But I assume you will tell me frankly anything you may know or learn in the way of direct evidence bearing on the matter?"

"That, certainly." But though Haviland's words were a definite promise, his tone and manner seemed hesitant, and a trifle vague.

"Am I to have the privilege of working with you, Mr. Stone?" inquired Hardy, his heart beating tumultuously lest he receive a negative answer.

"If you care to. And if you are willing to work in my way. I am somewhat impatient of interference or questioning. But, if you want to assist in investigating,

under my absolute orders, I shall be glad to have you do
so."

Nothing was further from Hardy's mind than to
interfere or to show any undue curiosity concerning the
work or methods of the great Detective. He was more
than content to watch silently, to run errands, and to
make himself useful in any way desired by his superior.
He said this, and Stone nodded indulgently.

"I shall begin with this matter of the arrest of Count
Charlier," said Stone, as he looked over his note-book.
"Either that man is the guilty party or he is not. If not, he
must be released. If so, it must be proven. What do you
know of his history, Mr. Haviland?"

"Very little, Mr. Stone. In the first place, I doubt his
right to the title he assumes."

"You do? And why?"

Haviland looked a little embarrassed. "I'm not sure I
know why. But he doesn't act like a real Count."

"Yes? And how do real Counts act, I mean in ways
that differ from this man's habits?"

"You're having fun with me, Mr. Stone," and Gray
blushed like a school-boy. "But I mean it. It's this way.
I'm not a Count, but if I wanted to pretend I was, I'd act
just as Count Charlier does. There!"

"Good! That's definite, at least. Now make it a little
more so by describing some of these actions."

"Well," and Haviland's brow wrinkled, "well, to begin
with, his manners are too slick and polished."

"A traditional trait of Frenchmen."

"Yes, if real. But his seem artificially, purposely,—oh,
fakely polished! Have you seen him, Mr. Stone?"

"No, not yet."

"When you do, you'll see what I mean. He has shifty
eyes, and he rubs his hands together, and if he's standing,
he half bows with every sentence he utters, and he smirks
instead of smiling, and his whole attitude is a fifty-fifty of
apology and bumptiousness."

"Bravo! You 've given a graphic picture of him at all events. I'll reserve further consideration of his personality until I have seen him."

"You believe implicitly all that story of Bates, do you, Mr. Stone?" and Haviland looked dubiously at the Detective.

"Yes, I do, at present. If anything turns up to disprove any part of it I may have to revise my ideas. But just now, it seems to me that Bates told the simple truth. To be sure, he only told it because he feared an accusation of murder, and he knew that to confess to the lesser crime would go far to help him deny the greater."

"You may be right. But might there not be collusion between Friend Count and Bates?"

"Collusion?"

"Just that," and Gray shook his head doggedly. "I've a vague idea that Frenchy is mixed up in this thing somehow. Now, he couldn't possibly have administered the poison, himself, personally, nor could he have struck the blow personally, but couldn't he have hired the man Bates to do it for him?"

"On the face of things, Mr. Haviland, does that look plausible? Is the Count, as you describe him, a man who would engage a burglar of the Bates type to commit a brutal crime? Again, if Bates were merely the Count's tool, would he not, when caught, pass the blame on to his employer?"

"He sure would! You are right, Mr. Stone, those two never hooked up together! It's out of the question. But as Estelle and Bates are in cahoots, why didn't she give Miss Carrington the poison, herself?"

"Well, she did fix the bromide, hoping to make her mistress sleep soundly. But the lady never took it. Now, if the maid had given or expected to give the poison, why the bromide at all?"

"But, look here," broke in Hardy, "mightn't it be that Estelle did do the poisoning and arranged the bromide as a blind, to put us off the track, exactly as it has done?"

"There's small use speculating about that poison," said Stone thoughtfully, "we must go at that systematically. We must find out where it was bought and by whom. People can't go round buying deadly poison without a record being made of the sale. We must inquire of druggists, until we find out these facts."

"There's no druggist about here who would sell aconitine," said Hardy, "it doubtless was bought in New York."

"That, of course, adds to the difficulty of tracing the sale, but it must be done. Mr. Hardy, I will ask you to do all you can to find out about that."

"You want to look up a French apothecary," advised Haviland. "That Count is at the bottom of this, as sure as shootin', and he's full clever enough to hide his tracks mighty closely. Why, that man is a fortune-hunter and an adventurer, and he wanted that ten thousand dollars, and he poisoned Miss Lucy to get it! That's what he did! And he was on deck that night, after the jewels, that's where he was! It was he in that room talking, it was he who left his glove there,—of course, he didn't know it,— and now you've got him under lock and key, I hope you'll keep him there, and not let this Bates discovery get him the slip. If the two were not working together, then, surely they are incriminated separately, and you want to look into the case of little old Mr. Count!"

"You may be right, Mr. Haviland," and Fleming Stone smiled at him, "but I think you are assuming a lot because of your prejudice against the Frenchman. Was he very attentive to Miss Carrington? Had he proposed marriage to her?"

"That we don't know. Of course, we had all been afraid he would—"

"Why afraid?"

"Oh, we didn't want my cousin to marry an adventurer. Of course, he only wanted her fortune, and as her business manager, I had a right to interfere, or at least, to look after her interests enough to prevent that."

"But was she not a capable woman, who could be supposed to know her own mind?"

"Ordinarily, yes. But, there's no use mincing matters. Miss Carrington greatly desired to marry. However, she paid no attention to men whom she did not consider interesting. There were several such, and she sent them packing. The Count, though, she took to at once, partly because of his title and partly because,—well, he has a way with him. He flattered her, and she took the bait like a hungry fish!"

CHAPTER 14: WHO GAVE THE POISON?

THOUGH Fleming Stone's acumen and quick perception had led to a swift apprehension of Bates, his next steps were not taken so rapidly. He spent much time in the boudoir of Miss Carrington, as if striving to make the walls tell what their traditional ears had heard.

The upset breakfast tray had been removed, but nothing else disturbed. Estelle had owned up, after Bates' arrest, that she did drop the tray, in her fright at the sight of the dead lady, and that she afterward denied it lest she be suspected of wrong-doing.

The plate that had contained sandwiches was still on the bedside table, but the glass of milk, with bromide in, had been carried away. Stone looked at the empty plate, and wondered. Had the poison been placed in the sandwiches? By Estelle? By anybody else? Who had had opportunity? Estelle had brought the sandwiches and milk to the bedroom, according to her usual custom, when she prepared the bed for the night. A tiny serviette had been over the sandwiches, and was still there beside the plate. Stone looked at it. A mere wisp of fine linen, with a monogrammed corner. The few wrinkles in it showed clearly to Stone's sharp eyes the dainty touch of fingers that had held the caviare sandwich. It undoubtedly denoted that Miss Carrington had eaten the sandwich. Had any one merely removed it, the napkin would have been uncreased. He had been told that she rarely ate this night luncheon, though it was always placed for her. Why had she partaken of it on that particular night? Had some one advised her to? Or urged it? Had the Count really visited her in the boudoir, and having previously arranged the poisoned sandwich, made sure that it would perform its deadly mission? Could he have entered the room unknown to the rest of the household? Stone went to the window. Yes, that matter was easy enough. A balcony outside the long French window was connected with the lower verandah by a spiral staircase. Any one could run up the steps and be admitted to the boudoir in perfect secrecy. Stone wondered for a moment why Bates hadn't entered that way, and quickly realized that for a marauder to appear at the window would have frightened Miss Carrington and caused an outcry. The entrance of the Count, however, whether expected or not, would be easily effected.

If the Count were really guilty, the circumstances were all explicable. Suppose Miss Carrington had made the appointment. Would she not, in her vanity, have donned the beautiful boudoir gown and the jewels to appear attractive in his eyes? And, supposing she had playfully caught his glove as he removed it, and had half-unconsciously continued to hold it. Then the conversation alleged to have been overheard by Miss Frayne would have been addressed to him, and the remarks would be, at least, intelligible.

The snake? Ah, yes, the snake. As to that there was no hint, no clue of any sort. But then, the thing was so inexplicable, that the explanation must be easy. A clue so strange, so bizarre, must lead somewhere. That could be left to the future. Now, he must decide on his first steps.

The decision took him to call on Doctor Stanton, and the physician welcomed him warmly. "Glad to see you, Mr. Stone," he said; "sit down, sir, sit down. I've been wanting a talk with you ever since I heard of your arrival. So you've ferreted out the burglar already! Great work, great work indeed! And now for the real murderer. You see, sir, I'm up to the minute in my information regarding this case."

"Glad to know it," returned Stone. "Now, Doctor Stanton, I hope you can help me. I don't mind admitting the thing has its baffling aspects. The burglar was easily traced, and easily disposed of. The real work, as you say, is just beginning. Will you, sir, tell me all you know of the poison that killed Miss Carrington?"

"Surely, Mr. Stone. The autopsy showed a fatal dose of aconitine. Aconite, as you of course know, is the herb, wolfsbane, of the Hellebore tribe, all the species of which are poisonous. Aconitine is an intensely poisonous alkaloid obtained from aconite. Taken in a moderate quantity, it acts as a powerful sedative, but the dose absorbed by Miss Carrington was undoubtedly fatal within half or three quarters of an hour."

"And she died at what time?"

"About two o'clock."

"Proving she took the poison at about quarter or half after one."

"Yes; thereabouts. It is not possible to fix these hours precisely, but the poison was administered positively between one and two."

"Administered? You do not think then, that she took it herself?"

"Most certainly not! Miss Carrington has been in my care, professionally, for many years. I knew her very well, and I know nobody more opposed to medicine in any form or drugs of any sort. It was a most difficult task to persuade her to take even the simplest remedy, and then she had to be assured over and over again that it was harmless. No, Mr. Stone, nothing could have made her take that dose of her own accord, nor could any one have persuaded her to take it, consciously. It was, without doubt, given to her secretly, by the clever ruse of the murderer. Of course it could not have been an accident. The marvelous part is, to my mind, how any one secured the poison. It is not an easy matter to buy aconitine."

"Then that ought to make it easier to trace. If the public could easily procure it at will, there would be greater difficulty in running down the purchaser."

"That is so; and yet, I think your search will be a hard one. How shall you go about it?"

"By canvassing the drug shops of the city, and of the small towns as well."

"It may be you can trace the sale. But if it was bought under promise of secrecy, and if that secrecy were well paid for——?"

"True, there is the difficulty. But what's a detective for if not to find out secrets?"

"Quite right. May your quest succeed."

"And now, a little more about the action of this poison. What are the immediate effects of a fatal dose?"

"In a few moments there occurs a tingling numbness of lip and tongue and pharynx. The numbness increases and affects all the muscles and death ensues inside of an hour. This paralyzing effect renders it impossible for the victim to cry out, and there are no convulsions. The body remains calm and undisturbed, and the eyes open. A dilatation of the pupil takes place, but the expression on the face remains as in life. This is why Miss Carrington continued to look happy and smiling—"

"And proves that when she took the poison she was happy and smiling, and therefore in no way terrorized or frightened into it."

"Exactly so. And that indicates that she didn't know she was taking it—"

"Or, that it was administered by some one she knew and loved and had all confidence in."

"It would seem so," and Doctor Stanton's fine old face showed a sad apprehension.

"How was it taken,—in what medium?"

"That we can't tell to a certainty. There were traces of the sandwiches discovered at the autopsy, but, though the poison could have been given her, concealed in a sandwich filling, it is improbable."

"Why?"

"Because the white granules or powder, which are soluble in water, would be more easily discerned in solid food."

"But, on the other hand, it could be unostentatiously placed in a sandwich, with little fear of detection; but to prevail on her to swallow a solution,—it is bitter, is it not?"

"Yes, slightly so. I admit, I cannot imagine any one inducing Miss Carrington to swallow such a draught. Therefore, it may well be, it was placed in a sandwich. The filling, they tell me, was caviare, which would disguise the bitterness."

"And does not all this, if true, point to some one exceedingly familiar with all the details of Miss Carrington's affairs? Some one who knew of her nightly sandwich? And, also, does it not imply the presence of some one who could and did insure her consumption of that sandwich?"

"It would indeed seem so, Mr. Stone; but when it comes to discussing such a question as that, I must ask to be allowed to retire from the field. It is my duty to tell all I know, from my medical experience, but further than that I am not obliged to express any opinions or voice any suspicions."

"You know, however, that Count Charlier is held pending investigation?"

"Yes, I know it. I have no opinion to express."

Fleming Stone rather admired this gentleman of the old school, whose courtesy was evident, but equally so his determination to say only what justice demanded of his profession. And then, like a flash, the reason came to him. Doctor Stanton suspected, or at least feared to suspect some member of the Carrington household.

Of course, this was not a new idea to Fleming Stone. He had mentally gone over the possibility of every one in the family and all of the servants at Garden Steps, but so far he had held his mind open for impressions rather than to formulate theories himself.

"Then, to sum up, doctor," he said, as he rose to go, "you assure me that you consider it out of the question that Miss Carrington took the aconitine herself, say, as a headache cure, or something, intending only a small curative dose?"

"Absolutely impossible, sir," exclaimed the old gentleman, almost angrily; "to begin with, Miss Carrington never had headaches, and if she had she would have borne any amount of suffering from them before she would have touched a drug or a medicinal remedy of any sort. And, aside from all that, how could she get aconitine? It is not to be bought for the asking at any druggist's! No, sir, my conscience makes me insist on that point, Miss Carrington never took that poison knowingly,—either by accident or design. It was given to her, without her knowledge, by a very, very clever villain."

"Again, then, could it have been given her innocently, by mistake? I mean, if some one, her maid, or any friend, had wanted to give her a sedative, and meant only a light dose, but by error in quantity—"

"No, sir! Not a chance! The amount given was too great to be an error. And every one in that house knows better than ever to have attempted to give medicine in any form or degree or for any purpose to Miss Lucy Carrington."

"It was crime, then," said Fleming Stone, "black crime. And as such, it must be discovered and punished."

"Yes," agreed Doctor Stanton, but he spoke with deep sadness and as one who feared where or toward whom such discoveries might lead. From the doctor's house Stone went to see the Count.

That elegant gentleman was highly irate at being detained against his will in such plain quarters as The Tombs furnished, but he was not as belligerent or vindictive as Stone expected to find him.

Hasty work on the part of the detectives from the District Attorney's office had resulted in his imprisonment, but the later development of Bates' share in the matter made it extremely probable that the Count might soon be released from custody.

Pleasantly enough the two men conversed, and Count Charlier gave the impression of one glad of help from an outside source.

"It is such absurdity," he declared, "to think I would in any way wish harm to the lady. Why, I admired her above all, and it was my hope that she would do me the honor to accept my hand."

"Honestly, Count Charlier?" and Stone looked at him with a man-to-man glance that caused the Count to hesitate in his protestations.

"Well, I was considering the matter in my own mind. You know, Mr. Stone, it is a great responsibility, this seeking a wife. And Miss Carrington was not—not in her first youth. Of a fact, her years outnumbered my own. So, I asked myself was it wise, was it altogether just to the lady to—"

"Never mind all that, Count," said Stone, a little impatiently, "just give me a few details of that evening, so far as your actions were concerned. You were at the house till midnight?"

"Yes, Mr. Illsley and I left together. We had spent the evening there at cards and music."

"You had had any private conversation with Miss Carrington during the evening?"

"Yes, we walked alone in the conservatory for a time,—"

"You proposed marriage?"

"Not exactly that,—but I may have hinted at such an event."

"And the lady seemed agreeable?"

"Entirely so. If I may say it, she met my advances half-way, and I could not misunderstand her feeling toward my unworthy self."

"She spoke to you of money matters? Of her will?"

"Yes, to my surprise, she told me she had bequeathed to me ten thousand dollars."

"Was not this a strange bequest to a casual acquaintance?"

"Oh, we were more than casual acquaintances. I have known Miss Carrington for two or three months."

"Which? two or three?"

"Perhaps nearer two," and the Count showed a slight embarrassment.

"Do your friends often leave you large sums of money on such short acquaintance?"

"It has never happened before," and now the Count's dignity was touched and he spoke shortly and coolly.

"Then, of course, it struck you as peculiar," and Stone's smile assumed an acquiescence.

But the Count returned: "Not at all. Miss Carrington was an unusual woman, and I never expected her behavior to be entirely conventional. When she told me of this I was simply and honestly grateful, as I should have been to any one who showed me such a kindness."

"You were glad to get the money, then?"

"Yes, indeed!" the Count exclaimed, with sparkling eyes, then realizing his slip, he hastily added: "that is, I was glad of the knowledge that it would come to me some day. Surely I did not want the lady to die, that I might receive it, but I was pleased to know she thought enough of me to make the direction."

"What did she mean by saying 'To-morrow all will be different'?"

"That I do not know. Could she have meant—"

"She did say it, then? You admit she said it to you?"

Breathlessly, Fleming Stone waited the answer. Miss Carrington had said this to the person who was with her behind her closed door at one o'clock! Could the Count be going to incriminate himself?

"Not to me only. She said it to all who were present. It was while we were playing bridge."

"She said it again to the man who killed her!"

"Of that I know nothing," said Count Charlier, politely.

"Bother!" said Fleming Stone, inaudibly.

CHAPTER 15: PAULINE'S PURCHASE

ALONE, Fleming Stone wrestled with the problem of the giving of that poison. The library at Garden Steps had been turned over to him for a study and no one entered the room unless summoned. Stone sat at the mahogany table-desk, but his eyes rested unseeingly on the beautiful fittings of polished silver and glass. On a memorandum block he wrote down the names of possible and probable suspects. To be sure, he thought, every one in the house might be deemed possible, as well as some who were not in the house. But each one must be taken into consideration.

To begin with the most important, Miss Stuart. It was possible that she poisoned her aunt, but so improbable as to make it exceedingly unlikely. True, she was heir to half the fortune, but well-bred, well-nurtured young women do not commit crime to inherit their money sooner. Except for that conversation reported by Anita Frayne, there was not a shred of evidence against Miss Stuart. And Stone did not place implicit confidence in that story of the talk behind closed doors. He had discovered that the two girls were not friendly and he knewAnita capable of making up or coloring a tale to suit herself. Pauline had told him that she was in the hall-window seat at one o'clock that night and had seen Anita coming from Miss Carrington's room. Or, to put it more carefully, she had seen her with her hand on the door-knob, in the act of closing the door after her. This Pauline had told to Stone, with an air of such verity and truthfulness that he was fain to believe her. However, in all honesty, he had to admit to himself, that Miss Stuart could have given the poison in some secret way, had she so desired. The same was true, though, of Miss Frayne, of

Haviland and of the various houseservants. But where could any of them get it?

Again there were the Count and Mrs. Frothingham to be considered. In fact, there were too many suspects to decide among, without further evidence.

"Any luck?" Stone asked of Hardy, who came in to report.

"No, Mr. Stone. I've raked the drug shops thoroughly, and there's no trace of a sale of aconitine. It's practically impossible to buy such a substance. I mean, for the ordinary customer."

"Yet somebody did."

"I suppose so. But doesn't it limit the field of search to realize that it couldn't have been a servant or either of the young ladies!"

"Why neither of the young ladies?"

"But how could they get it?"

"Why not as well as any one else? And somebody did."

"Then somebody stole it. Nobody bought it. I'm positive of that, now I've learned how impossible it is to make such a purchase. And how could those girls steal it?"

"I don't know, Hardy, but my point is, why couldn't they steal it if anybody could? You're denying their ability to steal the poison, because you don't want to suspect them. And neither do I, but we must look this thing squarely in the face. Somebody managed to get that aconitine and administer it to Miss Carrington secretly, and it is for us to find out who did it,—who could do it, in the face of almost insuperable obstacles. But it is futile to say this one or that one could or couldn't do it. Now, since you've found no trace of the poison sale, let's start from some other point. Surely, this case, with its unique circumstances, offers many ways to look for evidence. What strikes me most forcibly is the costume of the lady. Not so much the gown,—I believe she was fond of elaborate boudoir robes,—but the array of jewelry, the glittering scarf and the snake. Most of all, the snake.

That, of itself, ought to point directly to the true solution, and I believe it does, only we're too blind to see it. I 'm going to work on that snake clue, and to help, I wish you'd go at once to all the possible shops where it might have been bought. It may not be traceable and then, again, it may. And, the strange fact of her sitting idly before the mirror when she died! Whoever gave her the poison was there on the spot, must have been,—for it's sure enough that she didn't take it herself, according to the doctor's statements. Well, if the murderer was right there with her, and she not only made no outcry but continued to look smiling and happy, it was surely some one she knew and in whom she had all confidence. Perhaps this person urged her to eat the sandwich,—oh, pshaw, that's all plausible enough,—but, the snake! That's the bizarre clue that must lead somewhere. And it shall! I'll ferret out the mystery of that paper snake or my name's not Stone! Go to it, Hardy! Rake the Japanese shops and department stores, but find out who bought it. It isn't old. I observed it was fresh and new. Those flimsy paper things show handling mighty quickly. Find out who bought the thing, and we've a start in the right direction."

Hardy went off on his errand and Stone went over to have a talk with Mrs. Frothingham. The widow was amiable but non-committal. She was highly incensed at the arrest of the Count, but felt confident he would be liberated in a few days. She replied warily to Stone's questions, but admitted her presence in the house on the fatal evening.

"You see," she said, in a confidential way,

"I was lonely. The Count had gone so often of late to Garden Steps, and I was never invited, that I think I was a little jealous."

"Of Miss Carrington!" asked Stone, quickly.

"Yes," said Mrs. Frothingham, frankly; "and of Miss Stuart, and of the Count's intimacy over there. I had never even been in the house. So I went over there and looked in the windows. I saw them playing cards and

later strolling about the rooms. The great door stood a
little ajar and I cautiously stepped inside. It was vulgarly
curious, but it was no crime. As I stood in the hall I saw
some one approaching, and stepped up a few steps of the
staircase. It was all so beautiful that I looked at the
tapestries and decorations. I remember thinking that if
any one challenged me, I should tell the truth, and say
that I came in to look, as a neighbor ought to have a right
to do."

"Never mind the ethics of the case, Mrs. Frothingham,
stick to facts. Did you go upstairs?"

"No, indeed, only up four or five steps, just to the
turn of the staircase."

"But Mr. Illsley saw you coming down."

"Only those few steps. He couldn't have seen me
coming from the top of the stair, for I didn't go up so far."

"You spoke of being jealous of Miss Stuart. Why?"

"Because Count Charlier is in love with her."

"With Miss Stuart?"

"Yes; he was making up to Miss Carrington for her
money, but he is really in love with Miss Stuart."

Mrs. Frothingham shook her head doggedly, as if
determined to tell this, even though it should redound to
the Count's discredit. And it did.

"Then," said Fleming Stone, "that adds motive to the
theory of the Count's guilt. If he is in love with Miss
Stuart, might he not have been tempted to put Miss
Carrington out of the way, that Miss Stuart should
inherit the fortune, and be the bride of his choice?"

"Indeed, yes, that is a possibility," and Fleming Stone
saw at last, that this woman either suspected the Count's
guilt or wished to make it appear so.

Again, the sudden thought struck him, suppose she
was so jealous of the Count's attentions to Miss
Carrington, that she went to Garden Steps with the
intent of killing the lady. Suppose she did go upstairs,
although she denied it, and put the poison in the

sandwich. Surely, she had opportunity. Surely, she would now deny it.

Fleming Stone sighed. He hated a case where the principal witnesses were women. One never could tell when they were lying. A man, now, was much more transparent and his evidence more easily weighed.

However, if this woman desired to turn suspicion toward Count Charlier, it was either because she suspected him, or was implicated herself. In either case, her word was not worth much, and Stone soon took his leave to hunt a more promising field.

Returning to Garden Steps, he found that Pauline had received a letter from her cousin in Egypt.

"I am afraid," she said, as she handed Stone the letter to read, "that my cousin Carr will think we are not accomplishing much. Read the letter, Mr. Stone, and if you say so, I will ask Mr. Loria to come home."

Glad to read the letter from this half heir to the Carrington fortune, Stone took the sheet. It ran:

DEAR POLLY:

The awful shock of Aunt Lucy's death leaves me without words to tell you what I feel for you in your dark hours. What can I say in the face of such a horror? I wish I were there with, you to help you bear it all. For on you comes the brunt of the publicity and all the harrowing details that must be attended to. If you say so, I will return to America at once. But unless I can be of definite assistance or real comfort to you, personally, I would rather not go over just now. I'm just starting on a wonderful piece of work here. No less than excavating — but I won't take time to tell of it now. I'll write you about it later, if I don't go to you. This is a short note to catch the mail, and reach you as soon as possible. Remember, as I write, I have only your first two cables, and know nothing of details. I eagerly await your letters. Why don't you follow out your plan of coming over here in February? Leave all business matters in Haviland's hands, and get away from the scene of the tragedy. Of course, as I cabled Gray, get the best possible detective experts on the case. Spare no expense, and charge all to me. Surely, we want to find and punish the slayer of Aunt Lucy, and I repeat, if you, for any reason, want me to, I will come over at once. Cable, and I will take the next steamer. If you don't do this, do write me long letters and tell me everything that is happening. Poor Aunt Lucy. I know your life with her wasn't all a bed of roses, but I know how saddened you are now, and my heart goes out to you. Dear

Polly, command me in any way. I am entirely at your service here or there. If you come over here, I advise Haviland to stay there and look after things. I know the bulk of Aunt Lucy's fortune is divided between you and me, and I want Gray to see to all matters connected with my share. When he gets around to it, he can send me some money to further this work I am engaged on here. But let me know if you want me to come to you. With all loving sympathy and affection,

CABB.

Fleming Stone pondered over this letter. He had felt a certain curiosity concerning this absent cousin, who was heir to half the great fortune, and so would have had a possible motive for a crime that would secure his inheritance to him at once. But there was no possible way of connecting a man in Egypt with a deed committed in the victim's boudoir. Vague thoughts of Loria's employing somebody to do the deed for him formed themselves in Stone's mind, but were soon dismissed as untenable. The man Bates could not be a tool of anybody, and beside, he didn't kill the lady. The poison did that. The Count couldn't be a tool of any one. He was too evidently his own master, and whether guilty or not, was entirely on his own initiative. Oh, the whole idea was absurd. The letter itself was sufficient exoneration for Loria. He was absorbed in his research work and though thoughtful enough of Pauline's wishes, he was apparently not anxious to have his plans over there interrupted. He wrote like a good all round chap, and Fleming Stone could find no peg on which to hang a suspicion in his case.

"A good letter," he commented, returning it to Pauline; "what's your cousin like?"

"In looks? A little like me, but bigger and darker. He's a fine-looking man, and a kindhearted one. I shall advise him not to come home, for I know how interested he is in his work, and he can do no good here. Can he, Mr. Stone!"

"Frankly, Miss Stuart, I don't see how he can. I may as well admit to you, the case seems to me a most baffling one. The assault with the black-jack is, of course, accounted for, but I've have made no progress in the matter of discovering the poisoner. I feel that the solution of the mystery is closely connected with that paper snake. Can you give me any idea where the thing could have come from? Do you think Miss Carrington bought it herself?"

"I am sure she did not," returned Pauline, but her voice and intonation were such that Stone turned quickly to look at her. She had gone pale, and her eyes looked frightened. "Oh, no," she went on, hurriedly, "Aunt Lucy would never buy such a thing. She hated snakes."

"I know that, but she must have gotten it somewhere. It is easier to think she put it round her throat herself than to think she let some one else do it."

"Why do you say that?" and now Pauline looked angry. "It is incredible that she should have put that thing round her own neck! What could have induced her to do it?"

"There seems to be no theory to fit the facts," said Stone, wearily, "so we must try to get some facts that may suggest a theory. You think, Miss Stuart, that you saw Miss Frayne leaving Miss Carrington's room late that night!"

"I know I saw her with her hand on the doorknob," returned Pauline steadily, and just then Anita herself burst into the room. "That is a falsehood!" she cried, and her big blue eyes flashed angrily; "how could you see me, when you were yourself in Miss Carrington's room?"

This was what Stone had wanted, to get these two girls at variance; and he helped along by saying, "Were you, Miss Stuart?"

"Certainly not!" cried Pauline.

"You were!" Anita flung back. "Miss Carrington was talking to you! She said she wished her face was as beautiful as yours! To whom else could she have said that? Surely not to the Count! One doesn't call a man beautiful. And we all know that Miss Carrington admired your looks and lamented her own lack of beauty."

"All that applies equally well to yourself," and Pauline gazed steadily at the blonde beauty of Anita. "Why wasn't all that speech addressed to your own attractive face, and you repeat it to incriminate me?"

Here was an idea. Stone wondered if it could be that Anita was in the boudoir and to turn suspicion from herself tried to pretend she had heard Pauline in there.

"And she said you were fond of pearls!" went on Pauline. "Your admiration for my aunt's pearls is an open secret!"

It was. Often had Anita said how much she preferred the soft lustre of pearls to the dazzling sparkle of other gems.

"And she left you ten thousand dollars in her will," continued Pauline, more as if thinking these things over aloud than as if accusing Anita of crime.

"Wait, Miss Stuart," cried Stone; "what are you doing? Implying that Miss Frayne had anything to do with the tragedy?"

"I am implying nothing. I am trying to see how far the accusations she makes against me will fit her own case. You remember she said my aunt proposed to leave my share of the fortune to some one else, but Carr's share must remain untouched. Well, to whom else could she think of giving my share, but to this scheming girl who tried her best to get my portion, but did not succeed?"

Anita struggled to reply, but words would not come. So furious that she could not articulate, she gurgled hysterically, when into the room came Haviland and Hardy. Both looked exceedingly grave, and Gray went at once to Pauline and put his hand kindly on her shoulder. Then he suddenly caught sight of Anita and her evident distress, and leaving Pauline he went over to the other and put his arms gently round her.

"What is it, Anita?" he said. "What has upset you so?"

"Pauline!" was all Anita could say, when she was interrupted by Hardy.

"Let me speak first," he said, for he saw there was dissension between the two girls. "I have made a discovery. At Mr. Stone's directions I have been investigating shops where the paper snake might have been bought, and I have learned that one was bought at Vantine's recently by Miss Stuart."

"Ah," said Fleming Stone gravely, "did you buy one, Miss Stuart?"

Pauline hesitated. She was white as chalk, and her lips quivered.

"Of course she did!" screamed Anita, greatly excited; "she did, and she was in there talking to Miss Carrington, just as I said I And she put that thing round her neck to frighten her! And then she gave her the poison, and then she came away and left her to die! All alone by herself! The fiend!"

"There, there, Anita, hush," and Haviland tried to soothe the frantic exclamation of the girl.

Pauline stood waiting, in silence. At last she said, "When you remove that ranting woman, I will answer your question, Mr. Stone."

"You'll answer it now!" cried Anita. "In my presence, and at once."

"I think you must answer, Miss Stuart," said Stone, gently. "Did you buy a paper snake?"

"I did," said Pauline, and added in a low tone, "A long time ago,—this can't be the same one."

"The date of the sale is about a week before the death of Miss Carrington," went on Hardy, merciless in his statements.

"For what purpose did you purchase it?" asked Stone, a little sternly.

Pauline now drew herself up, proudly. "I bought it," she said, in clear, distinct tones, "because my aunt instructed me to get it for her."

There was a silence; and then, "Oh, come now, Pauline, you can't expect us to swallow that!" Gray Haviland said, with a tolerant smile at her. "Try again."

"That's the truth," said Pauline, but her voice trembled, and with a half-stifled exclamation of despair, she ran out of the room.

"Stop, Pauline, where are you going?" cried Haviland as he ran after her.

"Don't touch me!" she cried. "I'm going to cable Carr to come home! He's the only one who can help me! You're so wrapped up in Anita that you can't tell truth from falsehood. Carr will know what to do,—and I shall send for him."

"Wait, Miss Stuart," said Fleming Stone, gravely; "you may cable Mr. Loria, if you choose, but for a few moments I must claim your attention. It is, to my mind, of the greatest importance to learn the details of the purchase of that paper snake, and I must ask you to tell us the circumstances of your aunt's request for it."

"There is little to tell," said Pauline, in a hesitant way. "It was one day when I was going over to New York that Aunt Lucy just said, casually, to get her one of those Japanese paper snakes from Vantine's, and I did."

"That's enough!" cried Anita. "Miss Carrington never sent for a snake! never in the world! You'll be saying next she told you to get her some aconite to poison herself with!"

Chapter 16: The Two Girls

"Miss STUART," and Fleming Stone's voice, though gentle, had a ring of decision, "if I am to go on with this case, I must insist on your entire confidence, and absolute,—" he hesitated over the word, "truthfulness."

The two were alone. After the altercation between Pauline and Anita, Stone had requested the others to leave them, and he determined to get at the truth of this marvelous statement about the purchase of the snake.

"I understand, and you are quite right," murmured Pauline, her manner quiet, her tone even, but in the dark eyes raised to his Fleming Stone saw fear,—definite, unmistakable fear.

"Then explain, for I am sure you can, why you suppressed the fact of your own purchase of that paper snake until forced to admit it."

"I was afraid." The beautiful face was of a creamy pallor and the scarlet lips quivered. But this evident agitation on Miss Stuart's part did not deter Stone from his probing queries. "Why were you afraid? Afraid of what?"

"Afraid that if you knew I bought the snake you would think I was in some way connected with—with the crime—"

"But don't you see that to attempt to conceal the fact of your purchase makes any such suspicion more imminent?"

"You don't think I would—would—"

"I don't want to think anything about it, Miss Stuart. I want to know, and I want you to tell me all about your aunt's strange request for you to buy a thing she so feared and abhorred."

"I don't understand it myself. But Aunt Lucy was full of vagaries and would often ask me to buy strange or outlandish things for her."

"But not of a reptilian nature?"

"No, she had never done such a thing before."

"Did she give no reason for the request? Make no apology or explanation?"

"No. I was just leaving her, when she called me back, and said, 'Won't you stop in at some Japanese shop, and get me a paper snake?' and I exclaimed in surprise at the request. Then she lost her temper and said she supposed she knew what she wanted and for me to get it without further to-do. So I did."

"And when you brought it to her?"

"She merely took it and laid it in a desk drawer, without even unwrapping the parcel. I never saw it again till I saw it round her neck."

"And you do not think she placed it there herself?"

"I am sure she did not. The only reason I can ascribe for her wanting it, is that she might have thought her dread of them a foolish whim and determined to accustom herself to the sight of them by means of the harmless toy. That's all I know about that snake, Mr. Stone. But the truth, as I have told it to you, is so strange, so almost unbelievable, that I knew it would only serve to attract suspicion to me, so I denied it. You know Miss Frayne is only waiting to pounce on it as complete evidence of my guilt."

"You and she are not good friends?"

"We have never been really friendly, though always polite on the surface of things. But she is jealous of me, and tried in every possible way to undermine my aunt's faith and trust in me, and even plotted to have me disinherited and my fortune bequeathed to herself."

"An ambitious plan!"

"She is ambitious. She intends to marry Mr. Haviland, and she intended to have my half of the Carrington money."

"You don't suspect her of the crime!" and Fleming Stone looked up quickly.

"Suspect is too strong a word. But to me there seems room for grave inquiries. I was in the hall at the time she declares I was in my aunt's room—"

"Wait a moment, Miss Stuart, isn't this a sort of deadlock? You say you were in the hall, Miss Frayne says you were in the boudoir. Why should I believe one in preference to the other?"

There was infinite sadness in Pauline's eyes as she looked at her questioner. "That is so—" she said, slowly; "why should you? I have only my unsupported word. Nor has Anita any witness. But, Mr. Stone, I thought a Detective always looked first of all for the motive. What reason could I have for—for killing my aunt?"

"You put it plainly, Miss Stuart, and I will reply in an equally straightforward vein. The first thing we detectives think of is, who will benefit by the crime? Naturally, money benefit is first thought of. The greatest money benefit comes to you and your cousin in Egypt. The nature of the crime makes it impossible that he could have committed it. There is, however, a possibility of your own connection with it, so we must question you. But there are others who benefit in a pecuniary way by the death of Miss Carrington, so they too must be questioned. You surely see the justice and the necessity of all this investigation?"

"Oh, yes, and it seems to me also justice that you investigate the story of Miss Frayne. She, too, has only her own unsupported word as to that conversation she relates. May she not have made it all up?"

"She has a witness, Miss Stuart, a credible witness. Mr. Haviland has told me that he saw Miss Frayne at the door of the boudoir at about quarter past one."

"Gray saw her! He didn't tell me this. Mr. Stone, I hate to speak ill of another woman, but Miss Frayne can really wind Gray Haviland round her finger, and I have no doubt she has persuaded him to give this evidence, whether—"

"Whether it is true or not?"

"Yes, that is what I meant, though I hated to say it."

"Miss Stuart, it is often hard to tell when a man speaks the truth, but I have no reason to disbelieve Mr. Haviland's statement. He told quite circumstantially of being up and down all night. He was restless and wandered about in several rooms during the small hours. You know he told of seeing the maid on the stairs. And he gives me the impression of a truthful witness who would not lie outright, even at the behest of a woman in whom he is interested."

"Then they are going to suspect me?" Pauline's voice was so full of despair that Fleming Stone caught his breath as he looked at her. Her great eyes were wide with fear, her hands were clenched and her whole body tense with horrified suspense.

"Give me some good reasons why you can not be suspected," he cried, eagerly leaning forward in his chair. "Give me some proof that you were in the hall at that moment, or that you were in your own room, or—"

"That proves, Mr. Stone, that you do suspect me! Your assumption that I could have been in my own room shows that you do not believe I was in the hall,—as I was."

"Then why didn't Miss Frayne see you there?"

"How do you know she didn't? Why do you accept her words as truth, yet disbelieve mine?" Pauline had risen now and stood before him. Her tall slimness, her wonderful grace and her beautiful, angry countenance made an alluring picture. "I was not in favor of your taking this case, Mr. Stone, and I am even less so, now, that you refuse to believe what I say! I shall cable at once for my cousin to return. I do not wish Gray Haviland and Anita Frayne to arrange all this to suit themselves. I am mistress here, in Mr. Loria's absence, and if my authority is doubted I want him here to stand up for me!"

"Just a moment, Miss Stuart. You are not entirely just to me. It is necessary for me to question you, but you must see that your innocence—of which I have no doubt—will be more easily established by a policy of frankness on your part, than by futile anger toward Miss Frayne or Mr. Haviland. The incident of the paper snake, as explained by you, is not necessarily incriminating, and if you will wait a few days before calling your cousin home, I think very likely you will prefer not to do so. I understand that you do not wish him to come home, unless he can be of assistance to you?"

"Yes, that is his desire, to stay over there unless I want him. But, Mr. Stone," and now the lovely face was almost smiling, "if you mean what you said, that you do not doubt my innocence, then I will not send for Mr. Loria. I am content to let it all rest in your hands."

The girl's beauty now was dazzling. Color showed in her cheeks, her eyes shone, and the curve of her exquisite red lips was almost a smile. Stone looked at her in amazement. He had spoken truly, he had not doubted her innocence, but this sudden elation on her part puzzled him. What did it mean? Only, as she meant it to seem, that if he believed in her innocence it could be easily proved? Well, he would accept that diagnosis of her attitude, but he would move warily. This case was unlike any other he had ever engaged in, so he must attack it in a different way. And first of all, he must decide which of these two women was speaking the truth. Yet, how could he decide? If Pauline had been in that room when Anita listened at the door, she would, of course, try to prove that she was elsewhere. But, in such a case, why not say she was in her own room? It wasn't plausible that she should confess to being in the hall, if she were really in the boudoir. That, then, was in Pauline's favor. But the conversation detailed by Anita? That must be further analyzed.

These thoughts flew through Stone's quick-moving brain as he stood looking at his beautiful hostess.

"Puzzling it out, Mr. Stone?" and Pauline's smile was a full-fledged one now; "perhaps I can help you. If you'll accept my assistance without doubting my word, I'm sure we can do wonders in a detective way."

This was not in Pauline's favor. It was too much like bargaining with him to believe her innocent. Then, too, though all unconscious of it, Stone was influenced by the wonderful charm of the girl. Though her lips were smiling a little, her great dark eyes still held that look of fear, that hunger for protection, that desire for some one on whom to lean.

"And I won't send for my cousin just yet," she went on. "It's too bad to call him home when he's so busy over there. You know, Mr. Stone, that Mr. Loria is a wonderful man. His achievements in excavation have brought him fame and glory. And you mustn't think he's heartless because he doesn't return at once. You know it was all arranged for us to go over there next month and he had made all sorts of plans for us and for himself. He can't leave his work at a moment's notice, unless, as he says, I have need of him."

"Was he fond of his aunt?" inquired Stone, casually.

"He was her idol. To Aunt Lucy the sun rose and set in Carr. She was perfectly crazy to go on this trip to Egypt, in order to be with him. He was fond of her, yes. More so than I was, because she was always kind and goodnatured to him, while she was always unpleasant to me."

"Why was she?"

"I don't know. Well, I suppose I may as well tell you, one reason was because she was always envious of any one whom she considered better-looking than she was herself. This may sound strange to you, Mr. Stone, but it was the key-note of my aunt's existence. She adored beauty in every way,—pictures, clothes, everything,—but she was so sensitive about her own plainness, that a younger or prettier face made her, at times, irritable and even cruel. She would never engage a servant with any pretensions to good looks. Therefore, as she chose to consider Miss Frayne and myself of comely personal appearance, she was unkind to us both."

"And Mr. Loria? Is he not handsome?"

"Oh, yes, very. But Aunt Lucy liked handsome men. Carr Loria is like a picture. His father was of Italian descent, and Carr has the clear olive skin and dark beauty of that race. Gray Haviland is good-looking, too, but it was only feminine prettiness that stirred up Aunt Lucy's ire."

"Why did she ever engage such an angelface as Miss Frayne?"

Fleming Stone watched closely for a sign of irritation at this speech, and saw it. Pauline's smile faded, and she said, abruptly:

"Do you think her so beautiful?"

"She has the perfect blonde fairness usually typified by the celestial white-robed creatures on the old canvases."

"Yes, Anita is a perfect example of a blonde. Why, she is the daughter of an old school-mate of my aunt's, and so that's why Aunt Lucy took her, and then she proved such an efficient secretary and such a patient, meek thing to scold, that she kept her position."

"Miss Frayne doesn't seem so extraordinarily meek to me."

"No, indeed! She's not meek at all. But she always was to Miss Carrington. That, of course, to keep the position, which was both easy and lucrative. Easy, that is, except for my aunt's temper. That was vented on poor Anita, morning, noon and night."

"That, then, might give us a motive for Miss Frayne's desire to be rid of her cruel mistress and to get the inheritance that she knew would come to her at Miss Carrington's death."

Pauline shuddered. "I can't think of such a thing, Mr. Stone, but, if anybody in this house is to be suspected of the awful thing, it can be no one but Anita. She tried, I know, to supplant me in my aunt's affection, and to have my inheritance, or part of it, transferred to herself."

"You know this?"

"Yes. For some time she has been making insinuations and telling my aunt tales about me,—untrue ones,—that would make Aunt Lucy angry at me. I tell you this, Mr. Stone, because I want you to know Anita Frayne as she really is."

There was the ring of sincerity in the tone, there was a look of truth in the big, dark eyes, and there was a most appealing expression on the lovely face that gazed into his own, but Fleming Stone turned from the speaker with a polite but decided gesture of dismissal, saying, "Please ask Miss Frayne to come here a few momenta."

CHAPTER 17: THE OVERHEARD CONVERSATION

AWAITING the arrival of Anita Frayne, Stone thought rapidly. Forming his judgments, as always, more by impressions than by words, he found himself believing in Pauline Stuart. She had bought the paper snake, she had lied about it, but many women would have done the same. Knowing that the purchase of the toy meant definite suspicion, wouldn't any innocent girl have feared and dreaded that exposure? If she had been guilty, she would scarcely have dared deny the facts of buying it, lest it be proved against her, and make matters worse. Again, it was impossible to connect that magnificent woman with crime. If she were connected with it, it could only be as the criminal herself. There was no theory that admitted of her being an accomplice, or a tool. Stay, there was that Loria man. Stone couldn't rid himself of a vague idea of implicating the distant nephew by means of an accomplice on the spot. But the notion was not logical. If Pauline had killed her aunt under her cousin's instructions, she was just as much a murderer as if she had done it entirely of her own initiative. And if the two cousins had conspired or worked in collusion, it was Stone's duty to fasten the deed on Pauline, as the available one of the pair. Stone ran over in his mind the letter from Loria. It gave no hint of greed or cupidity in his nature. He was engrossed in the pursuit of his hobby, archaeology, and was only willing to leave his work if that would definitely please his cousin, on whom, he fully appreciated, the responsibilities of the occasion would fall. He fully trusted Gray Haviland to look after all business affairs, so he was not a suspicious or over-careful nature. He asked no immediate money and only desired some, in the course of time, to further his work. Whatever might be the truth, there was no reason to cast a glance of suspicion toward Carrington Loria. His opinion of Pauline's possible guilt Stone held in abeyance, and Miss Frayne entering, he greeted her with punctilious politeness and a confidential air, tending to put her at ease.

"Miss Frayne," he began, "the situation is a grave one. I am forced to the conclusion, tentatively at least, that Miss Carrington was deliberately poisoned by some one in her own household. It may have been a servant, but it is difficult to imagine how or why a servant could accomplish the deed. At any rate, I must first consider the members of the family, and in so doing, I must request absolute truth and sincerity from all."

"I'm sure I've no reason to equivocate, Mr. Stone," and Anita's voice was almost flippant.

"All I've told about what I heard at Miss Carrington's door is absolutely true, and I can repeat it word for word."

"It seems strange you have it so accurately at your tongue's end."

"Not at all. I went to my room and wrote it down as soon as I heard it. I often make such memoranda. They are frequently useful later."

Fleming Stone mused. This seemed a strange thing to do, at least in view of the later events, but then, if Miss Frayne had been the guilty one, and had made up all this story of overheard conversation, surely she would not have done anything so peculiar as to make that detailed memorandum; or if she did, would not have told of it.

"I have, of course, a copy of that memorandum," continued Stone; "what I want is for you to tell me again why you think it could not have been entirely a soliloquy on the part of Miss Carrington."

"For two reasons. First, I have lived with the lady for four years, and never have I known her to talk to herself or soliloquize aloud. Of course, this does not prove that she never did so, but I know it was not her habit. Second, nobody in soliloquy ever would use that definite intonation which is always used in speaking to a person. You know yourself, Mr. Stone, that a soliloquy is voiced slowly, mumblingly, and usually in disjointed or partially incoherent sentences. The talk I heard was in clear concise speeches unmistakably addressed to somebody present. She could not in a soliloquy use that direct form of address, even if talking to some one in her imagination. She would not keep it up, but would go off in a reverie or drop into impersonal thought. I wish I could make this more clear to you."

"You do make it clear, Miss Frayne. I know just what you mean. I quite agree that one could easily tell the difference between a spoken soliloquy and remarks addressed to a hearer. But you heard no replies?"

"None at all. But I hold that is not peculiar, for while Miss Carrington 's voice was especially high and carrying, an ordinarily low voice would not be audible through that closed door. You can prove that by simple experiment."

"I have," said Fleming Stone. "I have tried it, and as you say, an ordinary voice in a low tone is not audible. But Miss Carrington's must have been raised unnecessarily, to allow of its being heard."

Stone watched Anita's face as she listened to this. But she only replied, with a shrug of indifference, "I can't say as to that. I heard every word clearly, that's all I can tell."

"Suppose she had been talking to a picture of some one, say a photograph of Miss Stuart or of Mr. Loria, or of Count Charlier, would her tone of voice then be explicable?"

"Perhaps. But she would have had to imagine vividly the person there before her. And, again, Miss Carrington had no such photographs in her rooms. All her family photographs are in this library, in frames or cases. She was methodical in such matters. She has series of pictures of Miss Stuart and of Mr. Loria from their childhood to now, but they are all in order in the cases over there." Anita made a slight motion of her hand toward a mahogany cabinet. "No, Mr. Stone, whomever or whatever Miss Carrington was talking to, it was not a photograph of any of her relatives or friends. As you know, there was none discovered in her room, so what could she have done with it?"

"That's true, Miss Frayne. But hasn't the theory of a living person in there also inexplicable points? If somebody was there, it was, of course, some one well known and whose presence in the house was unquestionably correct. But her remarks, as I read them from your notes, imply different auditors. Granting for a moment that Miss Stuart was there, why would Miss Carrington say, 'Henri, Henri, you are the mark I aim at'?"

"I admit that must have been a soliloquy, or an apostrophe to the man she wanted to marry, though he was not present."

"You have no thought, then, that Count Charlier was present?"

"Certainly not! The idea is absurd. Miss Stuart was in there with her aunt, and I'm sure it was some remark of Pauline's, which I, of course, did not hear, that made Miss Carrington speak of the Count as if to him."

"How, then, do you account for the presence of Count Charlier's glove?"

"Miss Stuart put it there as a blind."

"And how did Miss Stuart get it?"

"Easily. The Count had been spending the evening here. He may have left his glove by mistake,—or—"

"Or?"

"Or Pauline may have abstracted it purposely from his coat-pocket during the evening with a prearranged plan to do all just as she did do."

"Miss Frayne! you can't mean to assert your belief that Miss Stuart so far planned the crime as to intend to cast suspicion on Count Charlier by means of that glove!"

"Why not? If Pauline Stuart is responsible for her
aunt's death, I assure you, Mr. Stone, she is quite clever
enough to prearrange all details, and to plan so adroitly
that suspicion should fall on some one else. Miss Stuart is
far more crafty and deep than you can have any idea of! I
have known her for four years, and I can tell you she is
far from ingenuous!"

"Suppose we leave the question of Miss Stuart out of
the discussion, and continue our first line of thought. Had
Miss Carrington ever spoken to you of changing her will?"

As was his frequent experience, Fleming Stone's
quick question caught his witness unaware, and she
stumbled a little in her speech, as she replied: "N—no.
Why should she?"

"Only because her frequent quarrels with Miss Stuart
might have made her wish to leave less of her fortune to
her niece. And in the conversation you overheard, Miss
Carrington touched on this subject."

"Yes, she did. But except for that reference, spoken to
her unknown companion, I have never heard anything of
such an intention on her part."

"You're fond of pearls, Miss Frayne?"

"Oh, I know what you're getting at now. That speech
Miss Lucy made about fondness for pearls. Of course, I
am. Who isn't? I often told Miss Carrington that I
admired her pearls far more than all her diamonds or
other glittering stones. But I wouldn't commit a crime for
all the pearls in the world! And, if I had, why didn't I
steal the pearls?"

Anita's voice rang out triumphantly as she put this
question, but Fleming Stone said quietly: "I haven't
accused you of crime, Miss Frayne, but since you ask
that, let me remind you, that if the crime were done with
intent of robbery, the reason that the robbery was never
accomplished is the same that kept the man Bates from
stealing. Few people can bring themselves to take
valuables from a dead body. However, I cannot think the

poisoning was done with any idea of direct robbery, but for the gain that would come by the bequests of the will."

"Then your search is limited by the list of inheritors?"

"It is, Miss Frayne."

"Then, Mr. Stone, how can you overlook or undervalue the weight of evidence against Pauline Stuart? Remember, she bought that snake herself. Miss Lucy never told her to buy it, never in this world! Pauline feared her aunt would disinherit her—"

"How do you know that?" the question was shot at her, and Anita fairly jumped as she heard it.

"Why—why, you know I heard reference made to it that night when—"

"When you overheard that conversation; yes, go on." Fleming Stone had gained his point, which was to prove that Anita did know of the proposed change in the will before that time, and to his own belief he had proved it.

"Yes, I cannot doubt now that Pauline knew her aunt intended to change her will, and so she was so desperate at the idea of losing her fortune, she—I cannot bear to put it in words—"

"She poisoned the lady," said Fleming Stone, very gravely.

"Yes." Anita's voice choked, but she enunciated the word. "Mr. Stone, you must think me dreadful to hold these suspicions, but you asked me to be frank—"

"And I wish you to be so. I am here, Miss Frayne, to discover the poisoner of Miss Carrington. It is my duty to get all possible light on the matter from any one I can. It is the duty of those whom I question to tell all they know, truthfully and straightforwardly. If these truths implicate or seem to implicate a member of the household, none the less must the investigation be carried on and the case be pushed to its inevitable conclusion. The great danger lies in mistaking opinions or imaginations for facts. Now you are telling facts as to the words you overheard, but you are giving only opinions as to whom those words were addressed."

"That is so," and Anita's gaze was a wondering one. "But, Mr. Stone, since the fact of that person in the room is undiscoverable, one can't help forming an opinion. Haven't you one?"

"I have."

"Oh, what is it?"

"I think those words were spoken to some inanimate object, not to a person. Suppose the remark thought to be said to Count Charlier was addressed to his glove, which she was undoubtedly holding at the time."

"I never thought of that, because I have assumed that Pauline put that glove in her hand after—after it was all over, to implicate the Count. And, any way, that's only that one remark,—or two. To what inanimate object was she talking when she said 'To-morrow all these jewels may be yours'?"

"That I cannot answer. That whole conversation is most mysterious."

"Indeed it is, Mr. Stone, under any other hypothesis than that of the presence of Pauline Stuart in her aunt's room at the time!"

"May I come in?" and Gray Haviland's good-natured face appeared, as he knocked and opened the door almost simultaneously.

"Yes," said Stone, "and I will ask you, Miss Frayne, to leave us. I am getting to work in earnest now, and I want to push things a little."

Stone watched the effect of this speech on Anita and was not surprised to see her look at him with startled eyes, as she unwillingly went through the door he held open for her.

"What's doing?" asked Haviland, in his breezy way; and Stone replied, frankly: "Lots. Those two girls are sworn foes, aren't they?"

"Of late they have seemed to be. The break came a month or more before Miss Carrington died. Two beauties never can remain friends."

"They are both beautiful women," agreed Stone. "Which do you think had a hand in the tragedy?"

"Good Lord! Neither of them! What are you talking about? That Count man is responsible for the whole thing, Bates and all."

"I know you think so, Mr. Haviland, but I can't agree with you. Now, look here, we've got to face things squarely. Take the story Miss Frayne tells, about that mysterious conversation. If it were all a figment of her brain—"

"What! Man, you're crazy! Anita Frayne make that all up out of the solid! Never, in a thousand years! If she said that talk was talked, it was talked, and that's all there is about that! Why or by whom it was talked, is another matter, and as I understand it, that's what you're here to find out. And, between you and me and the arc light, I don't believe you ever will find out."

"No?"

"No! And this is no aspersion on your powers. I believe that fool Count was in there, and as he'll never admit it, and you'll never believe it, how can it be proved?"

"Never mind that, now. Prepare yourself, Mr. Haviland, for some unwelcome questions. You don't want to, but I must insist on your answering them. Which do you consider the more truthful and honest of the two young women I've just been talking to?"

"Nixie! You can't get an answer to that question out of me! Why, I'd be a cad to say anything but that they are both impeccably truthful and honest."

"So you would, in ordinary circumstances. But you must realize, Mr. Haviland, that I'm here for the definite purpose of solving the mystery of a terrible crime, and I can only do it by inquiry and investigation. If you really refuse to help me I must learn what I want to know in other ways."

"But, hang it, man," and Haviland, impressed by Stone's manner, considered the question; "I do think they're both truthful,—that is, one of them—Oh, I can't say it! I can't talk against a woman!"

"You'll be obliged to tell all you know, sooner or later. If you tell me now, I truly believe it will be better all round."

"Well, then,—now wait, I've got to think this thing out; I believe,—why, blessed if I don't believe either of them would lie if she was in a tight place! There! you've made me say a nice, honorable thing, haven't you?" and Haviland looked utterly digusted with Stone and with himself too.

Chapter 18: Fled!

THE days went by, leaving the mystery unsolved. Count Charlier was released from custody, there not being sufficient evidence to hold him. Bates was in jail awaiting the action of the Grand Jury, but it was recognized that he was not the murderer of Miss Carrington.

Search for the poisoner had so far been fruitless, and the newspapers were clamoring for the arrest of somebody. But the Police Detectives were at their wits' end, and even Fleming Stone was baffled.

For hours, Stone sat thinking over the many peculiar features of the case. It was not in embarrassment that he felt himself unable as yet to trace the criminal, it was rather with a sensation of curiosity that he wondered what point he had overlooked. There must be some clue, some definite indication of what way to look, but so far he had not perceived it.

So interested was he in the search that he took no note of the passing of time or the growing impatience of those who watched him.

"It's this way, Hardy," he would say to the younger detective, "the mystery centres about that paper snake. When we find out the reason for Miss Carrington's sending for that thing, we've the whole story."

"You believe, then, that she did send for it?"

"Of course; why not?"

"We've only Miss Stuart's word for that; and it doesn't seem as if Miss Carrington would—"

"Nonsense! It doesn't seem, you mean, as if Miss Stuart would—Why, man, what possible sense could there be in Miss Stuart's buying that snake on her own account? If she set out to poison her aunt,—which she didn't,—she could have managed it in a dozen ways without lugging in that paper reptile. In fact, it never would have occurred to her to do so. Why would she do it?"

"In an attempt to frighten the lady to death?"

"Rubbish! The first effect of such a fright would be a fearful outcry on Miss Carrington's part, and immediate discovery of the plot. Moreover, if Miss Stuart bought that snake for any such purpose, she would have bought it secretly; at some little, obscure shop, not at a well known emporium. No, sir, the snake is the key to the puzzle, but how? That is the question. 'You see, the doctors are pretty sure that the thing was put round the lady's neck before she died. Therefore she was either unconscious at the time, or,—she was willing."

"Never! Everybody says her fear of the things would never let her have it put on her willingly."

"I know they say so, but they may be mistaken. I'm beginning to evolve a theory that will fit the facts, queer as they are. But my theory needs a whole lot of other facts to back it up, and those facts I can't seem to find."

"Does your theory implicate Miss Stuart!"

"It does not."

"I thought not."

"You thought quite right. It does not implicate Miss Stuart, because she is in no way responsible for her aunt's death. But she may have knowledge, or she may think she has, that is leading her to shield somebody else."

"Whom?"

"I don't know. She is rather a puzzling creature. Is she—is she in love with that cousin of hers?"

"Haviland?"

"No, the one in Egypt."

"Oh, Loria. I don't know, I'm sure. You read his letter to her, it wasn't in any sense a love-letter."

"No, but it was evidently a letter written with the idea of other people reading it, because of the circumstances. Of course, he wouldn't put any intimate talk in it. And it was typewritten, so I couldn't judge anything of the man from his chirography."

"Does handwriting mean much to you?"

"Yes, indeed. It is a wonderful expression of character. But I don't suppose it would declare his adoration of a lady, unless he put it in words also."

"You don't connect Loria with the crime in any way, do you?"

"I don't see how I can, unless in collusion or through the assistance of Miss Stuart. And I'm not ready to do that. I'm working now on that conversation overheard by Miss Frayne."

"You accept that whole, then?"

"Yes, for the simple reason that she would not have invented all that talk. Even if she were in the room herself, and the remarks were addressed to her, she might be trying to lay the blame elsewhere; to create that conversation out of her own brain is too preposterous. You see, Hardy, these things must be weighed in the balance of probability. If Miss Frayne had set out to invent a lot of stuff which she merely pretended to overhear, she would have had two sides to the conversation. It is that unusual effect of one voice only that gives her story the stamp of truth."

"But there must have been another voice, even though inaudible to her."

"That's just the point. There may have been,— probably was. But if the story was her own invention, she never would have thought of representing that second voice as inaudible. Now, either she did hear Miss Carrington say those things, or she didn't. I believe she did, because if she hadn't, she must have invented the tale, and if she had invented it, it would have been different. Likewise, Miss Stuart's snake story. If it were not true that her aunt asked her to buy that snake, Miss Stuart must have made up that yarn. And if she had made it up, it would have been different. That's always

my test for the truth of an amazing statement. If the
teller were falsifying, would he tell it that way? If so, then
it is probably a lie: if not, then probably it is a true bill.
Now they say Miss Carrington had a high, shrill voice.
Did you ever hear it, Hardy?"

"No. I never knew the lady. But I've heard a record of
it on the phonograph, and it is high, and rather thin."

"On the phonograph? How does that happen?"

"Gray Haviland is a dabster at that sort of thing, and
he has people sing for him and make records frequently.
And once I heard that they had a record of the dead
woman's singing, and I asked to hear it, merely out of
curiosity or a general interest. And it contained some
spoken words too, and her speaking voice is high and
shrill, just such as would carry through a closed door. You
can, of course, hear the record, if you care to."

"I do care to. I'll make a note of that. Now, here's
another thing. Miss Stuart has declared that she
obliterated a footprint which was noticeable in that
powder scattered by the dressingtable."

"Yes, I know it. And Haviland states that it was he
who wiped out that print! What do you make of that?"

"That Haviland did do it, and Miss Stuart fibbed
about it to shield Haviland."

"Oh, so it's Haviland you think Miss Pauline is
shielding?"

"I think it may be; at any rate, she suspects some one
dear to her and—"

"You're 'way off, Mr. Stone! If you'll excuse my saying
so, Miss Stuart has pulled the wool over your eyes until
you don't know where you're at."

Fleming Stone gasped. Pulled wool over his eyes! Over
the eyes, the gimlet eyes, the allseeing eyes of Fleming
Stone! What could the man mean? And this so-called wool
pulled by a woman! What unheard-of absurdity!

"Mr. Hardy," he began.

"Yes, yes, I know. Nothing of the sort, and all that.
But it's true, Mr. Stone. Miss Stuart is a siren from

Sirenville. She can make any man think black is white if she chooses. And she has been bullied and cowed by that old aunt of hers for years, and for my part, I don't blame her for getting to the end of her rope. If she—"

"Stop! Mr. Hardy, I know you think you're right, but you are not! Do you hear, you are not! And I'll prove it to you, and that soon! I'll ferret out this thing, and I'll do it on this new theory of mine whether you believe it or not!"

Hardy looked at the man in amazement. He had expected a different mode of procedure from this talented sleuth. He had looked for a quiet, even icy, demeanor, and magical and instantaneous solution of all mystery. And here was the great man, clearly baffled at the queerly tangled web of evidence, and, moreover, caught in the toils of a woman whom Hardy fully believed to be the criminal herself.

But he only said quietly, "What way does your theory point, Mr. Stone? I may be able to help you."

"You can't, Hardy, because you're so determined to find Miss Stuart guilty that you couldn't see it as I do. You consider the strange features of this case—and Lord knows they are strange!—separately, whereas they must be looked at as a whole. The gown, the quantity of jewelry, the smiling face, the glove, the overheard conversation,—all these points are to be considered as of one import,—as leading to one conclusion. And you think of them as implicating—separately, mind you—Miss Stuart, Miss Frayne, and the noble Count. Now, all those queer points are not only connected, but identical in their significance. But never mind that. Here's the place to begin. Miss Carrington was poisoned. She didn't poison herself. Who did?"

"Mr. Stone, you have put it tersely. I entirely agree that all we are seeking is the answer to that last question of yours."

"I will yet give it to you," and Fleming Stone spoke solemnly rather than boastingly. "The poison, the aconitine, was taken by Miss Carrington as she sat there at her own dressingtable. She took it willingly, smilingly—"

"Yes, because she didn't know she was taking it. When she ate the sandwich—"

"The poison wasn't in the sandwich. She took that poison in water. The tumbler and spoon that were used are even now on the glass shelf in her bath-room."

"You know this?"

"I know that in the glass that now stands there a chemist has found a slight trace of aconite. I took the glass myself to be tested, with that result. This is not a great discovery, it merely proves that the poison was administered in water, not in a sandwich."

"But it also means that it was given to her by some one who could persuade her to take the solution, unquestioningly,—not under compulsion. "

"It would seem so."

"And that points to Miss Stuart."

"Not necessarily. Hardy, I refuse to discuss these things with you if you avow everything to condemn her. Why does what I have just told you point to Miss Stuart any more than any one else in the house? Why not Miss Frayne? Or Haviland?"

"Pshaw! Nobody suspects Gray Haviland."

"But why not? If you're merely suspecting here and there without definite reason, why not include him on your list? And here's another thing. Whoever mixed that poison in the glass of water, afterward rinsed the glass and returned it to its place in the bath-room? This was either done at the time, that is, before the lady died, or later on, after death had ensued. In either case, it opens up a field of conjecture."

"It doesn't with me," said Hardy, bluntly. "There's no room for conjecture. It simply piles up the proof against Miss Stuart, and all your skill and even your will can't get her off."

A low moan was heard and a sound as of a falling body. Stone sprang to the door, and flinging it open, disclosed Pauline lying on the floor where she had just fallen. With a low exclamation, Stone picked her up and carried her to a couch. In a moment she sat up and cried, "What do you mean, Mr. Hardy? Do you think I killed Aunt Lucy?"

"There, there, Miss Stuart, don't ask foolish questions," and Hardy, deeply embarrassed, stood at bay. It was one thing to assert his suspicions to Fleming Stone, and quite another to have them overheard by this beautiful and indignant girl.

"How dare you!" Pauline went on. "I was at the door and I heard all you said. No, I am not ashamed of listening, I'm glad I did. Now I know what I have to fight against! And you, Mr. Stone, do you think me a murderer?"

Pauline cringed not at all. She looked more like an avenging goddess, as she confronted the two men, and her blazing eyes and frowning face challenged their replies.

"I do not, Miss Stuart," said Stone, quietly, but Pauline responded, "How do I know? If you did, you'd say you didn't! I have no friend, no one to stand up for me. I shall send for Carr. He will defend me."

With a disdainful glance round, she left the room. The two men looked at one another.

"Guilty," said Hardy.

"Never!" said Stone, and then the two went their different ways.

Hardy's way led to the Police Headquarters, and his report there, which included Stone's story of the tested glass, was heard with interest.

He demanded Miss Stuart's immediate arrest, claiming that only she could have persuaded her aunt to swallow the poisoned draught.

Inspector Brunt was not quite willing to order arrest, but he set machinery at work which he hoped would bring decisive results of some sort.

It did.

That same evening, Pauline went to Fleming Stone. The two were alone. Standing before him, in all her somewhat tragic beauty, Pauline asked: "You don't think me guilty, Mr. Stone?"

He looked deep in the great, dark eyes that seemed to challenge his very soul, and after a moment's steady glance, he replied, "I know you are not, Miss Stuart."

"Can you prove it?"

"I hope to."

"That means nothing. Are you sure you can?"

Fleming Stone looked troubled. Never before in his career had he been unable to declare his surety of success; but with those compelling eyes upon him he couldn't deny a present doubt. Shaking himself, as if to be freed from a spell, he said, at last, "Miss Stuart, I am not sure. I am convinced of your innocence, but the only theory of guilt that I can conceive of is so difficult, so almost impossible of proof, and so lacking in plausibility, that it seems hopeless. If determination and desperate effort can do it, you shall be exonerated. But there are many circumstances not in your favor. These I shall overcome, eventually. But, to be honest, until I can get a clue or a link of some sort to join my purely imaginative theory to some tangible fact, I can do little. I am working day and night in my efforts to find this connection I seek, but it may take a long time. Meanwhile—"

"Meanwhile, I may be arrested?" Pauline's voice was a mere whisper; her face was drawn and white with fear. To Stone she did not look like a guilty woman, but like an innocent girl, frightened at thought of unjust suspicion and terrorized by imagination of the unknown horrors that might come to her.

"Oh, help me!" she moaned, "Mr. Stone, can't you help me?"

"Pauline!" he exclaimed, taking her hands in his; "Pauline! Go!" he cried, tensely: "I will save you, but until I do, keep away from me! You unnerve me! I cannot think!"

"I understand!" and Pauline slowly drew her hands from his. "I will keep away from you."

Stone let her go. He closed the door after her, locked it, and threw himself into a chair. What had he done! Full well he knew what he had done. Hardy was right. He had fallen in love with Pauline Stuart! He realized it, quietly, honestly, as he would have realized any incontrovertible fact. His subconsciousness was that of a deep, still gladness; but, strangely enough, his surface thought was that since he had fallen in love with her, so undeniably, so irrevocably, she must be innocent.

Then on the heels of this thought, came another, equally logical: if he deemed her innocent, was it not only because he loved her? It was only after an hour of deep thought that Fleming Stone pulled himself together and realized with a conquering assurance, that he could go on with the case, and do his duty. If, as he was confident, he could prove his vague theory to be fact, then his love for Pauline would help him to good work and triumphant conclusions. If, instead, his further investigations showed his theory to be false, then he must push on, and if—it couldn't be, but if—well,—he could always drop the case. But,—and of this he was certain,—his heart should not only be kept from interfering with the work of his head but it should help and encourage such desperately clever work that success must come. Pauline did not appear at dinner that night, and on inquiry, Stone was told she had gone over to New York for a day or two.

This, then, was what she had meant when she said, "I will keep away from you." The next day came District Attorney Matthews to interview Miss Stuart. Her absence from home annoyed him and he asked for her New York address. This no one knew, as she had not informed any of them where she was staying in the city, and Mr. Matthews went off in a state of angry excitement. But the household at Garden Steps was even more excited. For this was the first sign of a definite action against Pauline. What it meant or how far it would go, no one could say.

And then, that afternoon, came a letter from Pauline herself. It had been mailed in New York that morning and contained the surprising news that Pauline had sailed at noon that day for Alexandria.

"Get her back!" roared Haviland, as he read the letter. "Wireless the steamer and make her get picked up by some incoming ship! Don't think of expense! She musn't run off like that! It's equivalent to confession of the crime!"

"Hush!" demanded Fleming Stone. "How dare you say that?"

"It's true!" cried Anita. "Why else would Pauline run away? She knew she was on the verge of arrest and she fled to Carr Loria. He will hide her from her pursuers."

"He can," said Haviland, thoughtfully: "maybe it's as well she's gone there. Of course, she did it."

"Of course, she didn't!" and Fleming

Stone's voice trembled in its very intensity. "And I shall prove to a lot of dunder-headed police that she didn't, but it will make my work much harder if you two insist on Miss Stuart's guilt. Why do you want to railroad her into conviction of a crime she never dreamed of?"

"Then who did it? " demanded Anita. "To whom was Miss Lucy speaking when she said those things I heard?"

"If you harp on that string much longer," said Stone, looking at her, "one might almost be justified in thinking she said them to you."

"No," said Anita, in a low, awed voice, and looking straight at Fleming Stone, "no, she did not say them to me."

And Stone knew she spoke the solemn truth. But she had not spoken the truth when she said she saw Pauline Stuart coming from the boudoir of her aunt.

CHAPTER 19: LETTERS FROM THE FUGITIVE

PAULINE 's flight was deemed by many a confession of guilt. The District Attorney declared his intention of cabling a command to hold her for examination at Alexandria. Or, he said, perhaps it would be better to intercept her course at Gibraltar or Naples.

The people at Garden Steps paid little attention to these suggestions, so absorbed were they in planning for themselves.

"Poor child," said Haviland, "she ran away in sheer panic. You don't know Pauline as we do, Mr. Stone; she is brave in the face of a present or material danger. When a gardener's cottage burned, she was a real heroine, and saved a tiny baby at risk of her own life. But always a vague fear or an intangible dread throws her into a wild, irresponsible state, and she loses her head utterly. Now, I may as well own up that I do think Polly committed this deed. I think that she had stood Aunt Lucy as long as she possibly could, and you've no idea what the poor child had to put up with. I think that when Lady Lucy threatened to send Pauline away, homeless and penniless, this panic of fear overcame her and she gave that poison, on an impulse—"

"But," interrupted Stone, "that would imply her having the poison in readiness. She couldn't procure it at a moment's notice."

"That's so," agreed Haviland, thoughtfully; "but, even so, it's my belief that that's the way it all happened. How Pauline got the stuff I 've no idea, but there's no other explanation that fits the facts. Aunt Lucy's aversion to drugs or medicines could have been overcome by few people, but Pauline could have wheedled her into taking it by some misrepresentation of its healing qualities or something like that."

"It must have been under some such misapprehension that she took it," said Stone.

"For I'm convinced she took it dissolved in a glass of water, and therefore, was conscious of the act, though not of the nature of the dose. But couldn't Miss Stuart have given it innocently by mistake, as a headache powder, or—"

"Miss Carrington never had headaches," returned Anita, "and, any way, Pauline couldn't make such a mistake. It isn't as if Miss Carrington had a medicine cabinet like other people, where drugs might get mixed up. No, Mr. Stone, there was no mistake."

"You think Miss Stuart administered the poison purposely, to kill her aunt?" It would have been a brazen soul indeed, that could have spoken falsely under the piercing gleam in Fleming Stone's eyes then.

"I am forced to think that," replied Anita, quietly. "And you know I was present when Miss Carrington denounced Pauline and told her to leave this house the next day. And I also heard Miss Carrington when she said, later, that half her fortune should not go to a niece who treated her as Pauline did—"

"Would she have used those words in speaking to Miss Stuart?" asked Stone, pointedly.

"Surely she would. Why not?"

"Never mind all that, 'Nita," said Haviland. "Polly's gone,—run away,—and it's up to us to do all we can to help her. If her flight means she's guilty, never mind, we must stand up for her, and deny anything that incriminates her. If she did poison Aunt Lucy, we don't want her convicted of it. She'll go straight to Loria, and he'll look out for her all right. But if we find anybody's going to head her off at Naples, or anywhere, we must warn her and help her to thwart their plans."

"Accessory after the fact—" began Stone. "Sure!" said Haviland. "You bet we'll be accessories after the fact, to help Polly out! Why, Mr. Stone, if she did this thing, the best possible plan for her was to vamoose, just as she did do. Carr Loria can hide her in Egypt, so nobody can find her, and after a while—"

"Mr. Haviland," and Stone's eyes gleamed, "I am surprised at your attitude. How can you so easily take Miss Stuart's guilt for granted?"

"No other way out. Now, look here, Mr. Stone, neither Miss Frayne nor I did this thing. We weren't tied to Miss Carrington's apron strings. We could walk off and leave her if we chose. But Miss Stuart couldn't. Her life was a perfectly good hell on earth. I know all about it, a lot more, even, than Miss Frayne does. I don't quite say I don't blame Polly, but I do say I quite understand it. She is an impulsive creature. She'll stand an awful lot and then fly all to pieces at some little thing that sets her nerves on edge. She's clever as the Devil, and if she procured that aconite, long ago, say, it was in anticipation of some time when she—well, when she just reached the limit. And it happened to come that night. That's all."

"Wrong, Mr. Haviland, all wrong!" and Stone's face was positively triumphant. "I've found an additional hint, in what you've just said, and I'm convinced I'm on the right track! One more question, Miss Frayne, about that conversation you so luckily overheard."

"Luckily?" said Anita, her great blue eyes showing alarm in their startled gaze.

"Surely! Most fortunate, to my mind. Indeed, it may well be that that carefully exact memorandum of yours may be the means of clearing Miss Stuart of all suspicion. Now, tell me this. You heard only Miss Carrington's voice, as if speaking to somebody. Did it sound as if she spoke always to the same person, or to more than one at the different times?"

"Well, it did sound as if she spoke to different persons, but it couldn't have been so. Surely, if there had been more than one I must have heard some other words than her own."

"Never mind your own surmises. You say, it seemed as if she addressed more than one person. Why?"

"Because she used a different intonation. At times angry, at times loving. But this is only an impression, as I now look back in memory. I haven't thought about this point before."

"Nor need you think of it again. You have told me all I want to know, and I assure you it will be of no use for you to mull this over or give it another thought."

"But I don't want you to think, Mr. Stone," and Anita began to cry, "that I want to suspect Pauline—"

"I am not considering your wishes in the matter," said Stone, coldly. "If you do not want to think Miss Stuart implicated in this matter, your words and actions are unintelligible to me, but they are equally unimportant, and I have neither time nor thoughts to waste on them."

With this somewhat scathing speech, Stone went away, leaving the angry Anita to be comforted by Haviland.

"What did he mean?" she cried, her cheeks pink with anger, and her blue eyes shining through tears. "Gray, does he suspect me?"

"No, Anita, of course not. But he's on a trail. Perhaps it wasn't Polly after all."

"But it had to be! It was somebody in the house, and it wasn't you or me or any of the servants."

"Well, you listen to me, girl. If they quiz you any more about that talkf est you butted into, don't you color the yarn to make it seem against Polly. I won't have it!"

"How cross you are! But I never did, Gray. I never made it seem to be evidence against Pauline."

"You never did anything else!"

"Don't you love me any more?" and the soft lips quivered as an appealing glance was raised to his face. Her eyes, like forget-me-nots in the rain, were so beautiful, Haviland clasped the lovely face in both his hands, and said as he held it: "I won't love you, 'Nita, if you go back on our Polly. I'm surprised at your attitude toward her just now, and I warn you I won't stand any more of it. I'm forced to think she did this thing, but I intend to admit that to nobody but you and Stone. If he can find the real criminal, and it isn't Polly, I'll bless him forever. But you know, as well as I do, why he is clinging to that forlorn hope. It's because he's—"

"Of course, I know! Because he's in love with her."

"Yes; and it's a remarkable thing for him to fall head over heels in love at first sight, like that."

"Well, of course, she is handsome," and Anita's grudging admission was real praise.

"You bet she is! And old Stone fell for her in a minute! Now there's the old adage of 'Love will find a way,' and if Fleming Stone has any magic ability, or whatever these wizard detectives claim, he's going to work it to the limit to prove Polly innocent. And I hope to goodness he succeeds. Great Scott! I wouldn't suspect the girl if there was a glimpse of a gleam of any other way to look. But, you hear me, Anita! Don't you say a word, true or false, that will help on the case against Pauline Stuart! I won't stand for it! And don't you say you saw her coming from that room, when you know you didn't!"

The postman came just then, and brought with him two letters addressed in Pauline's dashing hand.

"Well, what do you know about that!" exclaimed Gray, half glad and half scared at the sight. "One for me, and one for F. S. Here, Anita, take Mr. Stone's to him, while I eat up mine."

"I won't do it! I want to see what's in yours, first," and Anita stood by Gray's side to look over his shoulder.

"All right, then," and they read together:

DEAR GRAY:

I couldn't help it. You see, I was so frightened at what you all said, that I didn't know what to do. I came over to New York, with a vague idea of asking Mr. Price to help me. I stayed with Ethel all night, and somehow things seemed to look so black, I couldn't think of anything but to go to Carr. I went down to the steamer office to eee about changing my tickets for an earlier date, or something, and I found the Catalonia sailed to-day. I'm scratching this off to go back by the pilot. I had about two hours to get ready, so I bought a trunk and some clothes, went to the bank and got a letter of credit, and here I am. I don't know yet whether I'm glador sorry to be here. But I know I could not stand it at Garden Steps another minute, with you and Anita both against mel Mr. Stone doesn't believe I did it, but he is doubtful of being able to prove my innocence, so I'm going to Carr, and you can address me in his care. He's my nearest relative, and it's right for me to go there. I cabled him from New York to expect me, and to meet me at Alexandria, I'd write more, but it's most time for the pilot to go, and I want to send a word to Mr. Stone. Of course, you will look after all my bills and affairs till further notice.

PAULINE.

"Good Lord!" said Gray, "Think of that poor child going off like that, because she thought you and I were against her!"

"Well, aren't you?" asked Anita, an angry gleam in her eyes.

"No I never!" shouted Gray. "If Pauline is guilty a thousand times, I'm not against her! I'm for her, Anita, for her, first, last and all the time! Come on, now, let's take Mr. Stone his letter."

They found Stone in the boudoir, the room where the ghastly crime had been committed. He spent many hours here of late; it seemed necessary for the furthering of his theory, and yet, whenever any one was admitted to his presence there, he was found sitting staring at the room and its furnishings, as if waiting for the inanimate objects to speak.

"A letter? From Miss Stuart?" he said, eagerly. "I hoped for one, by the pilot."

He opened it, and after a glance handed it over to Haviland.

It said, only:

MY DEAR MR. STONE:

Thank you for your belief in me, and forgive me for running away. And, please,—oh, I beg of you, please drop the case entirely. Your further investigation and discovery can only bring sorrow and anguish to my already distracted soul.

I have no time to write more, but assume that I have put forth any or every argument that could persuade you, and at once cease all effort to learn who is responsible for the death of my aunt.

Sincerely yours,
PAULINE STUART

CHAPTER 20: IN THE BOUDOIR

APPARENTLY, Fleming Stone paid little attention to this letter from Pauline. Really, every word engraved itself on his heart, as he read the lines, and when he gave the paper to Gray Haviland, it was only because he knew he would never need to refresh his memory as to the message Pauline had sent him.

Stone also read the letter she had written to Gray, and his deep eyes clouded with pain at some of the lines. But he returned it to Haviland without comment, and then courteously dismissed the pair.

"He's bothered to death," said Gray, as they went downstairs.

"So'm I," responded Anita, "But nobody cares about me, it's all Pauline,—whether she's a—"

"Let up on that, 'Nita!" and Gray spoke warningly. "Don't you call Pauline names in my hearing!"

Anita, pouting, flounced away to her own room.

Fleming Stone remained in Miss Lucy Carrington's boudoir. He sat on a window-seat, and looked out across the wide gardens and the innumerable steps. There was not much snow now. Merely great wind-swept stretches, dotted with evergreen trees, and the carved stone of the terrace railings and balustrades. Long, Stone mused over Pauline's letter. For a time, he gave himself up to thoughts of her in which consideration of crime had no part. He knew he loved her, loved her with all the strength and power of his great nature; with all the affection and devotion of his big heart; and with all the passion and adoration of his deep soul. He knew she was not averse to him. Knew almost, with his marvelous power of knowledge, that she cared for him, but he knew, too, that if he let his mind dwell on such alluring thoughts or visions, he could not work. And work, he must. Ay, work as he had never before, with an incentive he had never had before. And Fleming Stone's mind was troubled to know whether this love for Pauline would help or hinder this work he must do. And he resolved, with all his mighty will-power, that it should help, that he would control this surging emotion, so new to him, and would force it to aid and assist his efforts, and to triumph over all doubts or obstacles.

Again he concentrated his whole mentality on the room and its contents. He swore to wrest from the silent witnesses the story of the crime.

This was not his usual method of procedure. On the contrary, he almost invariably learned his points from questioning people, from observing suspects, or quizzing witnesses. But, he realized the difference in essence between this case and any other in which he had ever engaged. He had no more questions to ask. He knew all any one could or would tell him. He knew all the facts, all the theories, all the evidence, all the testimony. And none of it was worth a picayune to him, except negatively. This case must be, and should be, solved by the application of his highest mental powers, by the most intense thought and, doubtless, by most brilliant and clever deduction from hints not facts, from ideas, not visible clues. To work, then! To the work that must bring success!

Leaving the window seat, Stone walked round the room, and finally drew up in front of the mirror the easy chair in which Miss Carrington had sat when she received the blow given by Bates. Whether she had sat here while taking the poison, no one knew. If Stone's theory was right, she had not.

By referring to the photographs taken of Miss Carrington after her death, Stone was able to reconstruct the scene correctly.

He placed the easy chair just as it had been when she sat in it. He assumed the position she showed in the photographs, and gazed at himself in the mirror, as she must necessarily have done.

Slowly, he went over that conversation reported by Anita Frayne. Never, for a moment, had he doubted the truth of that report. He was sure Miss Carrington had really said all the things Anita repeated, and the clear and indubitable explanation of those remarks would mean, he was sure, the solution of the mystery.

By way of interviewing his silent witnesses, he endeavored to reconstruct, in thought, Miss Carrington's movements that night. Pauline and Anita had left her, all three of them angry, at a little after twelve. Later, Estelle had left her,—that was about quarter to one. Then she had on her embroidered robe and some jewels. She was not then sitting at the dressing-table. Nor had she then, presumably, taken the poison. For the doctors insisted that she had swallowed the poison very near the hour of one, but after it rather than before, and had placed the hour of her death at two. So, Stone reasoned, Miss Carrington must have taken that aconite at pretty nearly the very time Anita heard her talking. It seemed to Stone incredible that there could have been a person present to whom Miss Carrington could have addressed those remarks, and who could have given or allowed her to take the deadly draught.

The idea that Pauline could have been this person was not among Fleming Stone's catalogue of possibilities.

Moreover, the fact of the one voice strongly impressed him. Another voice, however low, must have at some point of the conversation risen to an audible sound to a listener with normal hearing. Also, Anita had asserted that the speeches of Miss Carrington did sound as if addressed to different persons. It was not likely there were two or more intruders or visitors there at once, and slowly but surely Fleming Stone decided, once for all, that Miss Carrington was alone in that room at that time. This meant, not exactly soliloquy, the mode of address contradicted that, but it meant, to him, at least, that she was addressing some inanimate object or objects as if they were sentient. His task was to discover those objects. His first thought was, as he sat in the easy chair before the mirror, that the lady had spoken to her own reflection. But the speeches, of which he had a memorandum, precluded this hypothesis. She would not say to herself "You are so fond of pearls," or "You have a beautiful face."

Abandoning that supposition, Stone methodically searched for something that might have been addressed.

Clearly,—that is, if he were on the right track,—the words "Henri, you are the mark I aim at!" could have been spoken to the Count's glove, which she held in her hand. In the same vein, assuming that the glove, to her, represented the Count himself, might have been said the speech about the ten thousand dollars, and the remark that he loved pearls.

Accepting these possibilities as facts, Stone went on to discover more. His method was to repeat to himself her very words and strive to see or sense something to which they might have been addressed.

"You have the most beautiful face I ever saw," he quoted softly and then, scanning the room, went on: "I only wish mine were as beautiful."

His eyes lighted on the picture of Cleopatra, which hung above the mirror of the dressingtable.

"That's it!" he cried, with instant conviction. "She looked at that beautiful face and then in the mirror, at her plain features, and she involuntarily cried out for the beauty denied her! Poor woman, to live all her lonely, hungry life, surfeited with wealth yet unable to buy the fairness she craved!"

Not doubting for an instant the truth of hia conclusion, Stone checked off that speech and passed on to the next on his list. If he could account for them all, he would be sure Lucy Carrington met her death alone, and therefore by her own hand. Of course, she did not knowingly poison herself, but if persuaded that the prepared draught was some innocent remedy—oh, well, that was aside the point for the moment.

But, quoting the phrase, "To-morrow I shall be forever free from this curse of a plain face,—to-morrow these jewels may all be yours,"—even his ingenuity could suggest no meaning but a foreknowledge of approaching death. What else could free her from her hated lack of beauty? What but death could transfer her fortune of jewels to another? Of course it might be that marriage with her would give the jewels to Count Charlier, but the two speeches were consecutive, and the implication was all toward the fate that was even then almost upon her. The remark about ten thousand dollars was unimportant, as she had recently willed that sum to five different people, and the reference to a change in her will that should cut out Pauline might have been merely a burst of temper. At any rate, Stone ascribed little importance to it then. He felt that he had learned enough to assume positively that Miss Carrington was not talking to a human being when Anita Frayne heard her voice. Then, he conjectured, as the maid was free of all suspicion on the poisoning matter, and as the two girls had left the room at a little after twelve, the weight of evidence was in favor of the poison being self-administered, no matter for what reason or intent. Granting this, there must be some trace of the container of the aconite, before it was placed in the glass. This must be found. If not, it proved its removal by some one, either before or after the poisoning actually occurred.

Eagerly, almost feverishly, Stone searched. Exhaustive search had long ago been made, but again he went over all the possible places. The ornate waste-basket beneath the dressing-table still held its store of dainty rubbish. This had been ordered to remain undestroyed. Stone knew the contents by heart, but in hope of an overlooked clue, he again turned the contents out on a towel. Some clippings of ribbon, a discarded satin flower, two or three used "powderleaves," a couple of hairpins and a torn letter were the principal items of the familiar lot. Nothing that gave the least enlightenment. Stone got up and wandered around. What had that poison been in before it was put in that glass?

The ever-recurring thought that some one might have brought it to the boudoir after preparing it elsewhere, he would not recognize. A sort of sixth sense convinced him that if he kept on looking he must find that clue.

He went into the bedroom. The beautiful appointments, replicas of Marie Antoinette's, seemed to mock at his quest. "We know," they seemed to laugh at him, "we know all about it, but we will never tell!"

Untouched since Estelle's deft hand had turned back its silken coverlets, the bed seemed waiting for some fair occupant. With a sigh at the pathos of it, Stone suppressed an involuntary thought of the incongruity of that gilded, lace-draped nest, and its pitifully unbeautiful owner. There was a profusion of embroidered pillows, and across the satin puff lay a fairylike night-robe of gossamer texture, and coquettish ribbons. A peignoir of pink crepe lay beside it, and on the floor a pair of brocade mules waited in vain for feet that would never again slip into their furred linings.

There was nothing helpful here, and with a sigh Stone went on to the bath-room. Fit for a princess, the shining white and gleaming silver showed careful readiness. Embroidered towels, delicate soaps and perfumes were in place—all showed preparation, not use.

"If I were searching traces of Estelle, now," groaned Stone, despairingly, to himself, "I could find thousands. But Miss Carrington didn't come in here at all. But, whoever rinsed that glass did!" The thought caused Stone to start with eagerness. It was the fact of the glass being out of line with the other appointments of the wash-stand that had first attracted his attention to it. After the test, the glass had been returned to its place, now in strict position between a silver cup and a flask of violet water. "Spoon in it," mused Stone. "Shows carelessness on the part of whoever put it there. Don't believe a spoon was in a glass, generally, in this celestial bath-room. If —"

His ruminations were cut short by a shock of surprise. Under the wash-stand was a small waste-basket. Had this been overlooked by the searchers? Not surprising, for thorough search had not been made in bedroom or bathroom, as in the room where death had taken place. Stone mechanically looked over the contents of the little basket. There was only a scant handful of papers. But carefully spreading a towel on the floor he turned the basket upside down. Tremblingly he fingered the papers. The first was the wrapper that had contained a cake of French soap. At a glance, Stone saw the corresponding soap in its silver dish. Estelle had doubtless placed it there, casting away its paper. But among the scraps was another paper—two more. They were,—they surely were in creases like the folds of a powder paper! With lightest touch, Stone unfolded them. There was one, about four inches square, that had been folded as if to contain a powder. This was white, and of a texture like writing paper. The other was of a paraffin paper, exactly the same size and shape, and in similar creases. Also there was a bunchy ball of tin-foil, that, when smoothed out, proved to be of identical shape and size with the other two.

There was no room for doubt. These were unquestionably the wrappers of the aconitine! Stone detected on the inside of the paraffin paper traces of the powder itself, and knew that a test would prove his discovery a true find. Now, then, where did he stand? To his own mind, what he had found proved that Miss Carrington had herself gone to her bath-room, opened the powder, thrown the papers carelessly in the basket, and then, mixing the stuff with water, had taken it then and there and rinsed the glass and set it back on the shelf. It was all natural and plausible.

But, he well knew, others would say that, remembering her detestation of medicaments, Miss Lucy

Carrington never did such a thing. Also, they would say,
some one else, some one of whom Miss Lucy felt no fear,
had mixed the draught, and had administered it, by
means of some yet undiscovered but plausible
misrepresentation. And only too well he knew whose
name would be associated with the deed!

Heavy of heart, he returned to the boudoir and sat in
the easy chair, before the mirror.

New thoughts came surging. It was sure, now, that
Miss Carrington took the aconitine in a glass of water, in
her own apartments,—one of them,—and took it, if not
knowingly or willingly, at least without any great
objection or disturbance. Clinging to his theory that she
was alone, Stone visualized her taking the draught by
herself. Assume for the moment, an intended headache
cure,—but no! If she took the aconitine alone and
voluntarily, she knew it was poison, for she said "To-
morrow I shall be freed forever from this homely face."

Did it all come back, then, to suicide? No, not with
that glad face, that happy smile, that joyful look of
anticipation. A suffering invalid, longing for death, might
thus welcome a happy release, but not life-loving Lucy
Carrington. It was too bewildering, too inexplicable.
Again and again Stone scanned the powder papers. They
told nothing more than that they were the powder papers.
That was positive, but what did it prove? To whom did it
point? Frowning, Stone studied his own face in the mirror
before him. Desperately, he repeated again all the
sentences on Anita's list. At one of them he paused, even
in the act of repetition.

He stared blankly into his own mirrored eyes, a
dawning light beginning to flame back at him. Then, a
little wildly, he glanced around,—up, down, and back to
his almost frenzied, reflected face.

"Oh!" he muttered, through his clinched teeth, for
Stone was not a man given to strong expletives, "it is! I've
got it at last! The powder, the pearls,—the snake! My
Heavens! the snake! Oh, Pauline, my love, my love—but

who—? who—? Have I discovered this thing only to lead back to her? I won't have it so! I am on the right track at last, and I'll follow it to the end—the end, but it shall not lead, I know it will not—to my heart's idol, my beautiful Pauline!"

CHAPTER 21: FLEMING STONE'S THEORY

ALONE in the library, Fleming Stone and Detective Hardy were in counsel.

"I'm going to show you this thing as I see it, Mr. Hardy," said Stone. "I frankly admit it's all theory, I haven't a particle of human testimony to back it, but it seems to me the only solution that will fit all points of the mystery. And I shall ask you to consider it confidential for the present, until I can corroborate it by unmistakable proofs."

Hardy nodded assent, his eyes fixed on the speaker in a sort of fascination.

This young detective had not been at all idle of late, but his work had amounted to nothing definite, and though he was himself convinced that Pauline Stuart was responsible for her aunt's death, he seldom exploited that view before Stone, having learned that it was an unwelcome subject.

"Here's the theory in a very small nutshell," said Stone, "but remember, you're not to mention it to any one until I give you permission. Miss Lucy Carrington took that powder, thinking it a drug that would make her beautiful."

"A charm? a philter?" Hardy's eyes seemed to bulge in his excitement.

"I'm not sure whether it was a fake magic affair, say, from a clairvoyant or fortune-teller, or whether it was a plain swindle from a beauty doctor or something of that sort. You know such people play on the credulity of rich patrons and get enormous sums and a promise of secrecy for a so-called beauty producer."

"But why would the beauty doctor or the clairvoyant person give a patient poison?"

"They didn't. They gave a harmless powder, and some evil-minded person added the aconite, secretly, knowing of the beauty scheme."

"Who did it?"

"That's yet to be discovered, but it will be easier if we can trace the one who sold her the nostrum. Now, listen while I reconstruct the scene. Miss Carrington, having dismissed her maid, goes to her bath-room, and takes the powder dissolved in water. These powder papers, which I found in her bath-room waste-basket, carry out that idea."

Hardy stared at the papers, but did not interrupt the speaker.

"Then, joyfully waiting the effect of the charm, she sits in front of the mirror to watch her features become beautiful. This is why she said to her own reflection, 'To-morrow I shall be freed forever from this homely face!' She gazed at the picture of Cleopatra above her dressing-table, and said 'Yours is the most beautiful face I have ever seen. I wish mine were as beautiful.' The remarks concerning Count Charlier were addressed to the glove which she held in her hand, a sentimental part of the whole performance."

"Mighty interesting, Mr. Stone, but pretty fantastic, so far."

Fleming Stone gave his slow, grave smile, that always betokened a surety of his own statements. "Wait a bit, Hardy, before you condemn this notion. I haven't finished yet. Now Cleopatra figures pretty strongly in this scheme. Look at these photographs taken after death. They show the lady exactly as she looked when she sat there. See, she is gazing at the picture of Cleopatra, too intently to be merely a casual glance. And, what do you think of this? She gazed at Cleopatra, and, holding the Count's glove, her mind and heart full of the Count, who would adore her when she achieved this looked for beauty, she said, 'You are the Mark I aim at!' meaning, as Cleopatra had her Mark Antony, she, Lucy Carrington, aimed at the Mark of her choice,—the Count."

"If that's true, Mr. Stone, you are the wizard of the ages! How did you dope it out? What—"

"Now, wait a minute. This isn't the pipe dream you think it. But listen while I tell the rest in my own way."

"Listen! I should think I would I Go on."

"You know, these fakers give out these charms with all sorts of fool directions to impress the duped customer. As I say, I'm not sure yet whether it was a professional of the clairvoyant type, or a regular beauty doctor. But in either case, I've no doubt that Miss Carrington paid him enough to compensate for giving up his practice and leaving for parts unknown. For after the charm failed to work, of course she would expose the fraud."

"But the poison—"

"Never mind that for the moment, Mr. Hardy. Surely, if we can discover for certain how and why the dose was taken, it will go far to help us trace the criminal who added the deadly element to the powder. Now, continuing the Cleopatra idea, I am sure that the clever clairvoyante,—we'll assume that's what she was—"

"She?"

"Merely to designate this faker person. Somehow I seem to see her as one of those crystal-gazing, frowsy-headed kimonoed females, who prey on the credulity of rich and foolish women,—well, let's call her that for the present, this clever clairvoyante somehow conceived the idea of offering to make Miss Carrington as beautiful as Cleopatra. Perhaps she had been here to see Miss Carrington on the subject, and that beautiful picture of Cleopatra put it into her head. But, assuming something of this sort, assume further that she directed Miss Carrington to robe herself, in a general way, like the queen in the picture. Note the pearls! Wouldn't this explain Miss Carrington's getting her pearls from the bank for this occasion? And wouldn't it explain her speech, 'You love pearls,' as being addressed to Cleopatra, to whom she was talking?"

"Go on, Mr. Stone! Go on!"

"I will go on! Wouldn't that explain, as nothing else on this green earth can, the purchase of a paper snake by the woman who feared and abhorred the reptiles? Supposing the fool clairvoyante had told her that to become like Cleopatra she must have a semblance of a snake at her throat, as Cleopatra had the asp!"

"Good Heavens!"

"I tell you, Mr. Hardy, nothing else would account for that snake! And any one of these things might seem the result of a lunatic imagination by itself, but taken all together, the theory holds water! Why think of the Oriental scarf, the embroidered robe, the mass of jewels in addition to the significant pearls, and the scarabs! All point to the type of Cleopatra. If there had been a picture on the wall, say, of Helen of Troy, and Miss Carrington had been rigged up in a Greek costume, with a fillet in her hair, and sandals on her feet,—or if the picture had shown the Goddess of Liberty, and we had found Miss Carrington draped in an American flag, could any one have denied the significance? There can be no doubt,—no doubt in this world, Hardy, that the costume, the jewels and the snake all point to a connection with the picture of Cleopatra, and if so, what other connection is possible than the one I've blocked out? Answer me that! And, finally, the speech to the Count, whose glove she fondled, 'You are the Mark I aim at.' A pleasantry of wording inevitably suggested by the thought of the man Cleopatra charmed and the man Miss Carrington desired to charm. And a play on words too, not at all unnatural to her, for I'm told she was both witty and clever in conversation."

"Mr. Stone, I am carried away by your arguments. I can't deny their plausibility, but I am bewildered. How did you fathom this remarkable plan?"

"Simply because there is no other plan that will fit the facts. I believe Miss Carrington did say all those things Miss Frayne relates. I believe she was alone in the room when she said them. Therefore, they must have had some meaning, and the meanings I have just ascribed to them must be the true ones."

"They must be—"

"And I will further satisfy you that they are. Here is a memorandum I found in Miss Carrington's desk. It is, as you see, a list of items. Bead it."

Hardy's eyes stared more widely than ever as he read:

Green and gold boudoir robe.

Jewels, especially pearls.

Scarabs.

Scarf.

Snake.

Something belonging to H.

"Now, that," and Fleming Stone spoke in low, even tones, without a hint of boasting or pride in his achievement, "is a list in Miss Carrington's own writing, and is undeniably a list of things to be worn on the occasion which she hoped would mean a delightful change to the beauty she so desired to be, but which, instead, was a change to the cold stillness of death. I found that, after reaching my own conclusions about the Cleopatra business. If I had found it before, I would have known it must refer to her costume, but I couldn't have gleaned from it the conclusions I had already come to. Now, Hardy, are you convinced?"

"I am, Mr. Stone. And I am also puzzled. From all this knowledge, we start fresh, as it were, and we—"

"Wait a minute, Hardy. Let's go slowly. Now, here are two ways to look at this thing. I told you about the clairvoyante first, because that first came to my mind as the inevitable explanation. But, suppose, instead of a professional clairvoyante or beauty doctor, some friend or—" Stone set his teeth, but went on steadily, "or some one in the household, planned all this scheme, and pretended to get a powder that would accomplish this transformation, gave it to the unsuspecting lady to take by herself, and in reality this powder was the aconite."

Hardy jumped. "Then Miss Stuart—" he began.

"Ah," and Stone's face was white and his voice like cutting steel, "Why Miss Stuart? Why not Miss Frayne, who listened at the door? Why not Estelle, who knew all her mistress' secrets? Why not Haviland, who is openly enjoying his present responsible position as man of affairs? Why not Count Charlier, whose crafty cunning shows on his face? Of course, also, why not Miss Stuart, but why necessarily Miss Stuart?"

"Well, she has run away, you know—"

"So she has, because of unjust and unfounded suspicions! When clues point directly to her, I shall admit them, but when they may equally well point to half a dozen others, I shall patiently investigate them and learn the truth. Now, I ask of you, Hardy, as man to man, not to favor Miss Stuart unduly, but to give her a fair show, and remember her lonely position and her timid nature."

Hardy looked furtively at Fleming Stone, whose eyes were downcast and fastened on some papers he was holding.

"Count on me, Mr. Stone. I am at your orders. I subscribe to your theories, and I will do exactly what you tell me, and no more or less."

"Good, Hardy, and thank you. Now, look at these papers. They are the ones that contained the fatal powder. See, this paraffin one was inside; then one of tinfoil, then one of rather heavy writing-paper."

"That doesn't look altogether like a clairvoyante's work."

"Why not? It does to me. They are mighty careful to do up their goods in an elaborate manner to impress their customers. But, mind you, I don't for a moment suspect this clairvoyante individual of intended murder. Either the aconite was added to the parcel from the clairvoyante, or the whole affair was concocted by the murderer and under pretense of its having come from the clairvoyante."

"H'm," Hardy was clearly beyond his depth.

"So," went on Stone, "we must deduce what we can from these papers. What do you see peculiar about them?"

"Just plain little old nothing," Hardy declared after a good scrutiny. "I see, as you remarked, three papers, folded similarly, and of nearly the same size. What do you see?"

"Not much more," confessed Stone, gazing discontentedly at the papers. "And yet, there must be something to notice. Here's one point. These papers, if tampered with, I mean if anything was added to their contents, were manipulated very carefully. You know how difficult it is to unfold and refold a powder-paper without making it look messy. These, I would be willing to assert, have never been refolded, or, as I say, if they were, it was done very carefully."

"That isn't much of a clue," and Hardy smiled.

"It may be," returned Stone. "It at least indicates a possible elimination of the clairvoyante and an indication of the murderer preparing the powder alone. At any rate, Hardy, I've told you all this in order to ask your help. "Will you go and see what you can round up in the way of the clairvoyante of our dreams! Go to all you can find in New York City. That is the prominent ones. Get a line on beauty doctors, and generally look up this sort of thing. And keep it all under your hat."

"All right, Mr. Stone," and Hardy was off at once.

Fleming Stone put away the papers, and sat for more than an hour in a brown study. It must be admitted that a photograph of Pauline Stuart, which stood on a near-by table, held Ms eyes much of the time. And his gaze, as it rested on the lovely face, was now tender and now sad.

At last he rang for a servant. To the footman who replied, he made a request that a chamber-maid be sent to him.

The girl came, wondering.

"Mary!" said Fleming Stone, inquiringly.

"Jane, sir," returned the maid, quietly.

"Good," said Stone. "You have intelligence, Jane, as shown by your calm rejoinder. Now, I.want you to go to the various bedrooms or dressing-rooms of all the members of the family and of all the servants, and bring me all the manicure scissors you can find. I assume that some of the servants might possibly have them?"

"Yes, sir, some of them."

"Very well. Get all you can possibly find, and be very, very careful to remember which ones are whose. Understand?"

"Yes, sir."

"Then go. If anybody questions you, say Mr. Stone ordered it."

Jane returned with many pairs of the kind of scissors asked for by the Detective. Absorbedly, Stone took them from her, and one by one he used them to snip at a sheet of paper from the library desk.

At each test, he asked Jane whose the scissors were, and sometimes he wrote the name beside the cut and sometimes not. One pair in especial seemed to interest him. "Whose are these?" he asked.

"Those, sir, I took from Miss Carrington's dressing-table." Jane gave a slight shudder as if at the recollection of the tragedy of that table. "But these are of a different patterned handle from the rest of that dressing-table's silver."

"I don't know, sir, as to that. They were there and I brought them."

"Very well, Jane. Take them all back to their places. Mind now, don't mix them."

"No, sir. Thank you, sir."

A strange excitement seemed to seize upon Fleming Stone. Abruptly he left the room, and, flinging on his overcoat in the hall, he snatched his hat and went away, almost on a run. His steps took him to the garage and in a few moments he was in a swift little runabout being driven to the sanatorium where Estelle was still staying.

After a call there, he hurried to Police Headquarters. Thence, after a rather long call, to a telegraph office, to one or two shops and then back to Garden Steps.

Here he put several servants at work for him, packing his effects and such matters, then summoning Gray Haviland to the library, he said; "I'm sailing for Egypt this afternoon. May I ask you to make no further investigations till my return?"

"Egypt!" gasped Gray. "Good Heavens, man! what for?"

"In the interest of my work for you," returned Stone, gravely.

"Rubbish! You're chasing Pauline! We'll never see either of you again!"

Fleming Stone smiled. "I do love her, Haviland, I make no denial of that fact. And I do hate to have her alone in a strange land. So, if I can be of any help to her, an ocean or two to cross shall not keep me from her."

"And your detective work?"

"Will not suffer by my absence. I've been to the Police and to the District Attorney and they approve my plans as I've outlined them so far. The rest must wait my return."

"Ah, and when will you be back?"

"I don't know exactly, but I will keep you informed of my whereabouts. Say good-by to Miss Frayne for me, and please excuse me now, as I've heaps to do. By the way, where is that record of Miss Carrington's song that I have heard of? Play it for me, will you?"

"Thought you were in such a hurry!" laughed Haviland, but granted the request. "Wonderful!" commented the Detective, as he heard it on the phonograph. "It is a perfectly-made record. If you don't mind, I'll take possession of it."

"All right," said Gray, carelessly, and in another half hour Fleming Stone was on his way to the pier where the *Macedonia* was making ready to sail.

Chapter 22: Pauline in Cairo

ON the first of March, about mid-afternoon, the *Catalonia* steamed into the harbor of Alexandria. Pauline, at the rail, watched the clearing outlines of mosques and minarets, as the beautiful city became visible. It was a glistening, dazzling strip, between the deep blue of the sea and the azure of the sky, and, breathless with delight, she gazed at the shining sunlit picture.

Then the Arab pilot came aboard, and soon Pauline found herself in a shore-boat, swiftly making for the quay. She knew Loria would meet her at Alexandria, she had had a telegram at Naples to that effect, and she thrilled with pleasure at thought of seeing wonderful Egypt with him. Landing, she was bewildered by the crowd of strange-looking people, natives, tourists, officials and porters, all shouting, running and getting in each other's way. Luggage was everywhere, and the game seemed to be to present any piece of it to anybody except the owner. Pauline fell to laughing at the antics of a black man robed in white and a brown man robed in yellow fighting for possession of a small portmanteau, while its timid and bewildered owner desperately hung on to it herself.

Three or four Arabs gathered round Pauline herself, each asserting his claim to all the virtues of a perfect dragoman. In more or less intelligible English, each insisted he had been sent to her personally by Effendi This or That, of marvelous wealth and power. Greatly interested, she listened to their arguments, until, encouraged, they became so insistent that she was frightened. Seeing this, they waxed threatening, even belligerent, in their determination to be engaged, and just as one laid his brown, long fingers on her arm, and she drew back in a panic of fear, she saw Carr Loria's smiling face coming to her through the crowd.

With a wave of his hand and a few short commands, he sent the bothersome Arabs flying, and greeted Pauline with affectionate enthusiasm.

"Polly, dear! but I'm glad to see you! Have you had a good trip? But such questions must wait a bit. Where are your checks? Do you see your boxes?"

"There's only one, and some hand things. Here is—"

"All right," and Loria took the little sheaf of papers she produced from her handbag.

"Ahri, look after these."

A tall Arab glided to Loria's side, and took the checks. "Ahri is my dragoman and bodyservant and general factotum," said Loria, by way of introduction. "This lady, Ahri, is my cousin, Miss Stuart. Her word is law."

"Yes, Mr. Loria. Miss Stoort is queen of all."

The man made a salaam of obeisance and turned away to look after the luggage.

"He's a wonder, that Ahri," said Carrington Loria, looking after the retreating Arab.

"But be very haughty with him, Polly. He presumes upon the least encouragement. Treat him like the dust under your feet, and he'll adore you."

"That's easy enough," and Pauline smiled.

"I'm scared to death of these brown and black men. But your servant is so grand of costume."

"Yes, he's a very high-class affair. Handsome chap and fond of dress. But he's invaluable to me. Speaks almost perfect English, and knows everything there is to know,—and then some. Knows, too, everybody who has ever been in Cairo or ever thought of coming here. And he possesses the proud distinction of being the only dragoman hereabouts who hasn't a letter of recommendation from Hichens. You haven't that, have you, Ahri?" for the Arab had just reappeared.

A marvelous set of white teeth gleamed in the sunlight, as the response came quickly: "I had one, Mr. Loria, but I sold it. They are of use to others; Ahri needs none." His selfconceit was superb, and he spoke with the air of a prince. But warned by Loria, Pauline gave him no answering smile, rather a patronizing nod, and Ahri's respect for the newcomer went up several points.

"Come along, girlie," commanded Carrington and he took Pauline's arm as he hurried her to the boat-train.

Watchful Ahri showed them to the compartment he had secured for them, and soon they were on their way to Cairo.

"Now, tell me everything," said Can' Loria, as they sat alone. "This is a three-hour trip and I want to know the whole story. Just think, Pauline, I've had only a few letters, and they were—well,—they were almost contradictory in some ways. So tell me all, from the beginning."

Pauline did, and by the time they reached Cairo, Loria knew as much as she of the death of their aunt and the subsequent search for the murderer.

"Wasn't it strange," he mused, "that that Bates person should go in to kill her, the very night somebody else had the same intention?"

"Well, but, Carr, Bates didn't start out to kill her, you know; he went to steal the jewels, and he knew they were all in the house that night, because Estelle told him so. Now, of course, whoever gave her the poison, must have known it too—"

"Oh, I don't know. Why didn't somebody want to put her out of the way to get a bequest? Not necessarily the Count gentleman, but maybe one of the servants. Maybe that Estelle? Didn't she receive a legacy in Aunt Lucy's will?"

"Yes, but nobody has thought of suspecting her."

"Don't see why not. I thought of her first clip. I don't think that Stone paragon amounts to much. Hey, what are you blushing about? Sits the wind in that quarter?"

"Don't tease me, Carr. I do like him better than any man I ever saw, but—"

"And so you ran away and left him! Out with it, Polly. Tell your old Uncle Dudley the story of your life!"

"There's nothing to tell, Carr, about Mr. Stone. But I came to you, because some people suspect me,—ME—of—of killing Aunt Lucy—"

"Pauline! They don't! Who suspects you?"

"All the police people, and Gray and Anita Frayne,—"

"They do! You poor little girl! I'm glad you came to me. I'll take care of you. But, Polly, whom do you suspect? Honest, now, who is in your mind?"

"I don't know, Carr. I can't seem to think. But when they fastened it on me, I was so frightened, I just flew. Why, just think, every one at Garden Steps was suspicious of me! I could see it even in the servants' eyes. I couldn't stand it, and I was afraid—"

"Yes, dear, go on,—"

"Well, I was afraid Mr. Stone would think so, and I couldn't bear that, so I just ran off on impulse. I regretted it lots of times on the trip over,—and then at other times I was glad I came. Are you glad?"

"Sure, Polly. I wanted you to stick to your plan of coming over, you know. Yes, I'm glad you're here. Now, we'll soon be in Cairo, and you'll love it,—all the strange sights and experiences. You'll live at Shepheard's for the present. I've engaged a chaperon for you."

"How thoughtful you are, Carr."

"Oh, of course, a beautiful young woman, can't live alone in Cairo, and also of course, you couldn't live with me. So, Mrs. MacDonald will look after you, but she won't in any way bother you. Whenever you need a duenna, she'll be right at your elbow, and when you don't want her about, she is self-effacing. You'll like her, too, she's not half-bad as a companion."

At Cairo, Ahri handed them from the train. Again Polly was impressed with the Arab's dignified bearing and rich costume. His long galabeah, shaped like a well-fitting bathrobe, was of white corded silk, exquisitely embroidered. Collarless, it gave glimpses of other silken vestments, and over it he wore a correct English topcoat, short and velvet-trimmed. From his tarbush to his English shoes and silk hose, he was perfectly garbed and groomed, while the scarab ring on his little finger was the only bit of jewelry visible.

"That's nothing," laughed Loria, following her glance. "Wait till you see him in all the glory of his burnoose and other contraptions. Here, Ahri, take this duffel, too. And, now, Polly-pops, you'll see Cairo."

The ride to the hotel was like a moving picture in color. The street crowds were rushing by, a flare of bright-hued raiment and darkskinned faces. Everywhere, baubles were for sale. Street vendors carried them on their heads, in their arms, or thrust them forth with eager hands.

Post-cards, jewelry, scarfs, and fans. Flywhisks with dangling beads. Embroideries, carved ivories, brasses, sweetmeats, fruits and newspapers, all were successively and collectively offered for immediate, almost compulsory sale.

"And I want to buy every one!" declared Pauline, entranced at the sight of the catchpenny toys.

"All in good time, honey. To-morrow, Ahri shall take you to the bazaars, with or without Mrs. MacDonald, as you choose, and you can get a bushel of foolishness if you want to. Everybody has to cure that first mad desire to buy rubbish, by yielding to it. You soon get enough."

"Then I may go alone with Ahri to the shops?"

"Yes, anywhere, by daylight, except to social affairs. There, or to any in-door entertainment, you must take her. But she'll know all these things. Abide always by her decision."

"But won't you be with me, Carr? You speak as if I will be much without you."

"I'm awfully busy, Pauline; I'll tell you all about it this evening. Then you'll understand. Here we are at Shephcard's. Did you ever see such a horde of freaks?"

It was just about dusk. The last rays of the Egyptian sunset were lingering, as if for Pauline to get one glimpse of the picture by their rainbow lights. Many were at tea on the broad Terrace; the scarlet-coated band crashed their brasses; and Pauline entered the hotel, her whole being responding to the strange thrill that Cairo gives even to the most phlegmatic visitor or jaded tourist.

Later, at dinner, she met Mrs. MacDonald, a correct, tactful and diplomatic widow, who looked forward with pleasure to the chaperonage of the beautiful girl to whom she was introduced.

At Loria's advice, Pauline had put on evening dress; and she made a striking picture, in black tulle, devoid of all jewelry or ornament save a breast-knot of purple orchids her cousin had sent to her rooms.

At dinner, conversation was general, and the trio was made a quartet by the addition of an English friend of Loria's whom he ran across in the hotel lobby. Later, after they had had their coffee in the great hall, Mrs. MacDonald and the Englishman strolled away and the cousins were left alone.

"How beautiful you have grown, Pauline," Carr said, his eyes resting on her piquant face, crowned with its mass of soft, dark hair.

"Speak for yourself, John," she returned smiling up into the handsome, sunburned face of the man who scrutinized her. "You have acquired not only a becoming tan, but a new air of distinction."

"Glad you think so, girlie. Thanks a whole lot. How do you like the MacDonald?"

"Very much so far. She won't try to boss me, will she?"

"Not unless you make it necessary; but you must remember that English etiquette obtains in Cairo, and you mustn't try to be unconventional, except as Mrs. MacDonald approves."

"Oh, I won't disgrace you, Carr, I've common sense, I hope. Now tell me about yourself."

"I'm deep in a new project, Polly, a wonderful one. It's an enormous undertaking, but I shall put it through all right."

"What is it? Excavation?"

"In a way. But here's the story. Mind, now, it's a dead secret. Don't mention it to Mrs. Mac. I trust you with it, but it must go no further. Well, in a word, I've come into possession of an old papyrus, that tells of a treasure—"

"Oh, Carr, are you a treasure-seeker!"

"Now, wait till I tell you. This papyrus is authentic, and it's nothing more nor less than an account of a great hoard of jewels and gold sunk, purposely, by an old Egyptian king to save them from seizure. You wouldn't understand all the reasons that prove this is a true bill, but it is, and so you must take my word for it. All right. The old duffer saw fit to sink this stuff in the Nile, at a certain spot, designated in this papyrus thing, and all I've got to do is to dig her up, and there you are!"

Carr Loria's face lighted up with the enthusiasm of the true archaeologist, and Pauline caught the spirit, too, as she exclaimed, "How splendid! How do you get down to it,—if it's under the Nile?"

"It's a big scheme, Polly!" and Loria's eyes sparkled. "I've got to have a coffer-dam, an enormous one,—and, oh, and a whole lot of paraphernalia, and it will cost like fury, but the end justifies the expense,—and then, think of the glory of it!"

"Have you got a right to do all this? Can anybody dig wherever he likes in Egypt?"

"No, you little goose! But I've managed all that part. I won't tell even you about it, but I've—well, I've fixed it up. Now, listen here, Pollypops, you're to tell just simply nobody a word of all this,—not one, littlest, leastest mite of a word! See?"

"All right, Carr, of course I won't tell, if you say not
to. But will you be away from us? Out of Cairo?"

"Off and on. I'll be back and forth, you know. This
place is up the Nile a bit, and, of course, I have to be
there much of the time. But you'll be all right. I know
heaps of people, jolly sort, too, and Mrs. Mac will take you
round, and you'll have the time of your sweet young life!"

"I'm sure I shall. But, Carr, have you forgotten all
about America, and Aunt Lucy and—and Fleming Stone?"

"No, Pauline, I haven't forgotten those things. But, I
own up, aside from the awful circumstances, I'm not
terribly wrought up over Aunt Lucy's death. Poor old
thing, she wasn't so awfully happy, you know, and Lord
knows, she didn't make anybody else happy. Then, too,
you must realize that as I wasn't there, through, the
dreadful time, as you were, I can't feel the same thrill and
horror of it. In fact, I try to forget it all I can, as I can't do
anybody any good by mulling over it. So, if you want to
please me, old girl, you'll refer to it as little as you can."

"But don't you care who killed her? Don't you want to
find out the murderer and bring him to justice?"

"I want that done, Polly, but I don't want to do it.
That's why I put it all in Haviland's hands; that's why I
didn't want to go to America, unless, as I told you at first,
unless you needed me. I can't pay proper attention to my
work here if I have any such worriment as that on my
shoulders. And I tell you, Pauline, this chance that has
come to me is the chance of a lifetime, the chance of a
century! It means fortune, fame and glory for me. It
means—oh Pauline, it means everything!"

"All right, Carr, I won't interfere in any way with
your work. I'll do as you tell me, but—but if they continue
to suspect me,—"

"Suspect you! My dear girl! Let 'em try it! I'll see to
that! Don't you fear. If anything bothers you, just leave it
to me! Ah, here come our truants. Now, Polly, for my
sake, leave all those subjects for the present, and be your
own dear entertaining self."

And Pauline granted his request, and was so attractive and charming that the Englishman straightway fell over head and heels in love and Mrs. MacDonald was torn between throes of admiration and envy.

CHAPTER 23: TWO WILLS

FOR a few days Loria stayed in Cairo, and devoted all his time to the amusement and entertainment of Pauline. Together they visited the Sphinx and the Great Pyramids. Together they made trips to Old Cairo and to the Ostrich Farm. Together they saw the Little Petrified Forest. But the immediate sights of Cairo, the tombs, mosques and bazaars, Loria told her, she could visit with Mrs. MacDonald or with their dragoman, after he and Ahri had gone on their trip up the Nile.

Pauline was happy. At Carr's request she had endeavored to put out of her mind the horrors she had been through. Frightened at the suspicions directed toward herself, fearing that she could not successfully combat them,—and, for another reason,—she had fled to Egypt, and her cousin's protection. This other reason she had almost dismissed from her mind, and she gave herself up to the enjoyment of the novelty and interest of her present situation. After their sight-seeing each day, they returned for tea on the Terrace at Shepheard's or went to Ghezireh Palace for it, or to the house of some friend. Dinner was always a pleasant affair, and they had frequent guests and were often invited out.

As Pauline was wearing mourning, no large social affairs were attended, and under Mrs. MacDonald's guidance the girl pursued her happy way.

Nearly a week after Pauline's arrival, Loria told her that the next day he must leave her, and go up the Nile to attend to his work there. They were in the sitting room of Pauline's pleasant suite at the hotel, and Mrs. MacDonald promised to cherish most carefully her charge in Loria's absence.

"How long shall you be away, Carr?" asked Pauline.

"It's uncertain, Polly. Perhaps only a few days this time, perhaps a week. I'll be back and forth, you know, and you're bound to find enough to interest you. Keep me advised of any news from America. You can always reach me by mail or wire, or telephone if need be. And, here's another matter, Pauline. You know, this work I'm up against is more or less dangerous."

"Dangerous, how?"

"Well, there's blasting and danger of caveins and such matters,—but don't feel alarmed, I'll probably come through all right. Only, I want to make my will, so if anything should happen, you'll be my heir without any fuss about it."

"Oh, don't talk about such things, Carr. You frighten me."

"Nonsense, don't take it like that. Now, see here. You know my way. Touch and go is my motto. So, I've asked a lawyer chap to come here to-night and fix up things. Suppose you make your will, too. Then it will seem more like a business matter, and not as if either of us expects to die soon. Who's your heir to be, Polly?"

"Why, I don't know, I've never thought about it."

"But you ought to. You see, now you're some heiress, and it isn't right not to have a will made,—on general principles. To be sure, you may marry—"

"Oh, I don't think I ever will, Carr!"

"Nonsense, Pollypops, of course you will. But you must take your time and select a good chappie. Now, how does this strike you? Jeffries, my lawyer, is coming here, right away. Suppose we each make a will, leaving all our wordly goods to each other. Then, later, when you decide on your life mate, you can change and rearrange as you like."

"But I haven't any fortune yet. Aunt Lucy's estate isn't all settled, is it?"

"No matter about that. It will be, in course of time. I have every confidence in Haviland, he's as honest a chap as ever breathed. He'll fix up all our interests over there, in apple-pie order and don't you forget it! Humor me in this thing, Polly, and believe I know more of business affairs than you do, and it's best to do as I say."

Pauline was easily persuaded, and as the arrangement was conceded to be merely temporary, she agreed. Jeffries came. The two wills were drawn, signed and witnessed, all in correct form. Loria, in his, bequeathed to Pauline all he might die possessed of, and except for a few charities and minor bequests, Pauline left her fortune to Carr. The business was soon over, and Loria took both documents, saying he would put them in his Safe Deposit box for the present, as Pauline had no place for valuable papers. The next day, Loria, accompanied by the invaluable Ahri, went away to the site of his projected enterprise. This affair was conducted with such strict secrecy that even the location was not known to many. Actual work had not yet been begun, but negotiations and preparations of vast importance were being made, and secret conclaves were held by those most interested. Pauline had been emphatically adjured to give not the least hint to any one whatever of the project, and she had promised faithfully to obey Carr's injunctions.

The next afternoon, a telegram from Fleming Stone announced his arrival at Alexandria and his immediate appearance in Cairo.

Addressed to her, in Loria's care, Pauline received it duly, for her mail was brought to her at Shepheard's, and Carr's forwarded to him wherever he might be. She had had a cable from Haviland, but no American letters had yet reached her. Stone, having sailed just a week after Pauline's departure from New York, was arriving eight days after her own advent at Cairo.

The girl's first emotion was of joy. The thought of seeing Stone again, eclipsed all other thoughts.

"Oh, Mrs. Mac!" she cried, clasping that somewhat rotund matron round the waist and leading her an enforced dance. "Mr. Stone is coming! Will be here for tea! Oh, I am so glad!"

But her second thoughts were more disturbing. Why was he coming? What were his suspicions? Could he be tracking her down?

Though Fleming Stone had never said a word of love to her, Pauline knew, by her own heart's 'detective instinct,' that he cared. But, his sense of duty might make it necessary to follow where the trail of suspicion led, even at cost of his own affections. Then, too, could he suspect?—

But Pauline's irrepressible joy at thought of seeing him left her little time or wish to indulge in gloomy forebodings.

Singing, she ran off to dress for Stone's reception.

"Which is prettier?" she asked of Mrs. Mac, holding up an embroidered white crepe, of Cairo construction, and a black net gown, brought from New York.

"Wear the white, Miss Stuart. It's most becoming to you."

It was, and when arrayed in the lovely, soft, clinging affair, with a cluster of tiny white rosebuds at her belt, Pauline's unusually pink cheeks and her scarlet flower of a mouth gave all the color necessary.

Her beautiful hair, piled in a crown atop her little head, was held by a carved ivory comb, and beneath their half-drooped lashes her great eyes shone like stars.

For the Terrace, she donned a large white hat, with black ostrich plumes, and flinging a white cape edged with black fur over her arm, she descended to meet her guest.

Though little given to emotional demonstration, Fleming Stone caught his breath with a quick gasp at sight of her, and advanced with outstretched hands and a smile of a sort no one had ever before seen on that always calm face.

"How do you do?" she said, smiling; for, though thrilled herself, she remembered the unfailing curiosity of the Terrace crowds.

But Stone, having taken her two hands in his, stood looking at her as if he intended to pursue that occupation for the rest of his natural life.

"Sit down," she said, laughing a little nervously under his gaze; "this is our table. Will you have tea?"

"Tea, of course," and at last Fleming Stone took himself in hand and behaved like a reasonable citizen. "And how are you? And your cousin, where is he?"

"Mr. Loria is out of Cairo just now," and Pauline turned to give the waiter his order.

"But we are three, as I am under most strict surveillance—" she paused, realizing what that phrase meant to a detective! "Of a perfect dragon of a chaperon," she continued bravely, trying to control her quivering lip.

"Here she comes now."

The appearance and introduction of Mrs. MacDonald gave Pauline time to regain her poise, and a glance of pathetic appeal to Stone made him take up the burden of conversation for a few moments. And then, with the arrival of the tea, the chat became gayer, and, of course, impersonal.

The Englishman, Pitts, appeared, indeed, he inevitably appeared when Pauline was on the Terrace, and joined the group without invitation.

It was not Fleming Stone's first visit to Egypt, and he noted with interest the changes, and looked with gladness on things unchanged, as the kaleidoscopic scene whirled about him. Later, they all went up to Pauline's sitting room, and viewed the street pageant from second-story windows.

And then, Mrs. MacDonald, after a short and losing battle between her conventions and her kind-heartedness, insisted that Mr. Pitts must take her across the street to buy some imperatively necessary writing-paper.

Outwardly courteous but inwardly of a rampageous unwillingness, Mr. Pitts acquiesced in her scheme, and Fleming Stone politely closed the door behind them.

He turned, to see Pauline looking at him, with a gaze, frightened, but,—yes, surely,—welcoming, and not waiting to analyze the intent of the gaze more deeply, Stone took a chance, and in another instant, held her in his arms so closely that the intent of her glance was of little importance to anybody.

"Pauline!" he breathed, "how I love yon! My darling,—mine! No, no, don't speak—" and he laid his finger tips on her parted lips, "Just look at me, and so— tell me—"

The wonderful eyes raised themselves to his, and Stone's phenomenal insight was not necessary for him to read the message they held.

"You do love me!" he whispered: "oh, my little girl!" and after a long, silent embrace, he cried jubilantly: "Now tell me! Now tell me in words, in words, Pauline, that you do!"

Unhesitatingly, without shyness, Pauline, radiant-faced, whispered, "I love you, dear," and the vibrant tones filled the simple words to the brim of assurance.

Though it seemed to them but a moment, it was some time later that Mrs. MacDonald's tap sounded on the door.

"Come," cried Pauline, springing away from Stone's side, while he sauntered to the window. "Oh, Mrs. MacDonald, you must know it at once! Mr. Stone is my fiance!"

Mrs. Mac was duly surprised and delighted, and, after congratulations, sent Stone away to dress for dinner, and endeavored to calm down her emotional charge.

Later that evening, Stone and Pauline sat in the hall watching the people. Almost as much alone as on a desert island, they conversed in low tones, and Stone, between expressions of adoration, told her of his theory of the beauty charm.

With paling face, Pauline listened. "Who?" she whispered. "Who? Do you suspect anybody?"

"You don't know of your aunt ever having consulted any beauty doctor or any such person?"

"Oh, no! I'm sure she never did. Never!"

"And you don't know of any one who would give her poison, under pretense of its being a charm or beautifier?"

"Oh, don't! Don't ask me!" and, with a face white as ashes, Pauline rose from her chair. "You must excuse me, Mr. Stone. I am ill,—I don't feel well—. Really I must beg to be excused."

Almost before he realized what she was doing, Pauline had left him, glided to the elevator, and he heard the door of the cage clang to, even as he followed her.

"Poor child!" he said to himself, "poor dear little girl!" and going in quest of Mrs. MacDonald, he asked her to go to Pauline.

"You will perhaps find her greatly disturbed," he said, "but I assure you it is nothing that can be avoided or remedied. Please, Mrs. MacDonald, just try to comfort and cheer her, without asking the cause of her sadness."

After a straightforward look into Stone's eyes, which was as frankly returned, Mrs. MacDonald nodded her head and hastened away. As Stone had predicted she found Pauline sobbing hysterically.

"What is it, dear?" she queried, "tell Mrs. Mac. Or, if you'd rather not, at least tell me what I can do for you. Don't, don't cry so!"

But no words could she get from the sobbing girl, except an insistent demand for a telegraph blank. This was provided, and Pauline wrote a message to Carr Loria telling him that Fleming Stone had come to Cairo. This she ordered despatched at once. Then she begged Mrs. MaoDonald to leave her, as she wished to go to bed and try to forget her troubles in sleep.

Meantime, Fleming Stone left the hotel and proceeded straight to Carr Loria's rooms. He expressed surprise when the janitor informed him of Mr. Loria's absence.

"Well, never mind," he said: "he'll be back in a few days. But I'll just go in and write a note and leave it on his desk for him."

The janitor hesitated, but after a transference of some coin of the realm was effected, he cheerfully unlocked the door and Stone found himself in Loria's apartment. It was a comfortable place, even luxurious, in a mannish way, and the Detective looked about with interest.

As he had proposed, he went to the writing table and taking a sheet of paper from the rack, wrote a short note. But instead of leaving it, he put it in his pocket, saying to the watchful janitor that perhaps it would be better to mail it. Then, he stepped into Loria's bedroom, but so quickly did he step out again, that the janitor hadn't time to reprove or forbid him.

"All right," he said, as he started to leave. "When Mr. Loria returns you can tell him I called."

This permission went far to allay the janitor's fears that he had been indiscreet; for Carr Loria was not a man who brooked interference with his affairs or belongings.

CHAPTER 24: CONFESSION

CARR LORIA was at Heluan when he received Pauline's telegram. For a few moments he studied it, and then going to a hotel office, he possessed himself of a telegram blank which he proceeded to write on, by the use of a type-writer near-by.

With a preoccupied look on his face, as if thinking deeply, he called Ahri and gave him, a long and careful list of directions. And it was in pursuance of these directions that the Arab presented himself at Shepheard's at ten o 'clock in the morning and asked for Miss Stuart.

"What is it, Ahri?" asked Pauline, as she received the dragoman in her sitting room.

"Miss Stoort," and the Arab was deeply respectful, "Mr. Loria begs that you go with me to Sakkara to visit the Pyramids and Necropolis."

"Now?" said Pauline, in surprise.

"Yes, my lady. Mr. Loria will himself meet you at the station. Will you start at once, please?"

"But I am expecting a caller—Mr. Stone,—"

"Pardon, but Mr. Loria said if you hesitated for any reason, to implore you to go with me quickly, and he will explain all."

Pauline paled a little, but she said, simply, "Very well, Ahri, I will go at once."

Escorted by the silent, majestic-mannered Arab, Pauline was taken through the crowded streets to the station, and they boarded a train just as it was leaving.

"We did get the train, Miss Stoort," said Ahri, with his sad smile, "Mr. Loria would be greatly mad if we had missed it. Yes."

Pauline nodded at him, her thoughts full of the spoiled day, which she had hoped to spend with Stone.

Yet she longed to see Carr, she wanted to tell him what Mr. Stone had said about the beauty charm and—"

"You said Mr. Loria would meet us at the station, Ahri; you put me on the train so quickly I had no chance to speak. Where is he?"

"Not the Cairo station, my lady. The station at Bedrashein."

"Where is that?"

"Where we are going. We alight there to see the ruins of Memphis and the Pyramids of Sakkara."

Pauline looked puzzled, but said no more and sat silently wrapped in her own thoughts, now of Stone, now of Carr, and again of herself. At Bedrashein, they left the train. Pauline looked anxiously around but saw nothing of her cousin.

"I do not see him," said Ahri, gravely, meeting her inquiring glance; "but I obey his orders. He said, if he be not here, we go to the desert to meet him."

"To the desert? How? Where?"

"This way. Here are our carts." Ahri led the way to where two sand-carts stood waiting, evidently for them. They were a little like English dog-carts and drawn by desert horses.

"You take that one, Miss Stoort, and I this," directed Ahri, standing with outstretched hand, like a commanding officer.

Bewildered but knowing the responsibility of Carr's servant, Pauline got into the cart he indicated. She did not at all like the looks of the gaunt black Moor who drove her, but thought best to say nothing. She had learned never to show fear of the native servants, and she held her head high, and gave the driver only a haughty stare. Ahri, after she was arranged for, sprang into the other cart, and they set off. The road was through the village, through palm groves, past large expanses of water, and at last through desert wastes, among foot-hills that quickly cut off the view of the road just traversed.

Pauline's cart was ahead of the other, and looking back she could not see the other one, in which Ahri rode.

A strange feeling began to creep into her heart. Covertly she glanced at her driver. The hard bony face was not turned her way, but she had an uncanny sense that the man was grinning at her. Sternly she bade him stop and wait for the other cart.

"No Ingleese," he rejoined, with a dogged expression on his ugly countenance.

"I command you," and Pauline laid hold of his arm, "I insist that you stop!"

"No Ingleese," he repeated, and now he gave her a distinctly impudent look and spurred the horse to faster pace.

Pauline considered. She was frightened beyond words to express, but she knew she must not show fear. Haughtily she held her proud little head aloft, and tried to think what was best to do. Something was wrong, that she knew, but whether it was Ahri who was at fault, or this dreadful man beside her, or—or,—she stifled back the thought of Loria.

He would save her, she knew he would, cried her worried brain, but in her heart was black doubt. All the unadmitted fears she had knownof late, all the repressed suspicions, all the insistent doubts, these came flocking, clamoring for recognition.

On they went,—where they might be she had no idea. Nothing could be seen but the neverending hills, not high, but of sufficient height to cut off all view of anything but their sandy slopes. Miles and miles they traversed. The sun was under a cloud, and Pauline had no knowledge of the direction they were taking. But from the man's grim, stony face, and cruel eyes, she knew she was in dreadful, even desperate danger. Courageously, she insisted over and over that they stop. The reply was only a shaken head and a reassertion that English was an unknown tongue. This Pauline knew to be a lie, from his intelligent expression at her words. At last, desperately trying to control her trembling hands, she offered her purse, if he would stop.

To her surprise, he consented, and jerked his horse to a stand-still. Pauline handed over the purse, and the driver got out of the cart, indicating by gestures that she should also alight, and rest herself.

The cart was small, and the ride had been uncomfortable, so after a moment's thought Pauline jumped out. She reasoned that the man having her money, had no desire to prolong the trip, and in a moment they would go back to Bedrashein. Often had she heard of these robberies, and she felt that, cupidity satisfied, she had little to fear.

But no sooner was she on the ground, than the Moor sprang again into his cart, and whipping up his horse, sped away across the desert sand and in a minute rounded a hill and was out of sight.

Pauline looked after him an instant, and then, realizing to the uttermost what it meant,—that she was abandoned to her fate in a trackless desert,—fell in a little heap on the sands and fainted away.

It was about eleven o'clock on the morning of that same day, that Carr Loria went to Shepheard's Hotel and asked for Fleming Stone. The two men met, and eyed each other appraisingly. There was no light chat, each was of serious face and in grave mood.

Loria spoke first, after the short greeting. "I have a telegram from my cousin, Miss Stuart," he said, drawing a paper from his pocket. "I know why you are here, Mr. Stone, and I think best to show you this. Frankly, I am glad of it."

Stone took the message, and read:

I have run away again. I am afraid of F. S. Don't try to find me, I am all right, and I will communicate with you after he goes back to U. S. I positively will not make my whereabouts known as long as he is in Cairo. Don't worry.

POLLY.

"We may as well be honest with one another," Loria went on. "I gather, from your presence here, that you know my cousin is guilty of the death of her aunt; but you don't know, you can't know, what that poor girl had to put up with. I can't blame her, that in a moment of,—really of temporary insanity,—she let herself be tempted—"

"I'm sorry to cut short this interview, Mr. Loria," said Stone, in his quiet way, "but, truly, I've a most important engagement just now. If I could see you, say this evening, and talk these things over by ourselves—"

"Surely, Mr. Stone. I must return to my work to-morrow, but I'll see you to-night. Will you come to my place?"

"Yes, I will. About nine?"

"Nine it is," and Loria swung away, as Fleming Stone turned and hastened into the hotel. Straight to Mrs. MacDonald he went and asked where Pauline was.

"She went to visit Memphis and Sakkara with her cousin," said the smiling chaperon.

"That is, she went with her cousin's dragoman, and Mr. Loria met them at Bedrashein."

"Oh, did he! Now listen, Mrs. MacDonald. Miss Stuart is in danger. I am sure of this. I am going to her aid, but I may not—" Stone choked, "I may not succeed soon. Tell me of this dragoman. What does he look like?"

Graphically, Mrs. MacDonald described the statuesque Ahri, and almost before she stopped speaking, Stone was flying along the corridor, down the stairs, and out at the door.

He caught a train to Bedrashein, and the first person he bumped into at the little station was Ahri himself waiting for the train to Cairo.

Fleming Stone went straight to the point. "Look here, Ahri," he said to the astonished Arab, who had never seen him before, "what have you done with Miss Stuart?"

For once the phlegmatic Arab was caught off his guard.

"What do you mean?" he stammered. "I have not seen her to-day."

"Don't lie to me," and Stone gave him a look that cowed him. "Now listen. You're in Mr. Loria's pay. All right. He paid you well for the job you Ve just done. Now, I'll pay you twice,—three times as well to undo it. Moreover, I'll inform you straight that you'll never work for Mr. Loria again. He's a villain, a wicked man. Take my advice, Ahri, give him up and come over to me. By so doing, you'll not only escape punishment for your work to-day, but get a fresh start toward a good position. I don't believe you're a bad man at heart, Ahri. At least, I don't believe you'll continue to be if you're better paid to be good."

Stone was right about this, and the talk ended in another expedition of two sand-carts into the desert. Ahri in one, with a native driver, Stone alone in the other, driving himself. Ahri's cart was driven by the same Moor that had driven Pauline only two or three hours before. Stone followed them, the wicked driver easily bought over to betray the place where he had left Pauline.

And there they found her.

Crouched at the base of a small hill, worn out by weeping and despair, racked by fright and terror, she had fallen into a fitful slumber from sheer exhaustion. Jumping from his cart, Stone waved the others back and went to her. On her face were traces of tears. Her gloves and handkerchief were torn in strips by her agonized frenzies. Her shoulders were huddled as if in frantic fear, and her face was drawn and pinched with anguish. But in spite of all this, Stone thought he had never seen her look so beautiful. Stepping nearer he lifted her to her feet, and unheeding the observers, he clasped her closely in his arms, and whispered endearing words.

Pauline, her eyes still closed, murmured, "it's only a dream. I must not wake, I must not!"

"No dream, darling," said the strong, glad voice in her ear. "Does this seem like a dream?" and his lips met hers in a long, close kiss.

Then her eyes opened, wondering, and lest she should faint from very joy, Stone carried her to the cart and placed her in it. Jumping in beside her, he ordered the other cart to lead and they started back.

Neither Pauline nor Stone ever forgot that ride. At first, she was content to ask no questions, happy in his nearness and her own rescue from an awful fate. But, later, she inquired about Loria.

"You must know the truth soon, dearest," said Stone, gently, "so I'll tell you, in part now. Your cousin is a wicked man, Pauline, and you must grasp this fact before I go on."

"Carr wicked?" and Pauline paled and trembled as if struck with a sudden blow.

"Yes, it was his hand, his will, that sent you to be lost in the desert. He showed me a false telegram, saying you had run away from me!"

"What? oh, I can't believe it!"

"Well, don't try now," and Stone smiled at her. "It's all I can do to manage this fiery steed without trying to tell you unbelievable things at the same time. Let me tell you something more easy of credulity."

Pauline's smile was permission, and Stone had no difficulty in convincing her of certain selfevident truths.

By the time the trio reached Cairo, Ahri was as stanch a follower and as true a slave of Fleming Stone as he had been of Carrington Loria. At Stone's direction he returned to his former master, for the present, and gave no hint of the later development of the kidnapping scheme.

"All went off as planned?" said Loria, secure in his servant's fidelity.

"Yes, master," answered the devoted trusty, and Loria said no more on the subject. That evening when Fleming Stone went to Carr Loria's rooms, he was accompanied by Pauline and the Englishman, Pitts.

Loria started at sight of his cousin, but quickly recovered his poise and jauntily asked her where she had come from.

"No place like Cairo, for me," she replied in the same light tone, and they all sat down in Loria's den.

"More company than I expected," he said, as he bustled about, seating them. "Ahri, another chair."

Ahri obeyed the request, and then softly left the room.

"Mr. Loria," said Stone, directly, "there is no use wasting words, we are here to accuse you of the murder of your aunt and the attempted murder of your cousin."

Carr Loria's face blanched, but he tried to put on a bold front.

"What do you mean by this nonsense? Is it a joke?"

"By no means; I have all the proofs of your crimes and I ask you if you will confess here, or to the Police?"

"Friend Pitts, I believe, is connected with the Police," and Loria laughed grimly.

"Yes, he is. Have you anything to say?"

"Only to deny your accusations. Except that it's too absurd even to deny such foolish talk. What do you mean anyway?"

"That you poisoned Miss Lucy Carrington, wilfully and purposely, by sending her a dose of powdered aconite, under the pretense of its being a beauty charm that would bring fairness and youth to her plain face."

Carr Loria's jaw dropped. He looked at Stone as if at something supernatural. "W—what?" he stammered.

"You did it to get her money, now, to go on with your work in the bed of the Nile. Then, in order to get your cousin's share of the fortune, you sent her away to die in the desert, having first induced her to will you her money."

"Ha, ha," laughed Loria, feebly. "Poor joke, Stone, pretty poor joke, I say! Murdered my own aunt! Not much I didn't!"

"Carr Loria, listen!" Impressively Stone held up his finger, to adjure silence, and at the same time he bent on Loria a glance of accusation that made him cringe. But, fascinated, he stared into Stone's eyes, and in the death-like silence came a voice,—the voice of Lucy Carrington,—in a burst of ringing laughter! Loria's eyes seemed to start from his head, and the sweat gathered in great drops on his forehead, as the voice of his aunt spoke: "This song is one of Oarr's favorites," they heard, distinctly.

"I'll sing it for him."

Then, in Miss Lucy's high, clear notes, came the song, "Oh, Believe Me If All Those Endearing Young Charms."

Before the last strains came, Loria was raving like a maniac. He had never heard of the phonograph records of his aunt's songs, for they had meant to surprise him with them on his next trip home.

"Have mercy!" he cried: "stop her! Oh, my God! What does it all mean?"

"Confess," ordered Fleming Stone.

"I will confess! I do confess! I did send her the powder, just as you say. I wrote her to dress up like Cleopatra, and put on her pearls, and scarabs, and fasten an asp, a paper one, at her throat, and take the stuff, and it would cause Cleopatra's beauty to come to her. I told her to hold in her hand something belonging to the man she loved. It was a great scheme,—a fine scheme," Loria was babbling insanely now. "I don't see how any one ever found it out. I was so careful! I made her promise to burn all my notes and letters about it, before I would send the powder. Who suspected it? I planned everything so carefully—so carefully—Made her promise to burn everything,—everything—letters of instruction, powder-

papers, everything must be burned, I said—everything,—
and she said, yes, Carr, everything. Over and over I wrote
it . Told her that if she left anything unburnt the charm
wouldn't work, and it didn't. Ha, ha," with a demoniac
chuckle, "it didn't!"

"Take me away, I can't stand it," moaned Pauline.

Again there was a silence. The phonograph had
ceased; Loria sat, with his head fallen forward on his
hands, at his table. He was still, and Stone wondered if
he were alive. Then, suddenly, he lifted his head, and
cried out. "Yes, I did it because I was crazy, wild over my
Nile scheme. Ah, that wonderful work! It will never be
done now. When I heard Stone was here I knew it was all
up. I planned to lose Polly for a time,—not forever, no, not
forever—I would have found her some day,—some day,—
all dead, in the desert, all dead—"

Pauline fainted and Stone flew to her side. But in a
moment she revived, and he begged her to go home. She
consented, and Ahri, dependable now, took her to the
hotel.

Fleming Stone and Mr. Pitts attempted to get Loria
to calm down and talk more coherently. Shortly he did so.
He gave a full account of all the details of his crime, and
though he denied the intention of leaving Pauline to die
in the desert, his word was not believed by the two
listeners.

Finally, he rose and walked across the room. "You
see," he said, a little wearily, but quite sane, now, "I've a
bad streak in me. My father was a Spaniard and he killed
his own uncle. The Loria line is a series of criminals.
Aunt Lucy never knew this, for my parents lived always
abroad. But blood will tell. And my father, after he killed
my uncle, followed it up by taking his own life,—like
this,—"

Though Stone caught the gesture and sprang to
prevent it, Loria was too quick for him. He had snatched
a dagger from the table, and plunged it into his heart.

Both men leaped at him, but it was all over in an instant. Carr Loria had himself dealt the punishment for his crimes.

"Perhaps it's as well," said Stone, musingly. "A trial, and all that, would have been awful for his cousin, and the family connections. Now the matter can be disposed of with far less notoriety and publicity."

"Yes," agreed Pitts.

Fleming Stone waited till morning to tell Pauline of her cousin's death. She was wideand pathetically sad, but composed.

It is all so dreadful," she said, "but, Fleming, I knew it before I left New York. I didn't know it, exactly, but I felt sure it must be so, and I had to come here to see. Then I found Carr so gay and light-hearted I thought I must be mistaken, and I was glad, too. Then when you came, I couldn't make up my mind whether you suspected Carr, or whether—"

"Whether I came only to see you," supplied Stone. "It was both, dear."

"What made you think of Carr, in the first place?"

"Because there was no real evidence against any one else, though the police were making things dangerous for you, my little girl." Stone held her close, as if even yet there might be a hint of danger. "And I made Miss Frayne confess that she didn't really see you leave your aunt's room that night, though she did honestly think that you were in there, and your auut was talking to you. Nor you didn't see her actually leaving the room, did you?"

"I only saw her with her hand on the doorknob. That was my first glimpse of her, and I thought she was coming out."

"No; she thought of going in to apologize for her hasty temper. But, hearing a voice, she paused, and so thrilling was the talk she overheard, she waited there some minutes."

"And then, you thought of Carr?"

"I sized up all the people who had motive, and Loria was surely in that category. And then I found the powder-papers. Dear, those would have gone sorely against you if any one else had discovered them. I resolved to wrest the secret from those papers, and I did!"

"You did? How?"

"By studying them for hours; with magnifying glasses, and without. I found at last a clue,—a possible clue,—in the fact that the edges of the papers had been cut with the curved blades of a pair of manicure scissors. I had Jane bring me 'all the manicure scissors in the house,—thank Heaven, your scissors didn't come within a mile of fitting the edges! You see, the papers were faintly scalloped on every edge. They must have been cut by the little curved blades, and rarely do two pairs of manicure scissors make the same scallop. The great discovery was that Miss Lucy's own scissors did fit them! This, dearest, would have pointed to you in the eyes of these determined police, for you had access to your aunt's toilet appointments."

"So did Anita or anybody in the house!"

"Yes, but the police were hot on your track, and ready to bend any hint your way. Oh, thank God, that I could and did save you! Well, I further noticed that these scissors of Miss Carrington's were of a different pattern from the brushes and mirrors of her set. I went to Estelle, and she told me that the last time Carr Loria was at home he took a great fancy to his aunt's scissors and asked her to give them to him. She did, and when she tried to get another pair with that especial shaped blade, she could do so only by taking a different patterned handle! Do you wonder that I came straight over here?"

"No," and the lovely eyes beamed with admiration of Stone's cleverness, as well as with affection.

"Then, last night, I went to Loria's rooms, and found not only the scissors, that fitted exactly the scalloped papers, but found that the outside powder wrapper is undoubtedly a piece of his own writing-paper. It is the same color and texture. Moreover, as he confessed it all, there is no further room for doubt. Another hint I had was when I found some of Loria's letters in your aunt's desk. Not their contents, they were just such as any affectionate nephew might write his aunt, but the chirography. You know the letter from him that you showed me, was typewritten, and I judged nothing from it. But his handwriting, —I have studied the science, — gave evidence of criminal traits, and I felt sure then I was on the right track. I brought the phonograph record to frighten him into confession, and it did. Ahri started it, in the next room, at my signal."

"I might have known you would do it. When I came here, you know, I wrote and asked you to drop the case. I feared your investigations would lead to Carr."

"It had to be a question of his guilt or yours," returned Stone gravely. "You don't know, darling, how near you were to arrest! Let's not think of it ever again. I'll engage to keep your dear mind occupied with pleasant thoughts all the rest of our life. You don't want to stay in Cairo, do you? Shall we try Algiers for a honeymoon spot? Or, if you don't want Africa at all, how about Greece, or over to Algeciras? Whither away, my Heart 's Dearest?"

"Whither? Together, then what matter whither?" said Pauline, her eyes full of a love deep enough to drown the sorrows that had filled the past weeks.

"Together always," he responded, holding her to him; "always, my Pauline."

THE END

Other Resurrected Press Mysteries From Carolyn Wells

Resurrected Press Mysteries From Louis Tracy

The Albert Gate Mystery
Four men murdered and a fortune in diamonds belonging to the Turkish Sultan stolen, while the Foreign Office official in charge has gone missing. Was it a common jewelry theft or was it a case of international intrigue? This is the question that barrister detective Reginald Brett must solve.

The Bartlett Mystery
When Ronald Tower is murdered on his way to a bridge game on the yacht Sans Souci it at first appears a common crime. But as Rex Carshaw finds, a tragic case of mistaken identity leads to political scandal among the rich and powerful of New York.

The Strange Case of Mortimer Fenley
When the wealthy Mortimer Fenley is struck down by a shot from an express rifle on the steps of his mansion, detectives Winter and Furneaux of Scotland Yard must find the culprit. Was it the artist who claimed he was painting a picture at the time of the shot? The disaffected younger son? Or is there another suspect?

The Stowmarket Mystery
For five generations the Fergus-Hume family has been cursed. Each of the baronets has met a violent end. When the fifth baronet is found slain by a ceremonial Japanese dagger, suspicion falls on his cousin David. It falls to barrister detective Reginald Brett to prove his innocence and find the real murder in a case that spans two continents and as many centuries.

Resurrected Press Mysteries by J. S. Fletcher

The Orange-Yellow Diamond
When an elderly pawnbroker is murdered in the London parish of Paddington, a young, down on his luck writer is accused of the crime. But then it's found the pawnbroker had had in his possession an extraordinary South African diamond worth over eighty-thousand pounds —a diamond that's now missing. It falls to Melky Rubenstein to unravel the mystery and prove the young man's innocence.

The Middle Temple Murder
When an elderly man's body is found on the steps of chambers in the Midde Temple, one of the Inns of Court, it falls to newspaperman Frank Spargo and Detective-Sergeant Rathbury to solve the crime. The murdered man, for indeed it was murder, was found with no money or identification on his person except for a piece of paper with the name and address of a young barrister. Who is the victim? Why was he killed? Who is the murderer?

Scarhaven Keep
Bassett Oliver, the famed actor, has gone missing. When Oliver fails to show for a rehearsal, aspiring playwright Richard Copplestone finds himself sent to the small village of Scarhaven on the northern coast of England to track down the actors movements. What he finds is mystery. Find the answers as Copplestone unravels the mystery of Scarhaven Keep.

Visit www.resurrectedpress.com

Resurrected Press Mysteries by Fergus Hume

The Green Mummy

Professor Braddock hoped to compare the burial practices of the Egyptians with those of the ancient Peruvians with his latest acquisition, the mummy of the last Inca, Caxas. But on arrival, the packing case proved to hold not the mummy, but the body of his assistant Sidney Bolton. It falls to Archie Hope to discover the murderer if he is to marry the professors step-daughter, Lucy Kendal. Who killed Bolton and where is the mummy? Was it the sea captain Hervey? The mysterious Don Pedro? Cockatoo the Polynesian servant? The professor, himself? And what has become of the emeralds? These are the questions that Hope must answer amongst the secrets of the past in The Green Mummy.

The Mystery of a Hansom Cab

"Truth is said to be stranger than fiction, and certainly the extraordinary murder which took place in Melbourne Friday morning goes a long way towards verifying that saying." Thus opens The Mystery of a Hansom Cab, the best selling mystery of the nineteenth century. When a man is found dead in a hansom cab one of Melbourne's leading citizens is accused of the murder. He pleads his innocence, yet refuses to give an alibi. It falls to a determined lawyer and an intrepid detective to find the truth, revealing long kept secrets along the way. Fergus Hume's first and perhaps most famous mystery... The Mystery Of A Hansom Cab.

Visit www.resurrectedpress.com

Resurrected Press Mysteries from the Dr. John Thorndyke Series

Dr. John Thorndyke Lecturer on Medical Jurisprudence and Forensic Medicine. Before Bones, before CSI, before Quincy, M.E– there was Dr. John Thorndyke solving the most baffling cases of Edwardian London using the latest tools of medical science. Read about his cases in:

The Eye of Osiris
John Bellingham, noted Egyptologist has vanished not once but twice in the same day. Now Dr, Thorndyke must unravel the tangled claims on his estate, solve the riddle of the missing man and find the "Eye of Osiris".

The Mystery of 31 New Inn
When Dr. Jervis is whisked away in a coach with no windows to an unknown location to treat a man in a coma from undivulged causes it is Dr. Thorndyke who must come up with the solution.

The Red Thumb Mark
The first of Dr. Thorndyke's cases finds him trying to prove the innocence of a young man accused of being a diamond thief despite the fact that his finger print was found at the scene of the crime.

John Thorndyke's Cases
More cases of medical mysteries as told by his trusted assistant Jervis, M.D. Eight stories of crime and deduction in Edwardian London.

Visit www.resurrectedpress.com

Resurrected Press Mysteries by John R. Watson & Arthur J. Rees

The Hampstead Mystery

High Court Justice Sir Horace Fewbanks found shot dead in his Hampstead home, a butler with a criminal past, a scorned lover and a hint of scandal. These are the elements of the Hampstead Mystery that Detective Inspector Chippenfield of Scotland Yard must unravel with the assistance of the ambitious Detective Rolfe. But will he be able to sort out the tangled threads of this case and arrest the culprit before he is upstaged by the celebrated gentleman detective Crewe. Follow the details of this amazing case at it plays out across Hampstead, London and Scotland until it reaches a stunning conclusion in the courts of the Old Bailey.

The Mystery of the Downs

When Harry Marsland was caught in a sudden down pour he sought shelter at Cliff Farm. Met at the door by a young woman clearly expecting someone else he is only too glad to get inside to wait out the storm. When they hear a noise upstairs in the deserted house they investigate only to discover the body of the farm's owner, Frank Lumsden, dead of a gunshot wound. Who then, killed Lumsden, and why? Who was the woman expecting and did she have any roll in the murder? These are the questions that private detective Crewe must answer in The Mystery of the Downs.

Visit www.resurrectedpress.com

Other Resurrected Press Mysteries

Mysteries on a Train

Before the Orient Express there was:

The Rome Express by Arthur Griffiths

A man is found dead in his first class sleeping compartment on the express from Rome to Paris. Who was his murderer? The Countess? The English General? His brother the clergy man? The maid who has disappeared? Is the French justice system up to solving the crime? Read about it in The Rome Express.

The Passenger from Calais by Arthur Griffiths

Colonel Basil Annesley finds he is the only passenger on the train from Calais to Lucerne. That is until a mysterious woman shows up at the last minute to book a compartment. Who is after her? What is her secret? Is she a criminal or a victim? Read about it in The Passenger from Calais

Visit us at www.resurrectedpress.com

About Resurrected Press

A division of Intrepid Ink, LLC, Resurrected Press is dedicated to bringing high quality, vintage books back into publication. See our entire catalogue and find out more at www.ResurrectedPress.com.

About Intrepid Ink, LLC

Intrepid Ink, LLC provides full publishing services to authors of fiction and non-fiction books, eBooks and websites. From editing to formatting, from publishing to marketing, Intrepid Ink gets your creative works into the hands of the people who want to read them. Find out more at www.IntrepidInk.com.

www.ingramcontent.com/pod-product-compliance
Lightning Source LLC
Chambersburg PA
CBHW071302250626
47159CB00004B/1275